YES YES Y'ALL

BOOK 1

A Novel by

Latif Mercado

YES YES Y'ALL Book 1

Printed in the United States of America

First Printing, 2020

ISBN 978-0-9993189-3-5

Cover illustration by June ArcaMay

La' Entertainment

Monroe, NC 28110

www.LatifMercado.com

Dedication

Book One of Yes Yes Y'all is dedicated to my son, Adam Latif Mercado. My first born, and my only boy. The one who truly helped change my life. I wrote this book while Adam was still in his twenties.

If I wanted anyone to be able to go into my past, and take a glimpse of what my life was like, it would be Adam.

This book is indeed fictitious, but like all of my Fiction, it runs a tight parallel to my own life.

Like Dad, Adam's always had that entrepreneurial spirit. I understand him more than he would ever think.

Son, I dedicate this book to you. I love you, and God bless you.

Dad

Table of Contents

CHAPTER 1

A Perfect Picture

It's a hot summer afternoon in The Bronx, and 1983 is nurturing the birth of its youngest child... Hip Hop. With Boom Box's blaring on every street corner, one bigger than the next and as cool teens bop through the hood lugging their monster radios on their shoulders, they're greeted by friends and encouraged to chill, so long as the batteries remain fresh.

Regardless of the stifling 90 degree weather, teens still stepped out with the freshest gear.

Guys and girls shared similar fashions of colored Lee jeans and Addias with the fat laces.

Most of the black kids on my block still sported short Afros, or even Jheri Curls.

Puerto Rican hairstyles came in a wide array of selections. The girls kept them teased high, and the guys either had Afros or tight Cesar's. Oh, and for the white kids? Well, I don't really recall, as there weren't many who lived on my block on Plimpton Avenue in the Bronx.

Rap music was everywhere, a passing fad many thought.

King Tim The 3rd, and The Sugar Hill Gang introduced many of us to the sound, but it was the acts being cranked out through Def Jam Records that were setting trends, and little did we know, making History.

Kurtis Blow, Run D MC, and LL Cool J became bigger than the Beatles, and The Beastie Boys gave the White Kids, rappers to call their own.

CHAPTER 2

Hood Star

From the moment I learned how to write, I was writing poems, songs and short stories, but I wouldn't share with anyone because I thought they were corny, which is why when Rap became popular, it wasn't long before I filled several notebooks with lyrics, and shared freely with anyone who would give me a couple of minutes. It got to the point that whenever friends and family saw me, they would ask if I'd written anything new. Back in those days the lyrics were clean enough for even Grandma to enjoy, and that she did.

My voice was quite different than what people were use to hearing on the radio, but it made it interesting, and they enjoyed listening to me, not to mention my rhymes were pretty good.

Where most rapped about themselves, I on the other hand had stories to tell. From Cavemen, to Spacemen, and everything in between. I loved playing the game where someone would say a word and I'd immediately bust out into an entire Rap based on that word. Mailbox! Lamppost! Telephone! I once even Rapped about the only Jewish family in the neighborhood, when they were spotted walking down the block.

I rapped about the Cat Woman who seemed to spend all of her money feeding the neighborhood strays. Our drunk mailman, and of course the old lady who always yelled at us through her dirty screened window.

I had become the Star of my neighborhood, and when we didn't have any music, my boy Edwin, who was nice on the drums would simulate a cool kick and snare beat straight off the fender of an old park car, whiles others joined in completing our Ghetto Drum Orchestra.

Everyone would watch as I bobbed my head, waiting for that right moment to jump in, and when I did, I always began with the line; *Yes Yes Y'all - Yes Yes Y'all - a To The Beat Y'all - a To The Beat Y'all!* And at that moment everyone would smile because they knew… this was it!

Straight off the top of my head I would rap about anything that was immediately in front of me, including my boys. They loved when I did that, made them feel special. Every so often I'd say something that would cause oohs and aahs, and though I tried my best not to diss anyone, sometimes I just couldn't help it 'cause the shit was funny.

It would be dark out and mostly everyone was already home from work. Kids would settle at their windows for the evening's entertainment, and sometimes their mother's would join them. As   for the fathers, well there weren't many where I came from, and the few that did exist were either drunk or asleep by that time. Our performance usually ended when the owner of that particular car yelled from his window threatening to call the cops.

Why I didn't already have a record deal baffled most who heard me. Little did anyone know, I'd been going to auditions now for quite some time. Though I knew how much friends and family enjoyed my raps, they were just that... friends and family! But the many auditions I'd gone to sort of instilled in me, that I might be nothing more than a Hood Star.

CHAPTER 3

The Village Voice

Every Wednesday morning I'd catch the train to Manhattan. Days that the station was obviously being watched by police I'd pay the fare, but most of the time, I'd sneak through. Of course there was no Library like The New York Public Library. There I would grab one of the free copies of The Village Voice. I loved that paper, and would simply flip through the pages of weird stories and articles. Advertisements for everything Gay, as well as 900 numbers that would charge your phone bill $20.00 for 60 seconds of moans and groans. I wouldn't dare call it from my phone because my Grandmother would've found out. She inspected every bill and receipt, literally with a magnifying glass. There was no getting over on her, she was sharp. I did sneak a call once from a friend's house, just out of curiosity. Man, did he get in trouble.

My anticipated reason for grabbing a copy of The Village Voice every week was for the classifieds. You see, if you were a college graduate seeking a career in Engineering, Computers, or with some major corporation, then the New

York Times was where you looked, and if you wanted a regular job like cleaning toilets, or selling Vacuum Cleaners, The Daily News and The Post were your papers. But if you were like me, and sought an adventure, the ultimate dream job of working at a Night Club, Recording Studio, in Theater or Film, then The Village Voice was where it was at!

I was open to anything along those lines. I even applied as a Janitor at a local Adult movie theater. I lied about my age, and was surprised when I was hired. I looked at it as just another entry into the world of entertainment, but when that little old lady handed me a rag and a scraper, and then warned me not to touch *anything* with my bare hands, I realized why they were so desperate for help. I was the fuck outta of there! Then there was the Talent section of the classifieds. Individuals and companies looking for musicians, singers, dancers, comedians, and last but certainly not least... Rappers! Just looking at those ads put butterflies in my stomach. I would stare at it and read the ads over and over, the phone number I would memorize for no reason at all. I remember one in particular, it read: Rapper Wanted by Production Company with Major Label connections. Call for appointment.

As I sat there flipping through the paper, I couldn't help but notice the new girl working behind the counter. I'd never seen her before, 'cause if I had, I'd definitely remember *her*. She had long black hair pulled into a tight ponytail. Her light brown skin had a sort of gold hue to it, which made her light eyes glisten, and her lips were so perfect I feigned for a taste.

The high counter hid her body from where I sat, but any

girl that pretty had to have a body just as fine.

I turned back to the paper and tried to find where I had left off, then placed my pencil on it and walked over to her. I caught her just as she turned around, in perfect view of the body that I had anticipated... Damn, I was right!

She wore a tight pair of red Lee jeans that she could've modeled better than anyone. She turned and was surprised to see me standing there, noticing I was staring, she smiled a set of perfect teeth.

"Can I help you?" She asked in a soft and sensual tone. At least five corny pickup lines immediately came to mind, but thank God I didn't use any of them.

"Do you have a pencil I could borrow?" Was the only thing I could think of, "What's wrong with the one you have?" She asked, gesturing to where I was sitting.

"Oh, the point broke." I lied. Not a very good one at that. The girl looked at me, and I could tell, I was losing points quickly.

"Well, bring it here." She exhaled. "I'll sharpen it for you."

I took a couple of steps backwards and then turned and walked over to the table and grabbed the pencil. She was watching closely, so I didn't get a chance to break the point, so I just I handed it to her along with a smile.

The girl held it up and we both looked at the point. She smiled and shook her head before heading over to the sharpener. I noticed her glance over at the prudish looking woman at the other end of the counter, who was obviously head bitch.

"How's this?" She asked as she handed me back my pencil.

"Best point I ever seen..." I replied, then noticed her name tag. "...Charlotte." Charlotte shot back a smile, before turning back to what she was doing before I interrupted.

I sat back down to continue reading, but my mind just wasn't there. I looked again toward the counter and caught Charlotte staring in my direction, but then quickly turned away.

I finally came across an interesting ad, grabbed my things and left the Library. Just before exiting I turned for one last look at Charlotte. But she was gone.

From a phone booth just outside the Library, I called the number on the ad and spoke to a guy named James. We set up an appointment for the next day around 7pm. He would've done it early but said he would be busy in the studio most of the day. He sounded legit, and I couldn't wait.

I got to the location pretty early. It was a luxury building on 72nd Street in Manhattan. I still had over an hour, didn't want to get their too late, nor too early. I decided to take a walk. This was a part of the city I had never been to. The Village, Theater District, and Harlem were my regular stops, but this area was more residential. Residential for the wealthy that is, and I didn't know anyone wealthy. I felt strange walking around there. Half of me felt out of place, but the other half felt at home. Doormen from other buildings stood outside smoking cigarettes. They were the only ones who nodded when I passed. Of course they did, they weren't from around here either.

I didn't grow up riding in cars. Trains and buses were my only means of travel, when I could afford it of course. Walking however was it. I would zone out and day dream as I walked. I could walk for hours, no wonder I was always so skinny.

I suddenly snapped out of it when I realize the neighborhood had changed considerably. I looked up at the street sign that read 43rd Street. I couldn't believe I had walked over thirty blocks.

"Excuse me sir, can you tell me the time?" I asked a man in a business suite walking pass. "6:40" He cautiously replied, as that line is one used often by muggers.

"Oh shit!' I blurted out, before taking off running. I couldn't believe what I had done. Excitement had gotten me there early, and now I had twenty minutes to get back. What was I thinking? How could I be so dumb?" I ran as fast I could, slowing down as I crossed each of the streets. 44th, 45th… Taxi cabs hitting their breaks as I jumped out in front of them. Entering the 60's I noticed people stopping and staring at me, as if memorizing my description for when the cops start asking questions. But there wouldn't be any cops, because I wasn't doing anything but trying to get to this audition on time. 63rd, 64th. Good thing I was thin and walked a lot, a fat kid would've given up already. 71st, 72nd… I made it!

I located the apartment number on the directory and pressed the button. A few seconds later, a voice crackled from the intercom.

"Who is it?" He asked. "Reynaldo Rosario."

"How can I help you?" I looked around, to see if anyone was listening. "I'm here for the audition."

A long silence took over, and my enthusiasm was quickly deflating, I didn't know the time, but I knew I was late... I already fucked up. I didn't know whether to press the button again, or go home. But with three minutes already passing, I knew it was over, and I had no one to blame but myself.

With my head down, I turned and walked off, but about twenty feet out, I heard a buzzing sound and quickly turned toward the door. They're buzzing me in! I dashed toward the door, hoping that I could catch it on time, but it seemed as if I was running in slowly motion. It felt as though the buzz was about to stop ... But it didn't, and I got to the door, I pushed it with all I had, sending it slamming against the back wall with a loud echoey bang. It was the only building on the block without a doorman, but with the lobby as small as it was, I could see why.

From my reflection in the elevator's brass door as I straightened my light blue Kango, wondering whether or not this elevator ride would be the ride that finally changes my life. I fantasized about the day I would come home with some great news for Grams. She always believed in me and I didn't want to let her down.

The Buzzer rang again, snapping me out of my trance. I turned and looked at the door, and then realized that I had never pressed for the elevator. They were probably wondering where I was.

I pressed the button, and immediately the door slid open,

as it was sitting in the lobby all along. I stepped in and pressed the 6th floor.

Stepping out of the elevator I immediately I spotted a sign that said Front Line Productions, an arrow pointed to the left. As I got closer to the door, the sound of beats became clearer, and though they were a bit corny, they were no doubt beats, and that alone excited the hell out of me. I was about to ring the doorbell, when a woman suddenly opened. With a finger against her lips, she quietly waved me in and guided me to a seat inside a small reception area.

The walls were decorated with gold and platinum plaques, none of which I recognized any of the artists. It seemed as if all of their success stemmed from Rock music, but I could understand their sudden interest in Rap, as it was blowing up.

My heart jumped when out of nowhere I heard someone begin to rap over the beats that had been playing since I arrived. I listened intently, and as excited as I was, I still couldn't get past the fact that the beat, and the rap were both whack! The kid rapping had a pretty good voice, but nothing special. I didn't want to come across as cocky, so unless asked I would definitely keep my opinions to myself. I was just happy to be here.

After the song, I listened as others applauded and complimented the Rapper's performance. Man, if they liked *him*, this is gonna be a done deal! I took in everything they said. How much they loved him, his rap, his look. They kept referring him to the next LL Cool J. And made plans to meet up again.

The group closed with a scheduled meeting in a couple of days. I could hear everyone coming my way, and I prepared myself to give off a good first impression, even though I had no idea what that might be.

Leading the pack was a tall blond guy. He looked more like a Super Model than an executive. His suntan fresh, and he had the bluest eyes I had ever seen. His clothes looked as if they were made especially for him, fitting perfectly. He was talking to the rapper kid who walked beside him, nodding at everything he was saying. He wore a Kango like mine, except his was black. He also wore a pair Cazel's, something I always wanted but could never afford. The kid looked toward me as he passed, giving me a serious nod. He knew damn well that I came to bump him from the deal they might be considering.

"What do you call yourself again?" Asked the female who walked just behind them. The Rapper, still looking at me suddenly smiled and replied.

"Nemesis."

Everyone froze for a second, I can see Blue Eyes staring into the air, thinking. He then looked back at the Rapper and said,

"I like that."

The female partner, not making a move until her blond boss did, followed with a smile. "Sounds black" The boss added. "*Real* black!"

"Yes, it does." The woman agreed with a smile. The assistant, a chubby gay kid with a clipboard followed along.

After letting Nemesis out, the producers turned to me.

"Hey, how's it going. I'm James." Said Blue Eyes. "Reynaldo" I replied taking his hand into mine.

"Reynaldo? Hmm." James repeated, sort staring into the air.

"But you can call me Rey." I said hoping it came across a bit cooler.

"Okay… Rey" He said, unimpressed. "This here is my Co-Producer, Rebecca, and our Assistant, Michael." We took a moment and greeted one another. I couldn't help but notice Michael wipe his hand on his pants after shaking mine.

"So, how can we help you, Rey?" James asked. I found it to be a strange question seeing that they were auditioning, but I went along with it.

"Well, as I had mention over the phone, I saw your ad, looking for a rapper." James and Rebecca looked at one another, and then back at me.

"…And?" Asked James.

"Well." I began, thrown off by the odd question. "I'm a Rapper, and I'd like to audition."

The entire room went silent. James looked at me, then again at Rebecca. Then they both looked over at Michael who wasn't trying to look at anyone. Finally, in one loud and sudden burst, James started to laugh. I looked at him, trying to key into the joke, when Rebecca followed.

I glanced over to Michael who was trying to ignore what was happening. Instead he stayed focused on his clipboard and pretended to write.

I waited there; expressionless until James started to simmer down a bit as did Rebecca.

James pulled out his handkerchief and wiped his eyes, then folded the hanky and placed it back into his pocket, before turning back to me and laughing some more.

I was getting annoyed, but kept my cool.

"Rey, I'm really sorry, dude." James said, wiping his eyes again." But you said you're a Rapper?" I nodded, and watched James place his hand over his mouth.

"I go by the name, El Rey."

"El Rey?" Like the kid on the Jetsons?"

"No sir, that would be Elroy." Michael corrected. James didn't look as if he liked that. "It means, King." Rey added.

"Actually, it means *The* King!" Michael again corrected.

"El Rey? Hmm." James replied circling me as he stroked his chin. Could he have made me anymore uncomfortable?

James looked to Rebecca for some sort of response, and got it in the form of pity. She raised her eyebrows and held them there until James shrugged his shoulders, then they both then looked back at me. You can tell these two had been working together for quite some time, as they seemed to have the ability to communicate without actually saying a word.

"Okay." Rebecca said looking at her watch. "Let's hear what you got." She flashed the phoniest smile I had ever seen before waving us to follow her to the back.

You can tell this is where they held all their auditions, including the one they just had with that guy, Nemesis. I've been to quite a few of these auditions, but I must admit, this one was impressive. It was much larger and much more professional compared to the others. Photos with various celebrities shared the walls with Gold and Platinum plaques.

Rebecca pointed to an X that was painted into the floor, from which I would stand, as she and James sat behind a long white table, making it seem more like a judging contest than an audition.

"Want me to take your knapsack?" Michael asked. "It's alright. I got it," was my reply.

"You can give Michael your music!" Rebecca said. Catching me totally She caught me off guard. My face told them immediately that I didn't have music. They looked at each other then back at me.

I placed my bag on the floor, and unzipped it. I began pulling out notebooks, loose pages, pens and pencils, magazines, and folded Village Voice pages.

"You got everything in there, huh?" Rebecca asked.

"This bag has my entire career in it." I said, I unfolding sheets of loose-leaf paper to see what was written on them.

"You wouldn't happen to have a sandwich in there would you?" James asked jokingly. I stopped and stared up at him. I caught Rebecca's knee hit his from under the table, which immediately shut him up, which is when I stuck my hand into my knapsack and pulled out one of Gram's Peanut butter and jelly sandwiches.

I found what I was looking for and handed it to Michael who walked it over to the table. "Sorry, I only have that one copy." I told them. But you can look at it together.

Rebecca took the sheet of paper where I scribbled the lyrics to Yes Yes Y'all, and held it between her and James.

Michael then went over to a camcorder that was already mounted on a tripod and pointed it toward me. Rebecca saw my face and explained.

"I hope you don't mind. We video tape everyone so that we don't forget who's who."

I thought about it for a second because that seemed kind of weird, but then I nodded okay. Rebecca looked at Michael, and signaled him to begin.

"Rolling!" He called out. I looked at the camera and stared at the little red blinking light.

"You can look at me, Rey" Rebecca said. "And please, relax." I took a deep breath and then exhaled, before nodding that I was read.

"Okay, Rey, please state your name, address and phone number into the camera." Though I messed up a few times, I finally got it right. Rebecca again looked at her watch.

My hands were a sweaty mess and teeth chattered behind my lips. My legs felt as if they were about to give, and I was terrified that the moment I started rapping, nothing would come out.

"Whenever you're ready," Rebecca repeated. I've done many auditions in the past, but for some reason, this time I was really nervous. All I could figure is that it had to do with the camera. I took a deep breath and was about to begin when…

"Stop!" Michael yelled out. We all looked his way.

"Sorry. Tape ran out." He said to his bosses. They both looked annoyed, and stopped him before he started loading another.

"Forget the damn tape." James said, "Let's just continue"

Rebecca looked at him in disagreement. But James just waved her off as if he just wanted to get it over with. But now knowing that there wouldn't be any camera, I was put immediately at ease. So I smiled at my tiny white audience... and began!

CHAPTER 4

From The Top

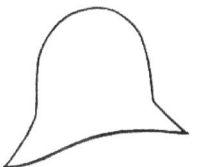

"This song is called Yes Yes Y'all" I said, as if anyone really cared. Then I began.

My first note was loud and awkward, and seemed to have startled Rebecca. Two lines in, the worst of the worst happened. Every performer's worst nightmare... I went blank!

Michael looked toward the floor. James yawned, but Rebecca sat back and smiled.

"It's okay Rey. Look, we're just three white people from Long Island. We don't know anything, so teach us". Rebecca had a knack for this job. She was able to place me in a comfortable zone. Rebecca then got up and dimmed the lights. I looked around, realizing just how cool this place really was. I hadn't noticed the blue lights inside the wall unit, nor the huge fish tank to the side of me. Several paintings on another wall seemed to glow in the dark. The vibe that was suddenly created did something to me.

"Now go 'head Rey!" Rebecca said, with a smile of

enthusiasm I didn't find in the other two.

I closed my eyes, placed a smooth beat in my head, and focused, trying desperately to block out the six eyes that were burning a hole right through me. I began tapping on my thigh, and bobbing my head. It felt like thirty piece orchestra suddenly possessed me, and upon the roll that my imagination finally drummed up … I began!

Half way through my song, which of course was much longer than it should've been, the lights turned on, and when I looked, it was James.

"What are you doing?" Rebecca asked him.

James reached into a crate on the shelf below the stereo and pulled out a cassette tape and placed it into the deck.

"Come on, James." Rebecca pleaded, but James ignored her, and pressed Play.

A beat suddenly kicked in, and James stood there bopping. He looked over at me and said, "Try it again, Rey.

"Try what?" I asked.

"Your Rap, from the top." I looked at Rebecca, and she nodded. I looked back at James, who gestured to me to listen to the music. I listened intently to the beat, trying to feel it out and find a place for my lyrics. When it finally felt right, well, sort of, I jumped in. Even Michael looked up from his notes and started paying attention. Rebecca looked at James, who gave her a huge smile as he swayed his body to the beat. The reaction I was getting was what I was hoping for. It was as if I was back on the block rapping for my boys.

I started to move with the beat, changing the pitch of my

voice just as I had written it. I had them. I could feel it.

My song ended with a repetitive hook, and James rolled his finger for me to continue repeating it as he walked over to the box and began fading out the music. I followed, fading my voice along with it, just as a record would.

When it was over they applauded so loud that I worried the neighbors might soon start banging on the walls. They all came up and congratulated me with handshakes, high fives and pats on the shoulder. I was getting choked up, and my eyes began to water. I couldn't believe what was happening.

"Man, that was incredible, Rey!" James said. "Thank you," I replied. "Thank you so much."

"Look, let me not pull any punches here and let you know we absolutely love it. "Thanks, man." I replied, trying to be as humble as I can.

"Do you, have more songs?" Rebecca asked.

"Songs?"

Rebecca and James both nodded..

"I have tons, at least two hundred. They looked at one another and smiled as if they hit the jackpot.

"Look, Rey, it's getting late. Let's meet back here on Friday, same time. We're going to go over the details, put together a contract, and make you a mother fucking offer.

"An offer?" I asked, in total disbelief.

"No, not an offer… A Mother Fucking offer!" He corrected. And we all started laughing.

This was crazy. I couldn't believe what I was happening.

How could it have been this easy? We shook hands as they escorted me to the door, just as they had done with Nemesis, a little earlier, except they didn't seem as excited with him than how they were with me.

Stepping out of the building, I was on cloud nine. The world was great, everything and everyone was beautiful. I could've hopped on the train, but I just had to walk, think, praise. I couldn't believe it. It was like a dream, or better yet, a dream come true! My eyes were flooded, but I really didn't care. All I kept saying to myself was… Thank you God! Thank you thank you thank you!

CHAPTER 5

My Queen

I couldn't believe that I walked all the way home from Manhattan. I was just way too excited to have to deal with the constraints of a subway car. The only bad thing about it was that it was now 1:30am.

"Where the hell were you?" Grams yelled. "What are you still doing up?" I replied

"You said you'd be gone for just a couple of hours. What are you up to? She yelled as she walked up to me staring me straight in the eyes.

Are you smoking pot? She asked, and though there were many more drugs in our hood worse than pot, that was the only one she knew about. Not to mention, nobody used the word pot anymore.

"Come on Grams, you know I don't mess with that stuff." I walked over to the sink and let the cold water run for a few seconds before filling my glass.

"You said you had a job interview. I was already concerned that it was so late what kind of job interviews at

Seven O'clock, except drug dealers.

"Grandma, please, you need to chill out." I took my glass of water and sat down at the kitchen table. Grandma walked up to me and slapped the glass off the table. It hit our wooded floor and shattered.

"What's wrong with you?" I yelled back, and immediately Grams started crying. I already felt bad that I had to lie to her about going on the audition, but we were so backed up on bills that that would've been the last thing she would've wanted to hear. I stood up and took her in my arms. She continued crying into my chest, before wrapping her arms around me as well.

"Papito, I'm old now, I'm not gonna be around too much longer."

"Stop talking like that." I told her. Grandma stepped back and looked me in the eyes. "Look at me!" I did as she asked, and she was right, she was getting old, but I remained in denial.

"It's all in your mind." I said waving her off.

"Yeah my mind, my back, my legs." You can try and pretend that it isn't happening, but it is, and my biggest fear is leaving you, alone and unprepared to take care of yourself," and though what she was saying was indeed humiliating, it was also a fact.

At 18 years old I've yet to work a regular job. I've been a dream chaser for as long as I could remember. Fame and fortune was all I thought about. The job hunts I went for were jobs I really had no business trying for. Like Studio Engineer,

A&R, Club Promoter, Booking Agent, Record Distributor. It was like my eyes could never see ads that were hiring Maintenance Men, Deli Clerks, or Factory Workers. Careers such as The Fire Department, Police, or Sanitation never appealed to me, simply because they seemed boring as hell.

Well, now was a better time than any to break it to my Grandmother. To tell her what I've been up to all this time, when she thought that I was out looking for a job, because now I finally made it. Hard times would be over shortly, and she could stop worrying about leaving her Grandson alone in this cold cruel world when she's gone.

"Grandma, sit down, I wanna tell you something." "Oh God, please, you're scaring me."

"There's nothing to be scared of, I'm okay. In fact, we're okay. "What are you talking about?"

"Grandma, you know how much I love you. I mean, you're my Queen, and whatever I do it's with thoughts of you."

"You didn't rob a bank did you?"

"No. Now stop it. Let me finish. You know how much I love music." Grams nodded. "It's all I ever dreamt of doing."

"Are you talking about the poems you sing?" "Yeah, Grandma. But they're called Raps."

"Yes, those."

"You see. I haven't been exactly straight with you."

"What do you mean?" She asked.

"I mean, I've been going on auditions."

"Auditions?"

"You see Rap is becoming really big these days, and everybody's looking for that next big star. Well, I feel that I can be that star. But unless I go out and look for that opportunity, it was never going to find me."

"Reynaldo, please, speak English."

"I haven't been looking for work!"

"You haven't?"

"No. I've been going on auditions, to be a Rapper."

"You mean the money that I've been scraping up for you to take the train to find a…"

"Exactly," I interrupted. "I've been going on auditions."

Grandma remained silent, staring down at the floor. I was waiting for her to jump up and slap the shit out of me, but she never did.

"Every day I went out there, and had to come back and tell you these stories…"

"You mean lies?" She corrected. I nodded.

"It killed me when I use to watch you kneeling inside your closet, trying to find enough pennies to buy me two subway tokens, and then go and make me a sandwich to take with me. I even lifted the couch so you can look under because you remember seeing a dime roll under it a while back. I hear you always negotiating with the electric company to keep the lights on, because the five dollars you told them you were short were the five dollars you held for me so I can go into the city every day to look for work."

I'm the reason your hands hurt Grandma. I'm why your back and legs hurt. I'm even the reason why your heart hurts, and now after hearing about how much I lied to you, I'm sure it's hurting even more. I'm sorry.

Grandma took a minute for it to all sink in. Not once did she look at me. She stood up, her eyes still staring out at the floor as she walked toward me. It felt like it was a set up, and I better brace myself for I was sure I was about to get my ass kicked. She took my face into her hands, tiptoed and kissed me on the forehead.

"I know."

"You know?"

"Yes. I told you. I know everything."

"But… but how?"

"I followed you." "You followed me?"

Grams nodded her head, and smiled. "Oh so I guess you didn't trust me?"

"Nope… and I was right not to. You never told me the truth."

I looked at my grandmother and then dropped my head in shame. "And I'm proud of you." She said. I looked up at her.

"Proud?"

"Yeah, I wanted you to aspire to be more than a Maintenance man, or a Deli Clerk. I was sad when you were telling me the jobs you were going for. You are way too young to settle, Mijo. I'm not here to help you fill a job application. I'm here to help you fill a dream!"

I couldn't believe what I was hearing.

"Do you know how disappointing it was to hear that you applied for a job as a Deli Clerk and never got a call back?" I had to laugh, because she was right, and I never thought of that.

"I feel so stupid."

"You should... Ever since you were a little boy I've always supported anything you ever wanted to do."

"You did."

"You wanted to join the Boy Scouts. So I gathered the money I needed, and signed you up. You went your first day with everything, your uniform, hat, new shoes. Shit you were the best dressed Boy Scout on the Team."

"Troop," I corrected, but she didn't care.

"And then you quit a week later. I borrowed fifty dollars from the Loan Shark across the hall so you can have your uniform, and you quit before I was able to pay him back."

"I'm sorry, Grams."

"It's okay sweetie, the important thing is, you gave it a try. You didn't like it so you moved on. That's the way it should be. If you're not happy somewhere, you need to move on. Life is too damn short. It was just the other day that I was sixteen, and now I'm sixty."

"That wasn't just the other day, Grams." I replied with a sarcastic smile. "You know what I mean!"

"And you never brought it up."

"Nope, neither did I bring up the football team, the Soccer team, The Wrestling team. All required registration fees and uniforms. But that was okay with me. What would've been disappointing is if you never tried any of those things.

Now you want to be a singer!"

"Rapper."

"A Rapper. How wonderful is that! So where do I sign?"

My Queen, my beautiful Queen. God may have taken away my parents, but then replaced them with this Angel, and if I had to do it all over again, I swear... I wouldn't change a thing!

CHAPTER 6

White Candles

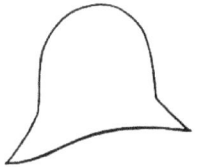

"That was good, Grams." I told her as I sat back and rubbed my belly. Grandma laughed as she took the plates from in front of me.

"Well I'm glad you liked it, Mijo, and I'm glad you had time to eat before you left.

"I'm so nervous, I didn't think I was gonna be able to eat."

"Well thank God for the nervousness, because thirds would've been out of the question."

Grandma and I laughed, then I watched as she walked over to her purse and pulled out ten dollars and gave it to me.

"What's this for?" I asked.

"Just in case you get hungry later."

"I really don't need it, Grams." I told her as I tried to give it back. But she refused. "It's only ten dollars, and this is an important night."

I looked at her and then stood up and placed the money

in my pocket. "If I don't use it, I'm giving it back."

"That's fine." She replied. I helped her clear the table, and then stood beside her as she began washing the dishes. I never really noticed her hands before, and I was a bit disturbed when I realized just how old and worn they looked, not to mention, the arthritis which had caused some deformity. Grams never complained, but at night, I could hear the moans that went on until her medication finally kicked in.

"So what do you think about moving?" I asked.

"Moving?"

"Yeah."

Grandma laughed, as if I had told her something so ridicules, so impossible.

"Where would I go, Reynaldo? This is my home."

"I'm talking about, somewhere nicer, maybe Long Island."

"Long Island?" She laughed. "Now what would I do in Long Island? You know you need a car out there. I wouldn't be able to just walk to the store.

"I wanna buy you a house."

"A house?" She asked, even more amused.

"Yes, a big one, white."

"White gets too dirty."

"Okay, brown!" Grandma laughed.

"With a fence that goes all the way around," my hand calling on her imagination.

"We'll have a great big oak tree in the backyard to give shade on those hot summers when you can sit out back, with a book and a tall glass of Ice Tea."

"It sounds wonderful. And I'm sure you're going to get it one day. But you need to get it for yourself, and your family."

"You *are* my family."

"One day you will have a wife, and kids, and a dog, and maybe a fish, who knows. That big tree out back would be a perfect place for a swing. You and your wife can sit back there, and watch the kids play with the dog, and live happily ever after… Now that's *my* dream, and all I want to see before I go."

Grandma had made that comment many times before. That she didn't want to leave this earth until she was sure that I could take care of myself. She wanted to see me with a wife because she didn't want to leave me alone. I understood that. I never commented, never wanted to hear it. But I understood it. Who knows, maybe subliminally I was afraid of being on my own for just that reason. That once Grandma saw that, she'd call it quits?

"I better start getting ready." I told her as I kissed her on the top of the head and headed for my bedroom to grab my things. On my way out I passed Grandma's room and watched as she lit a white candle next to a picture of me, and then stepped out and blessed me with a kiss. She congratulated me once again, and told me to be safe.

"I will Grams."

CHAPTER 7

The Look

The door opened and I was happily greeted by Rebecca who refused to shake my hand, but instead gave me a hug as if we had been friends for years.

"Come in." She so enthusiastically said as she stepped to the side. "Everyone's in the studio." I nodded, and continued toward the back.

"There he is!" Said James as he too came up and gave me the friendliest thug hug ever. Michael stood in the back, confirming his gayness with a shy smile and a three finger wave.

The only thing that threw me off a bit was when I saw that kid Nemesis. He was the only one not standing to greet me. He just sat there in a huge fluffy chair, staring. I couldn't tell whether his eyes were welcoming me, or dismissing me. Were we now label mates? Cause I just wanted to take his spot.

I did realize that he seemed to be wearing the same exact outfit he was wearing the day I saw him, while I wore all fresh gear, which included a Maroon Kangol pulled down over my Fro, a white hoodie, black Lee jeans and a pair of maroon suede Adidas.

"Rey, I'd like you to meet Nemesis." James said as he guided me toward him.

"He's signing on to the team today as well." I extended my hand, but Nemesis just nodded, and said, "Waddup!" James looked at Rebecca, and they both laughed, as if it was okay. Though to me, it was a diss. But that's cool too, now I won't feel bad when I bump his ass up outta here.

"Sit, sit down Rey." James said as he directed me into the metal folding chair that sat beside Nemesis. I couldn't stop wondering why they would want to sign two rappers. I was really hoping for some special attention, now it seems I'd have to share that with this Run DMC reject that sat beside me. I heard a click and a bright flash lit the room. I turned and saw Rebecca smiling at me as she held up a camera and snapped another.

"Just act like I'm not even here," she said as she snapped some more.

"I feel since we are about to make history, that we should document it." James added, and at that moment he pulled out two contracts, and placed them down on the table. The first thing I noticed was the heading where it said PRODUCTION AGREEMENT, and at that very moment, my sleeping butterflies awoke.

"Okay fellas... Let's do this!" James said as he handed us each a pen. Rebecca was snapping like crazy. I glanced over to

Nemesis who had already begun signing and initialing pages.

"Are we supposed to sign this *here*?" I asked. Nemesis stopped and looked at me, James and Rebecca at each other.

"Of course, Rey, it's a standard agreement." I looked at him, then over at Nemesis who shook his head and continued signing. I felt odd. I hadn't technically joined the company and I was already being a problem. I looked back down at the contract, then back at James and Rebecca.

"What's wrong, Rey?" James asked. I turned and watched Nemesis hold up his contract and smile for another photo.

"It's just that, for as long as I've been studying the business, all I ever hear people talk about is how not to just sign without a lawyer.

"Of course," James replied, "and I bet every one of those books that told you that were written by a lawyer." He was right, they were.

"You have a lawyer, Rey?" James asked. He had me there. Of course I didn't. Shit, I couldn't afford the ink on this contract, let alone a lawyer.

"No, I don't. I just didn't expect this all to happen so fast. I figured I'd have time to at least read it myself.

"It's fifteen pages, of industry mumble jumble, Rey." James said. "Are you really going to know what it all means?" Most of it wouldn't even apply unless you became a millionaire. By then you'd be able to afford an entire staff of lawyers to read over it. That's your worst case scenario, Rey. You become a millionaire." I looked at everyone, and then over at Nemesis who acted as though I was wasting his and everyone else's time.

"What is it you want to know, Rey?" Rebecca asked. "I can probably save you attorney fees, and save us all a lot of wasted time." I thought long and hard to come up with a few questions, and finally the obviously emerged.

"What kind of money am I looking to make?" They all looked at each other.

"We're a production company, Rey. We will pay to make a record, then shop the record to a few of our major company connections. If we sell the record they will give us an advance which we will use to recoup our expenses, and what's left over will be used for promotional services. Your money will be made from the record company in the form of royalties, mechanicals as well as performance." This shit was still mumble jumbo to me. I knew all the words, but applying them now to my own deal made my mind turn completely blank.

"And what is it exactly do you expect from me?" I asked.

"We expect you to write, Rey!" James answered. "Just write and write, and write." I looked at him. A bit confused.

"No, I mean, as an artist. What do you expect?" James turned and looked at Rebecca. They both looked as confused as I was. Nemesis sat back and pulled his Kangol over his eyes and laughed to himself.

"We don't expect anything from you as an artist." Rebecca replied. "Nemesis is the artist."

"I'm sorry?" I asked, shaking my head for clarity.

"We're signing you on as a writer." Rebecca said.

"A writer?"

"Of course, what did you think?" James replied. "Look, it's a super sweet job, Rey. You get your own office, a typewriter, not to mention all the coffee you can drink."

I sat there in silence, while my head spun. Trying to figure out where I misunderstood them.

"You okay?" Rebecca asked, but I didn't answer. I just stood up and rubbed my head.

"So you were never interested in me being an artist for you?"

"Well, writing *is* an art form..." Rebecca began, before I cut in.

"...You know what I mean!"

"Rey, Nemesis is a great rapper, and you're a great writer. Together you guys will rule the world. What we need from you are hit records. This is a dream job, Rey. Kids all over the world will be singing along to your lyrics. And the money? Oh my God! Writers make the most." James emphasized. I was silent. All I can think was that these people never had any intentions of signing me as an artist. They wanted me to *write* for the artist. And that artist was Nemesis, and frankly... he sucked.

"Look Rey." James continued. "Nemesis wanted to write his own raps, but we explained to him that we felt you were a much better writer and that his career would be much better off, and he was fine with that." I glanced over at Nemesis who was still tucked under his Kangol. "You guys are going to be a monster team."

"Hey, no offense," I said turning to Nemesis, "but I feel that I'm a better rapper than him too."

"Fuck you talkin' 'bout?" Nemesis snapped back as he pulled back his Kangol to reveal his ugly face and bloodshot eyes through the scratched up lenses of his Cazals.

"Okay, okay. You're right, Rey." James replied, holding his hand out to Nemesis to allow him to handle it. You *are* a better Rapper.

"What?" Nemesis responded.

"It's true." James continued. "Rey, you're a better Rapper, and a better writer, than Nemesis. I'm not gonna lie"

"Man, I'm getting the fuck out of here!" Nemesis huffed as he stood up. Rebecca rushed over to him and whispered something in his ear that made him sit back down.

"Rey, you have the sound, and you have the lyrics."

"So what's the problem? Why can't you sign me as a Rapper?"

"It's the look, Rey!" James said. I went silent and turned to the huge mirror on the wall trying to figure out what the fuck he was talking about."

"What look are you talking about?" Rebecca looked at everyone and then took a deep breath before finally letting it out.

"The *black* look!" She said, with a slight gesture toward Nemesis.

"You gotta be kidding me!" I replied.

"That's the look everyone's after these days." James

added "Nothing personal."

"He's got that look because he *is* black. Why didn't you just say that in your ad?"

"Well, legally, we can't." Rebecca answered. "But I agree, it would save a lot of time."

"Look," James began as he stepped forward, "now that we got it all out in the open.

Sign the contract, Rey, and let's get to work!"

"You know what, fuck you James!" I said, and then pointed at each of them. "Fuck you, you," and then at Nemesis, "and you too!" I took the contract and ripped it in half and placed it back on the table before storming out of the apartment. I can hear them calling me back, but I didn't care. I made my way to the stairway because I had no patience to wait for the elevator.

CHAPTER 8

The Subtle Buzz

I stood just outside the door of my Grandmother's apartment. I looked up at the apartment number 3A, reminiscing on the day she stuck them up there herself. Everyone else had the same plain white numbers. Gram's was gold and in a much fancier style. Those were some special times, and now the gold was more of a mustard color, and the corners were curled.

It was well after 1:00 am and I was hoping she wasn't awake, because I didn't feel like explaining what happened. I placed my key in the top lock, and slowly turned. I never realized how much noise that shit made. Then the second lock down by the knob, just as loud as the first. Other than the noise I was making, the rest of the building was dead silent, except for the subtle buzz of the fluorescent light fixture that hung over me.

I opened the door, and just as I stepped inside the lights flicked on, and Grandma jumped out from behind the wall.

"Surprise!" She yelled out, followed by a blow of one of

those annoying paper party horns. She scared the shit out of me. Little did she know, she nearly got knocked the fuck out.

Grandma stood there, laughing in one of those large pointed party hats. Still in the pink robe and fuzzy slippers I got her a few Christmas' back. The palms of her hands pointed at me, with her feet apart and knees bent, as if she was playing the offensive line. My eyes glanced over her head and there on the wall was a huge homemade banner that said congratulations!

"What are you doing?" I asked with a smile and a slight laugh.

"I was too excited to sleep." She said as she hugged me, then took me by the hand and led me over to the cake that she baked for me. Grandma was the worst at baking, and like most of her chocolate cakes, this one looked like a mound of chocolate horse shit, though it was the most beautiful mound of horse shit I've ever seen. All I could picture was Grams rushing to get all of this together before I got home, then sitting in the dark until she heard the door open. I looked back at the banner on the wall and asked…

"How'd you get that up there?"

"Oh, I just moved the couch, then slid the kitchen table over and climbed up. Smart huh?"

"No, it wasn't!"

"Aaah!" Was her reply as she waved me off.

"Go wash your hands and let's eat some cake while you tell me everything." I gave my Grandmother a kiss, then went into the bathroom to wash up. I stood there looking at myself in the mirror. My eyes kept filling with water and I just kept rinsing my face. What was I to do now? It isn't like she understands anything about the music business, and to her this would be just one more job that I didn't get.

"I told you to wash your hands, not take a shit!" Grandma yelled out as she knocked on the door. I opened up and stepped out. "I was washing my face." I replied as I followed her out into the kitchen.

"So, sit down and tell me everything."

Grams had already sliced me a piece of cake, and filled a glass with milk. I scooped a piece into my mouth, thankful for the icing that supplemented the extreme dryness. *Bless her heart for trying.* I chewed slowly, buying some time to help me come up with a story that would make her intended celebration not seem a waste, though the only thing I could come up with was yet, another lie!

"Everything went wonderful. These people really have it together."

"Are they, black or White?" I looked at Grams and shook my head. "They're white Grandma."

"Oh that's good!" She replied with a sigh of what sounded like relief. Grams was seriously old school Puerto Rican, so no sense asking what she meant by that.

"So, do you get paid on Fridays?" "Um, no Grams, it isn't like that." "No?"

"No, and here I held out the ten dollars she gave me earlier. "What's this for?"

"That's the ten you gave me this morning. I didn't need

it." "How did you get to the city?"

"I had enough to get there, and then I walked back."
"You walked?"

"Yeah, no biggie, I've done it before." Grandma stared at me. Or should I say… Through me! She wasn't dumb, and she knew me better than anyone.

"You hold on to that, Mijo." She said as she placed the bill on the table in front of me "That way you don't have to walk." I hated taking money from her, and now after lying I felt even worst. She knew something was wrong and didn't want to torture me anymore with questions, so she yawned, gave me a kiss and said goodnight. Just as she was about to go into her room, she turned and looked at me with a smile.

"Congratulations Mijo."

I sat there finishing off my cake, and thinking. Did I make the best decision? And I'm not talking 'bout the signing. I'm talking 'bout the lying.

CHAPTER 9

A Star is Born

Though I didn't feel like I was actually lying to my Grandmother, I was in fact not telling her the truth. The only way I thought I could fix this problem before it dominoes, was to head out and try and secure a deal so that way all I have to tell her is that I landed a better deal elsewhere. Bam! That would be it! And all of this deceit would be over. So every morning I was out by 8:00 a.m. and back in the city. On Wednesday mornings I would grab a copy of The Voice and write down all of the ads in a notebook, and then with a handful of quarters, I would call from a phone booth. It really sucked when an answering machine would answer, because it would charge my quarter, and I didn't have a number t leave them, so I would have to try them again later.

The one's I did manage to reach scheduled me in to audition. But after the ordeal at Front Line, I realized that this was my main problem. It seemed everyone was enthusiastic to meet with me when I called, but when they saw me, their disappointment was obvious. Like opening a huge Birthday gift and finding inside nothing more than a pair of socks.

I remember this happening even before Front Line, I just couldn't wrap my finger around it.

They said things like, I was incredible, my rapping was better than the best, and that I told *Real Stories.* But when it came to signing me, I wouldn't even get a call back. I guess everyone felt I didn't have the look.

Every few days it killed me to have to ask Grandma for carfare to get to and from the city. She was no fool though, she knew what was up, and just the fact that she didn't say anything, was torturous. She never again asked me about when I got paid or any particulars that only a person who "Really" worked at a label would know. She simply asked about my day.

How's the city? Is it as congested as they show on the News? How are the trains running? The way she handled this was ingenious, as it really put the hustle behind me.

Days that I couldn't land an audition, I went into office buildings and copied their directories into my notebook. I had my own personal listing of where every record, production, publishing, studio and management company was. Only the smaller companies I was able to visit, as the bigger ones had their lobbies secured with absolutely no access without an appointment.

But walking into even an independent company with nothing more than a sheet of paper with lyrics on it, I began to realize, was a pretty bad first impression.

It was becoming more and more evident that my only reason for not getting a deal as an artist is that every label seeking Rappers felt that unless you were black, your music would not be taken serious.

I even had one guy walk me to the door after I auditioned. He praised me even more than Front Line did, and told me he didn't think a Rapper at my level even existed, that my writing was genius. When we got to the door, I turned and looked at him and asked. "So what should I do?"

"Come back when you're black!"

I stood there, in awe as the old guy shut the door in my face, another confirmation that the only thing that stood in my way was my skin color. Puerto Ricans came in many shades, from milky white with blonde hair and blue eyes, to the blackest of black. I, unfortunately sat somewhere in the between, with a bit more emphasis on the white side, minus of course the blond hair and blue eyes. I somehow inherited these big ass curls that didn't allow me to do much more than just pick it out, which of course made them look even bigger, and always a bit lopsided.

It was Wednesday again, so I decided to stop into the Library to pick up my free copy of The Voice. I sat down and took my notebook out of my knapsack to take my notes, when my heart nearly burst out of my chest. The cover page read in huge letters, "A Star Is Born!" and below it, a full page head shot of none other than… Nemesis.

CHAPTER 10

In Every Aspect Of The Word

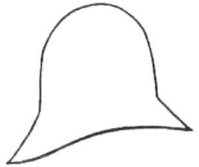

It felt as if I was suddenly hit in the stomach with a baseball bat. I couldn't breathe, and when I looked up from the paper, everything was spinning. Whispers of those around me echoed loudly, yet I was unable to make out what they were saying. I could feel eyes on me as I awkwardly stood up, and my noodled legs, gave me a hard time to walk, but I had to get out of there.

"Are you okay?" One of the Librarians asked as I made my way through the isle knocking over chairs and books. I couldn't answer her, my mouth seemed paralyzed, and MY face covered in pins and needles. I never realized how big this place was, as the Exit sign seemed a mile away. I needed to get air, cause for sure I was about to pass the fuck out.

I burst through the door, and stopped just outside to take a deep breath. I was so embarrassed that I wouldn't dare look back. Instead, I took off running.

A Star Is Born! That's all I kept hearing, and Nemesis's' life sized picture on the cover, was what I kept seeing. His old raggedy black Kangol exchanged for a brand new white one, and his black Cazal frames switched to gold.

"How could they?" I kept saying to myself. I couldn't understand it, that guy was wack in every aspect of the word. His sound was wack, his raps were wack, he even dressed wack! The only reason they chose him was because of his black skin, and that shit was wack too. I kept envisioning that day he walked past me at Frontline, turning and giving me that obnoxious look. This was *my* dream, and he just came by and stole it. I didn't know this guy, but God knows, I hated his fucking guts.

I must've run at least a mile, when I finally stopped abruptly and threw up in the garbage can at the corner. In my peripheral vision, I could see people stepping away from me, yet still watching. No offers to help, or even ask if I was okay. I guess I wasn't white enough either.

I wondered, did I make the right decision? Or did I mess up an opportunity of a lifetime?

Maybe writing for Nemesis was my way in and I was just too stupid and arrogant to see it. I should've listened to them. They obviously knew what they were doing. They took a bum and turned him into a Star... FUCK!

CHAPTER 11

My Bag

At the table I didn't say much, nor did I eat. I just sat there, my fork rearranging the food on my plate. Grandma could tell something was wrong. Anyone could for that matter. Grams had enough and placed her fork down.

"Talk to me, Reynaldo." She said. I looked up at her.

"About what?"

"About whatever it is that's bothering you."

"It' nothing."

"Please don't tell me it's nothing. I know you better than you know your own self."

Grandma was right, she did know me well, and yeah, probably better than I knew myself. But just talking would place more dominoes on the table, new lies that I would have to tell her in order to support the old ones I told her yesterday. She got up and walked over to me and placed the back of her hand on my forehead, then told me I was probably coming down with something. Yeah, it was bullshit, but it was her way of changing the conversation and rescuing me from having to lie some more.

"Go take your shower and go to bed. You'll probably feel better in the morning."

I looked at my Grandmother and wondered if they were all like this. Then got up and gave her a kiss.

My Showers were usually borderline cold, but tonight I needed a hot one. Everything in my body ached. It felt like I just climbed Mount Everest, with Grandma on my back, odd visual, but a perfect description. I placed my head under the shower and then started to cry. I tried my best to muffle the sound. I think I did pretty good, at least, I hope I did!

I wanted to pinpoint whether the pain I felt came from, anger, disappointment, jealousy, or humiliation. But I couldn't… I guess it was all of the above.

Staring up at the same cracked up ceiling I've been staring up at since I was little my eyes were stuck on open. I had not an ounce of sleepiness in me and my mind raced a mile a minute.

A dash of light from the streetlight just outside my window forever kept my room from ever being totally dark, comforting when I was a child, annoying as an adult. I remembered how as a child I would go to sleep with these vivid images of fame and fortune that would eventually continue in dreams as I dosed off. I tried to reapply that technique to help me get some sleep, except my thoughts were haunted by the images of Nemesis on the front of that paper.

What a horrible night it was. It seemed as if every time I dosed off and would begin to dream, Nemesis would show his ugly face. In one of my dreams, Grandma made Mofongo, a Spanish dish she knew I didn't like. And when asked why she'd made it, and she tells me, "Because it's Nemesis's' favorite. I woke up!

No sooner than I finally fell asleep, daylight woke me back up. I turned and looked at the clock. It was 8:30 am. I didn't want to get up for nothing. I laid on my back and stared up at the ceiling for a second before getting up. I knew I couldn't just bum around today, so I reached for my knapsack to see if I had enough money to get to the city, when suddenly my heart dropped.

"My bag!"

CHAPTER 12

Wack-Ass Shit

I jumped up and started searching my room when I suddenly stopped mid-action, and realized that I had left it at the Library.

"You want coffee?" Grandma asked as I rushed past her. "No thanks, I gotta go. Be back later!"

When I got to the station, I dashed upstairs and waited until I heard the train coming.

When it finally arrived I hoped turnstile.

As soon as I entered the Library, I rushed over to where I was sitting, and frantically started searching the area. I looked everywhere, even asked a few people if they would please stand so I could make sure they weren't sitting on my shit.

"Fuck!" I said, probably louder than I should've. I headed for the front desk and noticed one of the girls nudge another when she spotted me approaching.

"Excuse me." I began. "Is Charlotte in today?"

"No I'm sorry, she's off, can I help you with something?"

I hesitated for a moment but knew I needed to find my bag.

"I was in here yesterday, and left a bag over on that table. Did anyone turn it in?" "I could check the lost and found." The young woman replied.

"Would you please?" She nodded and went to the back.

"Are you feeling better?" The older Librarian asked. "You seemed a bit distraught yesterday."

"I'm fine now, thank you." I really didn't feel like even lying about it. Thank goodness the girl came right out, however all she had was a small pink book bag.

"This wouldn't be it, would it?" She asked. I shook my head, disappointed, and then grabbed a pencil and a piece of paper that was in the little basket on the desk, and wrote down my name and number.

I described my bag to them, and handed them the paper with my information.

I stepped outside the Library and stood at the curb. It was lunchtime in the city and the streets were packed with people rushing to and from work. I went to take a step into the street when a car zoomed by nearly hitting me.

"What the fuck!" I yelled and when I looked, I couldn't believe who it was. Nemesis, sat behind the wheel of a brand new Mercedes convertible. Two other guys were in the car with him. He looked at me for a second and when he finally recognized me he looked back at his guys.

"Yo, that's dude right there!"

The guys looked at me and sort of laughed to themselves.

"Roy, right?" He asked. He knew my name, and was just being an ass. "Rey," I corrected.

"That's right, Rey, So what's up? Last time I saw you, you ran up out of the office like a little bitch. So I assume you got a better deal?

"I got better options!"

"Options? That's what it's called these days?"

"Okay, so you got your little deal, but shouldn't you be in the studio somewhere, recording some of that wack-ass shit you call rap?"

"Wack-ass shit?"

"Of course, why else would they be begging for me to write for you? Your shit sucks!

"They ain't sign me for my writing, They signed me for my skills."

"They signed you for your black face, that's it!"

Nemesis' boys were about to get out the car. I stepped back ready to swing at the first mother fucker who stepped toward me, but Nemesis stopped them.

"Look homeboy, all bullshit aside." Nemesis began. "There's still an opportunity here for you, and it's important that you see it. Now, I'm not asking you to write *for* me… But what about writing… *with* me?

"You talking about, a collaboration?"

"Call it whatever the fuck you want, it's work! I can give you a few bucks on the side." No long term contracts, people don't even need to know you're involved. We can even start with some of your older shit that you don't really like. You know, put it to use. It's a win win situation."

I remained silent as Nemesis and his boys just sat there, waiting for me to respond.

"Nah, I'm good." I finally replied.

Nemesis looked around, then dropped his head and took a deep breath. He then placed his car back into drive and peeled off.

I crossed the street, once again, my head spinning. There went another decision that I had hoped I handled correctly. My biggest problem right now is money, and even though I keep getting offers to solve it, I keep turning it down.

Seeing Nemesis in my favorite Newspaper was bad enough. Seeing him in person, flaunting his new found fame and fortune, his new car, new clothes, and old friends who probably just crawled out of the wood work, was worst!

CHAPTER 13

Big Man

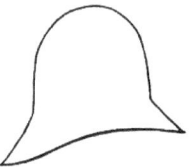

I spent a couple of weeks rewriting as many Raps as I could remember. Many I figured out, some I ended up making changes, but so many I knew were lost forever.

I never even copyrighted any of it, and I was terrified of somebody stealing my shit. Though I felt like staying in bed most days, I still forced myself out of the house.

I continued my regular routine of going to the Library every Wednesday to grab The Voice, and then I would go on auditions from there. The sickening part however was the many ads who now referenced Nemesis as to what they were looking for. NEMESIS-LIKE RAPPER SORT BY PRODUCTION COMPANY. I hated seeing those ads, and would usually skip over them, until it got to a point where *every* ad now referenced him.

I began going to auditions already expecting to be rejected. The only thing I hadn't done yet, but was about to, was tell them over the phone that I was Puerto Rican, and not black. *That* I thought would at least, save me the trip, not to mention the carfare.

Help Wanted signs that I never before noticed, began appearing everywhere. Were they always there, or were these signs from God telling me to give it up and find a normal job?

This gave me a bit of an idea. 48th Street and 8th Ave, is called Restaurant Row, and as its name depicts, it is an entire street lined with famous Restaurants, frequented I heard, by lots of industry folk. If I were to get a job at one of them, the chance of meeting someone who could help me was very likely. I decided that would be my move. I had no job experience, no resume, nothing, just my High School Diploma which if they needed it I'd bring by tomorrow. It was still pretty early so I took the walk, and the more I thought about it, the better an idea it seemed.

I imagined myself waiting on an executive from a major label. I would have on my best personality, and even give him a recommendation from the menu. I'd top off his drink a couple of times on the house, and when he's ready to go, I'd bust out with a short but ingenious farewell Rap. I've heard of many actors who had been discovered waiting on tables, and now I will be the first ever rapper to be discovered this way.

I got to the corner of 48th and 8th, and looked up toward 9th. Both sides of the street, lined with some of the finest restaurants on the East Coast. I started my way up, my eyes in full focus, but not once did I spot a Help Wanted sign.

I spotted this tall thin man coming my way. He seemed to be in a rush, and his uniform made it obvious that he work at one of the restaurants.

"Excuse me, sir." The man abruptly stopped and looked

at me. "Would you happen to know if any of these restaurants are hiring?"

"The only way of ever knowing is to walk in and just ask," was his heavily accented reply before turning and rushing off. I stood there, a bit overwhelmed by the task ahead. I walked back to the corner, took a deep breath and starting with the first restaurant on my right, I began.

Workers rushed back and forth as they prepared for the lunchtime rush. I stood there waiting for someone to greet me, but that never happened. I glanced over at one distinguished looking gentleman who wore a black suit and tie. He was standing behind a podium studying a menu. I walked up to him and stood there, waiting for him to be done with whatever it was he was doing, and when he was, and before I could say a word, he quickly turned and ran to the back yelling at cooks in the kitchen about something that he noticed on the menu.

I felt really awkward standing there. It was like they were hinting to me that they were too busy to even ask what I wanted. The gentleman in the suit stepped back over to the podium, this time with the Chef, yelling at him about the description of one of the meals. Man, did this seem like the wrong time to ask him anything, and before I got a chance to, the gentleman looked at me and in some strange foreign accent, rudely asked.

"What do you want?" Catching me off guard, I began to stutter as all of the chaos suddenly came to a halt, and everyone looked our way. After finally clearing the enormous knot that was lodged in my throat, I asked.

"I just wanted to know if you were hiring," And in a cold and uncalled for way, the gentleman yelled out a flat...

"No!" Before turning and proceeding to the kitchen as the rest of his staff followed with a bit more enthusiasm than before.

This went on at every restaurant I visited. Sometimes they wouldn't even open the door. They'd just wave me away through the glass, as if they knew why I was there. I made it to all of them, except one, but I was hesitant since lunch had already begun and customers were coming in and out. I turned around and started walking back to the avenue when after about twenty feet, I stopped. All I thought was what if this was the one that would hire me? After going to each and every restaurant, and experiencing rejections of every type, what harm could this last one possibly do? But if I didn't go, it would surely haunt me. This is where I would've been hired. This is where I would've waited on that one executive who saw something in me, the one who would slip me his business card along with a hundred dollar tip, the one who would sign me, and make me a star. The one that will help me bump Nemesis from his undeserved spot.

I turned around and headed back to the restaurant. It was packed, and every customer in there looked the part of *that* executive.

I opened the door and walked in. Another gentleman stood at a podium. At first he smiled at me, but after eyeing me up and down, he rolled his eyes and looked away. I walked up to him and just stood there until he noticed me.

"What is it you need young man?" He asked in a much

deeper and darker accent than the others.

"Sorry to bother you, but I was just wondering if you guys were looking for any help?" "Not today!" The man said then turned and began scolding one of the busboys. My eyes scoured the room as I made my way to the Exit. Opportunity seemed to flood this place, and I was saddened that I would not be a part of it.

"Hey boy," the man yelled out. I turned and spotted him waving me over.

"This here is Gustavo." He said gesturing to the man with the grumpy face standing beside him. "Whatever he needs, you do." I dared not ask any questions, instead I enthusiastically nodded and then followed Gustavo to the back where he handed me a white uniform, hat, and big rubber boots. He pointed to a locker for me to put my things then told me to meet him in the kitchen when I was done.

There I stood alone in a tiny dark locker room. The first thing I pulled out of my back pocket was the small spiral notebook where I had been rewriting my Raps. A bit hesitant to part with it, I knew I had to.

I placed it under my clothes where I felt it would be safe, and then finished putting on the uniform. I was hoping to be a waiter so that I would have the opportunity to mix and mingle with important customers, but by the look of my white uniform, it was obvious… I was being hired as a Chef! The only problem was… I couldn't cook!

I entered what seemed like the busiest place on earth, the kitchen of one of the world's most famous restaurants. It was long and narrow place with an ensemble of Chefs, Cooks, Waiters, and Busboys, all shuffling around like a professionally choreographed musical. An orchestra of commanding yells and kissing plates adding perfectly to its oddly syncopated background.

"Boy!" I heard someone call, and when I looked, it was Gustavo way at the other end, waving me to come over.

I felt like a contestant in a game of Frogger, as I tried to side step the rush and make my way along the kitchen.

As I approached, I noticed he was standing with another younger guy, this one dressed in the same Chef's uniform as I was, except he had on yellow rubber gloves and a scrub brush.

"You go with him, he show you what to do." Gustavo struggled to explain before waving me and the guy away as you would to an annoying fly. *He* didn't speak English at all. Either that or he was advised not to get friendly, because when I introduced myself, he seemed to have an attitude.

We walked up to a huge stainless steel sink, with hundreds of pots, pans dishes and utensils that apparently needed to be washed. He appointed me a spot alongside another young man who also minded his own business.

The young guy began demonstrating what I had to do, making it clear that I was in fact *not* being hired as the chef.

The three hours I spent washing pots, pans and dishes, felt like twelve. We were all given a break and I followed my team of dishwashers out to the back alley. Each and every one of them lit up cigarettes and began talking to one another. I couldn't figure out the language, let alone what they were saying, but what I noticed with all of them was, they all sounded angry, so I had no idea what they were talking about. I felt so weird and awkward, just standing there. Kind of made me wish I smoked cigarettes too.

I knew they were talking about me because whenever one would look my way, so would the others. I could just imagine what they might've been saying. I noticed one guy kept looking at his watch, good thing because I had no idea how long our break was. Another man came out into the back, I had never seen him before, but he was obviously a big shot. He was at least 6'5", and an easy 300 plus pounds. He wore a black double breasted suit that he could probably break out of like The Incredible Hulk. He walked up to one of the cooks and began yelling at him. Everyone started to back up, I followed.

Big Man was really scary, and his loud roar made him double in size. He turned and began yelling at everyone else. His tone seemed threatening. He then pointed back inside, making it clear in any language that break time was over.

I watched as each of the workers hurried back inside, Big Man slapping each of them in the back of the head as they entered.

I myself couldn't move, and when the last person went in, I stood there, Big Man standing by the door waiting for me, I assumed to slap my head also. I knew I had to go in, but my legs weren't cooperating. Maybe they knew something I didn't. After waving me over a few times, and me not moving, he decided to come to me, and the moment he stoop that first step toward me, I did the same, except my step was the fuck outta there!

CHAPTER 14

Walk of Shame

I swore that Big Man was chasing me, and when I got to the end of the alley, and turned around, I was relieved to see that he wasn't .

Everyone stared as I walked hurriedly down the street, but of course, look what I was wearing. This was so humiliating, walking through the city in this Dishwasher's getup, complete with the little white cap, and extra-large rubber boots. All that was missing was the yellow rubber gloves I left on the sink before I went on my break.

"Goddamnit!" I said out loud when I got to the station and realized that not only did I leave my money in my pants which was left in the locker, but also the notebook that I spent so much time rewriting my raps. I couldn't believe this shit happened again, and even contemplated going back. It wasn't so much the embarrassment of quitting the way I did, but rather running into Big Man. That dude was creepy.

At Grand Central Station there were lots of people, *and* lots of cops. This was definitely not the place to try and sneak in, but I had to get home. I thought about asking a cop to let me through, but if he said no, because they could be dicks like that, I'll be stuck, and they'd be watching me.

Trying to blend in with the crowd would be difficult, as not a set of eyes passed that didn't look my way. I walked over to the large subway map and pretended to reading it until I felt comfortable. I turned around and looked at the token clerk, I caught her looking back, 'cause she knew something was up. Finally she was distracted by a customer who was claiming she gave him the wrong change, and it was at that moment that I leap frogged over the turnstile and took off running toward the staircase that led down to the platform where I would catch my train.

It was just too much excitement for one day, I thought, as I watched the train pull into the station. I stepped in and immediately took a seat. I put my head back and closed my eyes to try and relax. I heard the doors shut and exhaled a sigh of relief. I heard some light laughter in the background and when I opened eyes, floating in front of my face was a police badge.

"Get up and turn around." said one of the two undercover cops that stood over me.

"Excuse me?" I tried.

"Don't waste our time, get the fuck up!" said the other cop, embarrassingly loud.

"You must have me confused with someone else." I tried again as they frisked, and then cuffed me behind my back.

"Well, as soon as we find someone else dressed like you,

we'll let you go."

The cops escorted me to the door where we stood while the train pulled into the station. I tried not to look around, but I could hear people making jokes and laughing.

I glanced up and noticed an advertisement that ironically said, *Jumping The turnstile is a crime. Pay your fare!*

The cop noticed the sign too, "Good advice, huh?" he said.

We stepped off the train and continued down the platform, I was so embarrassed. This uniform already drew a lot of attention, but it was these handcuffs that made it interesting. All I could do was look down. It seemed as though each person we passed was a comedian, as the cops tried to add their own corny twist to each joke. I pretended not to be paying attention, though I was only fooling myself.

Think that they were taking me to one of those little rooms where I would sit until they figured out what to do with me, instead, they took me up and over to the other side of the crowed station, where we would wait for the train to take us back.

My face felt as if it was burning red with embarrassment. This walk of shame could easily take the place of a jail sentence, and be more effective.

I entered the train to more stares and jokes, and though we were only going one stop, this ride seemed an eternity.

We entered a small room where I took a seat on an old wooden bench. There was already another undercover in the room. He seemed to be on a break, kicking back reading the

Newspaper. I had to laugh to myself when I spotted, Nemesis's' photo on the back of the cops paper, I swear he was laughing at me.

"Something funny?" the cop reading the paper asked. "It's just been one of those days." I replied shaking my head.

"So," began one of my arresting officers, "how long have you been jumping turnstiles?"

And though I've been jumping them for as long as I've been allowed to ride the trains, of course I wasn't telling *him* that.

"This is my first time, Officer."

"So what brought you over to the dark side?"

"Well, I just started working at this restaurant on 48th street. They had me washing dishes, as you could probably tell. Well, during the break, the boss came out back acting all crazy, and attacked one of the workers."

"So you ran off!" One of the officers said, cutting my story short, so I nodded.

"And left my things in the locker, including my wallet."

"What's your name?"

"Reynaldo."

"Reynaldo what?"

"Rosario."

"Where do you live, Reynaldo?"

"Bronx."

"Still with your parents?"

"My Grandmother, she raised me."

The two officers looked at each other, and the one who arrested me stood me up and removed my cuffs as the other ripped up the paperwork and dropped it into the trash can.

CHAPTER 15

Yo Soy Vieja

Now an even bigger task lies ahead, getting past my Grandmother without her noticing the outfit. I placed my ear to the door and could hear the television which meant she was in her room as we had no TV in the living room.

Gently, I unlocked the door and carefully opened it, timing the creaks so that they happened only during the speaking parts of her Novella. I made it in and didn't even close the door all the way to avoid the noise.

Gram's bedroom door was partially open and just as I was about to try and make it past, she stepped out.

Grams let out a loud yell that startled me more than *I* did her. She stared at me, trying to figure me out, and couldn't. But of course, what I told her I was doing for work, in no way coincided with the way I looked.

"What is this?" She asked as her eyes panned up from the oversized rubber boots, and though a thousand stories came to mind, I was done with all that, it was time to come clean. How could I keep lying to the only one in this world who has my back?

I walked over to the couch and was about to sit, when Grams stopped me, and instead slid over one of our wooden kitchen chairs.

"You smell horrible." She said waving off the lingering stench as she herself took a seat on the couch.

"Grams!" I began. She pried her eyes from my outfit and looked up,

"I'm not working at the record company." I just blurted out. She looked at me, but remained silent. I hated when she did that, and so prepared for her wrath. But this time it never came. In fact, all I got back was...

"I know," annd said like it was no big deal.

"You know?"

"Yo soy Vieja, no pendeja!" She said. And I should know this, because she's been telling me that my whole life.

"I'm sorry. I didn't want to let you down."

"You let me down by lying to me."

She was right, and I couldn't say anything so I just dropped my head.

"Since when have you ever felt like you couldn't talk to me?"

I shook my head and shrugged.

"So, what happened?" She asked. But just as I was about to speak, she stopped me, and made sure to emphasize..."The truth!"

I hid the truth for so long that I was having trouble finding it.

"They loved my Raps, Grams. But they said I didn't have the look."

"The look?"

"I'm not black."

"What?" She asked, her head snapping back. "Now that is the dumbest thing I ever heard in my life. Reynaldo, I lived my whole life with three strikes against me." Holding up the first finger she began to count them off. "I'm a woman. I'm Puerto Rican. And my skin is black!" In fact, I can even add a fourth strike if I want... Because I'm, *very* black!

She was so right, and made my problem seem like nothing more than some crybaby shit.

"And what about this?" She asked, pointing to my outfit.

"I took a job at a restaurant in hopes of meeting someone in the business. I didn't know I would be in the back washing dishes...

Grams started laughing hysterically, and why shouldn't she? That was some really silly shit! I joined in.

"Reynaldo, as long as I'm alive, I'll help you. But once I'm gone, Papi, you're on your own."

I smiled and got up, but when I went over to give Grams a kiss, she pulled back.

"Ay fo!" Go take a shower, and take all that shit you have on and put it outside in the garbage.

CHAPTER 16

Knocking Books

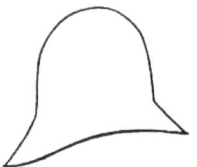

As I entered the New York City Library for my ritual Wednesday morning copy of The Village Voice, my eyes automatically turned toward the front desk in hopes of seeing Charlotte… And there she was! I know she saw me too, but she quickly dropped her head and continued doing what she was doing. I took it as though it was because her boss was standing beside her.

I went directly to the back and grabbed a copy of The Voice from the stack of freshly delivered papers. I took my regular seat and opened up my new notebook to a clean page.

I always enjoyed skimming the entire paper before heading over to the classifieds, but seeing Nemesis' mug on just about every other page, now made it painful.

His face made me cringe, and I felt the hype surrounding him was way too much. How many stories can you possibly read about this guy? His career had just begun. What the fuck could he be possibly telling them? I had no idea and no interest, and therefore flipped over the entire paper and started from the back.

It seemed like more ads seeking Rappers were beginning to appear, if only they'd stop using the phrase "Nemesis-Like Rapper." Where's the originality? It's like producers were scared to try something new, a light-skinned Puerto Rican Rapper for instance.

I looked back over at Charlotte and noticed that her boss had left, so I quickly snapped off the point of my pencil, and headed her way.

She played as if she didn't see me coming, so I just went along with it, and stood there until she looked up.

"Hi." She said with the most beautiful smile. Her eyes and teeth in perfect contrast with her golden skin, and a long straight ponytail pulled back tight.

"So, any luck finding your bag?"

"Nah" I replied.

"Well, next time maybe you should leave it where it belongs." I looked at her and tilted my head.

"Your back!"

We both laughed, but then Charlotte abruptly stopped when her boss rolled up behind me with her book cart.

"Is there a problem here?" She so obnoxiously asked, so I held up my pencil with the broken point.

"I'll take care of that." Charlotte said, snatching it from my hand.

I couldn't help but watch as her ass shook in those tight jeans, cranking the old fashioned pencil sharpener. Not until I felt the heat on the side of my face from the boss lady as she stood there just staring at me. I smiled… She didn't!

Once done Charlotte turned and headed my way. "They don't make'm like they used to." I said, trying to be cute.

"Or you just don't know your own strength." She replied, and she didn't even have to try to be cute… she was!

I inflated my chest a bit and thanked her as I took a couple of steps back, but just as I turned to head back to my table I accidentally ran directly into Boss Lady's book cart, knocking the whole thing over with me landing on top.

"For God's sake!" The Boss Lady cried out, watching me struggle to untangle myself from the mess. "Get up!" she yelled out, violating #1 of the library's top ten rules. Once on my feet, I attempted to pick up the shelf, but Boss Lady shoved me out the way.

"Leave it!" She demanded, then called Charlotte over to help. I felt horrible, and grabbed one more book before Boss Lady snatched it from my hand. I could've sworn that bitch's eyes turned red, and when I looked over toward Charlotte she gave me a subtle shake of the head, so I took the hint and left!

I stepped out of the Library and began walking down the steps when I noticed a huge crowd of people gathered below. This was Manhattan, and there was always something going on. As I descended upon the crowd, I couldn't believe what I was seeing. It was Nemesis once again, and this time he was standing there signing autographs. I quickly turned away and headed toward the subway.

How could this be a coincidence? Here's a guy who, just

the other day I was up against at an audition. He took my spot, invaded my favorite paper, and now I keep running into him. I fuckin' can't shake this dude. He's everywhere. In people's conversations, in ads, on magazine covers, and now I can't even walk anywhere without running into him. I couldn't help but think, Damn! Doesn't this guy have something to do, a studio session, a tour, something? It was starting to feel like someone was intentionally fucking with me.

CHAPTER 17

El Barrio

Dreaming is a great thing, but when you dream too much, it can be dangerous as I somehow daydreamed my way past the subway station, and ended up walking all the way over to101st and 5th. Aka Spanish Harlem, or to its residents... El Barrio!

I lost most of the day, so I decided to just catch the train and get home early so that I can start rewriting my Raps back into the new notebook before they are lost forever. As I was walking, for some reason I found myself thinking about one Rap in particular. Yes Yes Y'all. The song I performed at my last audition. I didn't realize what brought that particular song to mind until it smacked me across the face... Yes Yes Y'all had been echoing in the far distance throughout the neighborhood. I stopped in my tracks and scanned my soundings, trying to figure out where it was coming from, but couldn't pinpoint it exactly. I thought maybe I was just buggin', considering all the shit I'd been going through lately.

I even stopped to listen carefully, to make sure it wasn't

something that just sounded like mine, but no way, it was definitely mine. This one however wasn't being rapped, it was being sung, like a song, but from where, and by who?

People must've thought I was crazy as I hurried down the street, from 101st to 98th, my eyes locked on the top of the buildings that surrounded me. The piano that accompanied my song had a sort of strange Latin swing to it, and a male voice, thick and raspy sang my hook over and over, each time changing its rhythm slightly. It was obvious, he was trying to make it his own, and not only was he stealing my song, he was fuckin' ruining it. I couldn't figure out where this shit was coming from, and each time I thought I got it, it switched up on me, and would begin echoing in from another direction.

I tried asking people if they knew where the music might be coming from, but they quickly shook their heads and kept walking. I couldn't blame them. I looked like a damn nut. I hurried over to the next block and the music there was just as loud. It was the afternoon, and the streets were unusually calm.

My neck was aching and my eyes teary from looking up for such a long time. It was hot outside, so most of the windows on the tops floors were open.

I thought I had figured out from where the music might've been coming from and proceeded in that direction. I was crossing the street without looking, sending a couple of cars to a screeching halt, when suddenly... The music stopped!

I stood there like a fool. Completely still, hardly

breathing, waiting for the music to start up again so that I can continue my search, but it didn't.

"Get the fuck out of the street you asshole!" Was what snapped me out of my trance only to discover that I was standing right in the middle of an intersection.

I looked at the drivers and waved an apology as I made my way back to the sidewalk.

People were laughing; other cars being held up honked their horns with middle fingers up at me.

I walked around the same area for over an hour, hoping the music would start up again. But it was getting late, and I already wasted most of the day. I headed home, but I would in fact be coming back, and soon I will find the mother fucker who stole my shit. And when I do…

CHAPTER 18

Que Dios Te Bengida

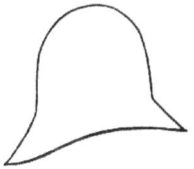

The knock on my bedroom door woke me, and I sat up a bit disoriented. I hadn't slept too well, I dreamt that Yes Yes Y'all had become this huge hit, but not with me Rapping, but instead it was Nemesis, and he wasn't Rapping it, he was singing it, just like the strange voice I heard yesterday. He was in his car, following me through the streets as I looked for the subway station, a flock of pretty girls followed behind him. I seemed to recognize every girl in the flock, two of them being Charlotte, and … My Grandmother!

"Reynaldo!" My Grams called out from behind the door. "Yeah?"

"Teléfono!" "Who is it?" "Un Donald?"

Donald? I didn't know any Donald.

"He said you called him yesterday." And then it clicked!

"Oh shit! Grams, tell him I'll be right there!" I got up and threw on a pair of shorts, then dashed into the living room, picking up the phone from the counter. Immediately I did what Grams always hated, I began to pace, stretching the cord to its limit, then back. That bugged the shit out of her, but she was gonna have to deal with it this time. She tried gesturing me to stop once, but realized that this must be important. She stayed there doing her fake ass reading, while she was really just listening in on my conversation.

"Hello?"

"Yes, is this Rey?"

"Yes it is."

"Hi Rey, this is Donald D with Funky Junky Productions!" He began, excited and enthusiastic. "You called about auditioning for a Rap project we are about to begin."

"Um… Yes, I did."

"Well, no sense in getting into it over the phone, besides, we're looking for a little more than just a good Rapper."

"What do you mean?" I asked.

"Well, it's gotta be the right look!" He replied. "But I rather not talk about it now, can you get in here sometime tomorrow. Let's say around noon?"

I agreed to meet with him, though his mention of *The Look* sort of deflated my enthusiasm a bit.

"So?" Grams asked.

"Just another audition, no big deal" I replied calm, and sort of disappointed.

"Just another audition? But this one called YOU!"

"They were just returning my call."

Grams got up from her seat and walked over to me.

"So, is it a Rap audition?" I nodded my head. "You don't seem too excited."

"He said he couldn't give me any info over the phone."

"I wonder why?"

"He said he rather see first if I had what they were looking for?"

"What do you think?"

"I think you might have a better chance of landing this than me." Grams knew exactly what I was saying.

Why don't they just say they want a black person?"

"Because that's discrimination, they could get in trouble."

"That's stupid." She replied. "Discrimination should be letting you waste your time and money, just to find out they don't want you because of your skin color!"

And her point was valid.

"Or why don't you just tell them before you go?"

"I thought about that, I just always feel like I'm losing the opportunity, as most people will turn me away without even hearing me."

"I understand Mijo, and this would be my advice. Don't walk in there thinking that they're going to turn you away, walk in there confident, like you're doing *them* a favor, and if they pass? Well, then that's their loss.

"But as soon as they see me, they seem so disappointed, and then they just pacify me. It's draining."

"I sat here and listened to your conversation." Grams

began. "The guy on the phone was loud and seemed very excited. But you? You talked as though you were already defeated. You can't do that, Mijo."

Wow, this old owl was indeed wise. I had no augment, she was right.

"What time do you have to be there?"

"Noon"

"So it's simple. You have two choices. Call him back and tell him what to expect when he sees you, or… "Just go down there and just get the fuckin' job!"

Grams wasn't just making a whole lot of sense, she was cursing, which meant, she was serious, laying it down the way it supposed to be. I guess when you get older, you don't want to waste time, so getting to the point is important. Sometimes I feel that she should've been a motivational speaker, 'cause so many times in my life, she's been my motivation.

"Now, go take shower, and wash off all that malo, get to bed early, and tomorrow, go get your shit!

And there she goes… cursing again!

I came out to a glass of orange juice and a Pop Tart she had prepared for me. I was never big on breakfast and even this was pushing it. Under my glass she placed a five dollar bill.

"I don't need this, Grams, I still have money."

"You're gonna get that job today and you might have to stay late, so at least if you get hungry…"

Grams was sure I was getting this gig, so much in fact, that I was beginning to feel it too. I took the money and stuffed it into my pocket, and then downed my juice. With my Pop Tart in a napkin, I gave her another kiss and hug and rushed out the door, and just as I was about to enter the staircase, she called out.

"Hey!"

I stopped and turned round as she stood there with her hands on her hips and a puzzled look.

"Oh, I'm sorry, Grams" I said with a smirk. "Bendicion!"

"Que dios te bendiga!"

CHAPTER 19

You're It. Mother Fuckin' It!

The door opened to some white girl on roller skates. She was about my age, wore two pigtails and a pair of tight yellow basketball shorts with the white stripe on the sides. She was cute.

"Welcome to the Funky Junky." She said with a big smile, gesturing for me to enter. I stepped inside and was in awe of what I saw. This place was huge, and the lights and bright colors gave it a sort of 70's feel. Huge beanbags in assorted colors were scattered about.

Teenagers and young adults scurried busily, some on foot, others on skates. "Come on." said the girl rolling up ahead of me.

Wasn't hard to tell that she was pretty new at skating, and the few times I swore she was gonna fall, I grabbed her. She laughed a bit embarrassed, but she was having fun. Pinball machines and other arcade games were scattered throughout the facility. The music that filled the air was like nothing I've ever heard before. Though the beats were typical rap beats, the music that layered on top was of another dimension.

We entered a room way in the back, this one way cooler than the others, but of course, it belonged to the Boss.

"Take a seat, Mr. D will be right with you." The girl said before skating off. I watched her bang her shoulder hard against the door frame, but I quickly looked away so as not to embarrass her any more than she had already been.

The only seats available were more Bean Bags. I went over to a purple one that seemed appropriate as it was the one closest to the desk.

Had I known how deep this thing went I probably would've chosen to stand, but it was too late, this thing literally consumed me. It was comfortable as hell, though I felt like a complete idiot sitting in it. I tried to sit up, but that was impossible. God, if I had to get up in a hurry, I'd be in big trouble. I tried to relax, my eyes exploring the office and the extraordinary artifact displayed throughout.

Donald D, read the sign on his desk, wondering what the D might actually stand for, and of course the only thing that came to mind was Duck. Wouldn't that be something?

I heard the door open, and tried turning to see who it was, but this bean bag made that impossible.

"Relax." Mr. D said as he walked in front of me and extended his hand. I took it into mine and looked up at his extreme blue eyes.

He was really tall, with an athletic build. He had huge mop of curly black hair, and wore wire framed glasses. His skin was so white it seemed transparent, and a few freckles covered his nose. He had on a white dress shirt with a bright florescent green tie, jeans and white sneakers. His long lanky handshake overstayed its welcome, and he looked at me as if my entire life was written on my face.

I tried again to sit up, but looked even sillier when I lost my balance.

Mr. D noticed, and helped me up, as if I was a damsel in distress, when in reality I felt more like a little bitch. You can tell this guy was smart, and I believe this entire scheme was part of a plan, even down to these goddamn beanbags.

Either way, that simple gesture broke whatever ice might've been there and the moment I was on my feet, business had commenced.

I followed Mr. D over to a tall barstool that I hadn't even notice. I sat down and watched him walk around the counter and begin whipping up some nasty looking shit that he called Wheat Grass. He passed me a little in a shot glass and we cheered before downing it. He told me about himself, and though it was obvious, he was rich, he made it clear.

After drinking his liquid garden, which made me now have to shit, he suddenly asked to hear my stuff.

I really thought that once he saw me, he'd come up with some sort of excuse to hurry me the fuck out, seeing that I didn't have *The Look* that everyone seemed to be looking for.

I have to admit, I got excited, and the green stuff seemed to give me a bit of a lift. Either this guy was really good at faking it, or he was genuinely interested… in me!

He got up and gestured for me to follow him over to this huge colorful Boom Box.

"You have music?" He asked, and of course I shamefully shook my head, though it didn't seem to matter.

"That's fine." He said. "I have some pretty cool beats I could play, or if you like you can just go Acapella?"

"Acapella!" I opted.

"Perfect!" Mr. D happily replied, and then put out his hand as if offering me the floor. I took a few steps back and looked at him. Mr. D stood there, staring at me with this huge smile that made my already uncomfortable state even more so.

Whether it was my nerves or that green shit he gave me, my stomach grumbled loud, and I could feel beads of sweat developing across my hairline. I took a few deep breaths trying to slow my heart beat, and the moment I felt ready, I began!

Of course Yes Yes Y'all was the song I chose. It was the one I always chose. The one I was most proud of, not to mention the one I knew would be the hit that would launch my career, and make a fortune for the one who would dare take the risk.

Anybody who heard Yes Yes Y'all loved it, and most memorized the hook after only one pass.

I didn't want to look at Mr. D, but I couldn't help it He had this magnetic thing about him. He knew how to show interest, and to make you feel like you are the most important person on the planet. He crossed his arms, but not in an intimidating way, but more so, to be relaxed. His smile was as pure and sincere as I've ever seen one, and his head and body bounced in a white boy sort of way that it reflected my own energy right back to me, but with a little extra spark that it picked up from him.

By the second chorus, Mr. D was already singing along, adding with it a little two step, that had I seen him doing that shit in a club would've had me dying. But I gotta admit. He had me hyped, to the point that I focused so much on his reaction that I nearly fumbled my words.

As I got to the final chorus, I wanted to give it that ending record effect, so I continued repeating Yes Yes Y'all with a fade out.

As soon as I was done, I noticed Mr. D standing there. His eyes focused on the floor in front of him. He stood completely still, and for an uncomfortable amount of time. I didn't know what to do, so I just stood there, staring at him, waiting. I was now becoming nervous. Was this him assessing the fact that though my Rap was probably the freshest shit he's ever heard, that I really didn't have the look, and so the story continues?

But then suddenly, as if this guy was either on something, or just one of them weird ass white boys, started jumping up and down like a fucking cheerleader. Spinning and dashing around the room. He kept saying *Oh, My God! Oh, My God!* I was just hoping, that was a good thing.

He then halted, and looked at me and said.

"You're it. Mother fuckin' it!" His eyes lined up behind

the finger he pointed dead at me. He scared, and excited me at the same time, and again he said it, but this time, with a little more emphasis. "You - Are - Mother Fuckin' - It!!! And I'm gonna make sure, the whole world knows!"

Mr. D. walked back over to his juice bar and refilled both our glasses with the green stuff. Just looking at it, made my bowels shift.

"We gotta toast." He said as he handed me my glass. He held up his, and I followed.

"To mother fucking Rey! The new King of Rap" He then downed his drink of nastiness in one take. Me? Well, I sipped and gagged.

As terrified as I was to even ask, I had to, I had to be clear.

"So, You liked it?"

"Liked it?" He answered. "What I don't understand is, why hasn't anyone picked you up yet?

Now that question I dared not answer, and so I just shrugged my shoulders.

"What was it?"

"Man, the whole package!" You got exactly what I was looking for.

I couldn't believe what I was hearing. This was way too easy, and he was way too convinced that I thought something was up. I was waiting for Grams to pop out of a closet or something, because I swore this was a joke.

"But!" Mr. D suddenly blurted out, his finger now pointing upward, and there it was, that dreaded *But*, the part that will soon take this entire moment and send it crashing into the ground. I knew it was too good to be true.

I stood there, and waited for him to tell me something that I wouldn't be able to change, wxcept this time he didn't say The Look. Instead he said…

"An image!"

"Image?" I asked, puzzled, thinking that was the one thing I did have down.

"Yeah, you need an image that says something."

"What's wrong with what it's saying now?" I asked, striking a slight pose.

"That's not an image, Rey. That's just you, and we don't want just you. Nobody does. You see, fifty percent of an artist's success, is his music. But the other fifty, well, that's his image, and right now you're only at fifty percent, and that's is not acceptable. At least not here at the Funky Junky!" I remained quiet, and just listened.

"Just think about it. Michael Jackson, Madonna, Prince. You see, not only did they have great music, but also great images"

I started to get a little worried, because I truly felt that Mr. D was hinting to something, in fact, what I really thought he was going to suggest, was that I perform in Black Face, or something absurd as that. This guy was truly off the wall, so of course I had to think that his ideas would be just as much.

"So what do you have in mind?" I asked. Mr. D squinted as he circled me. "I wear Kangos." I said.

"So does LL Cool J, and Nemesis."

"Cazals?" I said, pointing to mine.

"DMC already got that"

"Look Rey, *I* understand , however, when the fans see you, we want them to think of you, not anyone else. Rey, I'm going to need you to trust me one hundred percent. I'm going to come up with things that might be heard to explain, and you might not always agree with, but it's going to be because you don't understand them. But in order for this to work, I need you to trust me."

I took a moment to think about what he was saying. In fact, it might've been a bit longer than a moment, but Mr. D allowed me that time. I guess he wanted to make sure that I was committed, before he was, and then finally I smiled.

"You got it. One hundred percent!" I assured him.

I noticed a sudden change in his demeanor, as he went from this sort of goofy white kid to this serious business man, and began laying down a few hard rules.

"I'm going to expect your full cooperation. I will need you to listen to me, and only me? Though I'll do my best, I can't always explain to you everything that I'm doing. You just need to do as I say, and see for yourself, the outcome."

Again, I nodded.

"So, Mr. D. Before we go any further, I really need to ask you this. Is this gonna cost me anything. I mean, right now, things are kind of tight and…"

"… Rey!" Mr. D interrupted.

"Look, the absolute only thing this is going to cost you, is time and energy, and lots of it, now, can you afford that?"

When it came to time, I was a millionaire, and so I nodded.

"Great!" He said with a smile and a single clap. "Here's some paperwork, take it home, read it, let your lawyer read it, your mother, the plumber, whoever you feel will be real with you, and if you are satisfied with what you read, sign it, and bring it back tomorrow so we can get started immediately.

"So I can actually take this home?"

"Absolutely, I don't want you to be a part of anything you don't want to be a part of. I love what you are doing, but I want this to be a great experience for the two of us."

And at that point I was convinced. This shit was real... It was all real!

CHAPTER 20

Thug Knows No Age

I was on such a cloud that I decided to walk to 42nd and catch the train from there.

Everything seemed perfect and I was so happy. I smiled at everyone who looked my way, even stopped at a newsstand to give good ol' Nemesis a wink as his photo graced the cover of yet another magazine that hung over the counter.

I was in my glory, even thought about going over to the library, pulling Charlotte over the front desk and carrying her off into the sunset. But, without a car, that would've been one long-ass walk. I waited for the light to change, and then joined about a hundred people as we all crossed the wide street to the other side, when suddenly... there it was again! Yes Yes Y'all, being sung by some strange person. My day had been going so good, that I totally forgot about this entire fiasco. I immediately stopped and looked around, trying again to figure out where the Hell that shit was coming from. A loud honk woke me from my trance, leaving me a bit disoriented, and not realizing that I had stopped in the middle of a busy intersection.

"Get the fuck out of the way, idiot!" One driver yelled out.

"You're gonna get yourself killed!" A woman shouted. The rest just threw up their middle fingers. I made my way back to the curb and looked up and around as my song echoed throughout the city.

"Can you tell where that music is coming from?" I asked a young man unchaining his bike. He stood up straight and listened.

"Sounds like it's coming from down there," he said, pointing downtown, and without even a thanks, I took off in that direction. I could still hear the music, but it wasn't getting louder, or lower. It just seemed to linger overhead. I stopped again and asked a woman waiting to cross the street.

"You hear that music, right?" She nodded. "Can you tell where it's coming from?" She looked around a bit then pointed back to where I had just come from. I took off again, a light jog up the block, the music still playing. I picked up speed and crossed another street. I came upon another woman, this one was around my grandmother's age.

"Excuse me miss, but can you tell where that music might be coming from?" I asked with my finger directed toward the sky. But her face told me she didn't speak English. Either that, or she was hard of hearing.

"Yo money!" A voiced called out from behind me. I turned around and saw a suspicious looking guy leaning against a building. *Wha'cha need?* He mouthed. I quickly shook my head and continued on. Not realizing it, I had ended up in one of the rougher parts of the city, and knew I'd better get the hell out.

Out of nowhere, this young kid suddenly appeared in front of me. He couldn't be more than nine or ten years old, however, the Newport he had wedged behind his ear sort of threw off my equilibrium.

"Who you running from, homeboy?" He asked, looking to see who might've been chasing me.

"Nobody," I replied. Shorty crossed his arms and sucked his teeth in disbelief.

"Don't worry, Yo, this my shit." He said, gesturing out at the surrounding neighborhood. "Ain't nobody gonna fuck with you here." It was hard for me to take this kid serious, and the curses coming from this little boy's mouth was fucking me up.

His voice had the pitch of what a nine year old should sound like, except for the raspiness that sounded as though he'd been smoking since three.

"You hear that music?" I asked pointing to the sky. The kid looked up, and then nodded, "any idea where it's coming from?"

"Of course," he confirmed. "I just told you, ain't shit happenin' around here that I don't know about.

"I need to speak to him." I said, watching the kid stroke his smooth baby-like chin.

"I can do that!" He said, then waited for what I guess would be an offer. It was kind of sad that a kid his age had to resort to husting.

"Don't worry I'll take care of you." I assured him, as if he was your typical nine year old, but I should've known better.

The kid raised his chin and took a step toward me. His chest pushed out, and eyes locked on to mine. I realized that I might've made a mistake, this kid seemed fearless, but I don't know if that would be something to boast. I mean, what might've happened to him to put him in that state may very well had been horrific.

"Fuck I look like to you, nigga?" His voice wasn't actually loud, but it was piercing. To be honest, this little mother fucker kind of scared me.

I had to think fast and try and diffuse this little M80.

"Come on kid, help me out here, please. That's my song they're singing, that person stole it and I need to talk to him.

"That dude sings that dumb-ass song every fucking day. I'm tired of that shit, wack-ass song!"

"So you know who it is?"

"I told you, this my shit nigga! Ain't nothin' goes on around here without me knowing about."

"So what can you tell me?"

"Depends on what you can afford."

I looked at him, shook my head, and just waved him off.

"I'll figure it out myself." I turned and walked away, hoping that maybe there was a heart behind that baby chest, but I should've known better, these street kids don't care about anyone.

I turned and saw he was walking away. "Shit!" He was the closest I've gotten toward solving this problem.

"Hey kid!" I called out. He turned and looked at me, so I waved him back. As he approached I asked.

"What's your name?"

"You made me walk all the way back over here to ask me that?"

"No, I'm just trying to be friendly. My name is Rey," I said extending my hand toward him, but he ignored it.

"They call me, QUENEPA!" He proudly replied, and for the obvious of course.

"Quenepa?" I asked, trying my best to not even smile. He just nodded.

Look man, here's a dollar. But you gotta take me all the way to his door." QUENEPA looked down at my hand, and when he reached out for the money, instead of taking it, he slapped it out of my hand.

"What was that for?"

"Fuck I'm supposed to do with that, wipe my ass?" He said, a bit louder than was necessary. I looked around to see if we had attracted any attention... and of course we did! I bent down and picked up my dollar.

"I thought maybe you just wanted to get some candy or something."

"Candy? I don't want no fuckin' candy." He said even louder than before, except this time, that reference to candy, wasn't looking too good, and a few of the adults walking by, stopped to watch.

He kept yelling as I tried to calm him down. I couldn't believe this kid's mouth. I was at least twice his age, and still hadn't used some of those words that rolled so comfortably from his lips.

"Okay okay, So what do you want?"

"More than a fucking dollar!"

I dug into my pocket and pulled out everything I had, a five, a few coins and some lint. Quenepa reached out and snatched it all, as if he had owned it all along.

"Okay, so can we do this?" I asked, my own patience starting to run out.

"Yeah, come by tomorrow!" Quenepa suggested.

"Wait! Tomorrow?"

"Yeah, tomorrow we'll take care f it. I have shit t do today."

"But I just gave you money."

"Yeah, but this shit don't cover express delivery."

The music suddenly stopped.

"Shit!" I said as my eyes darted toward the sky. I stared up at the top floors of all the buildings that surrounded me, waiting for the music to start again, but it never did. And when I looked back down …Quenepa was gone!

My eyes quickly scanned the immediate area. I ran to the corner, checked behind a building. It was no use, he was gone, and so was my money. I noticed the few adults that had stopped to see what was happening, began to walk away.

There was no sense in asking them.

That was all the money I had. I didn't even have enough to get home, which meant I had to walk. What a waste of time, what a waste of money. I should've known better. That little bastard got me good. Even if I catch him, what am I gonna do? I turned and headed back uptown, and just kept saying to myself, "Little bastard!"

The music started up again, and I became furious. I decided to walk around the neighborhood a bit in hopes of spotting that little crook. Each time I heard that man sing out my hook, I cringed. What nerve he had, taking someone else's song and trying to pass it as his own. It was sickening, and what was even more sickening was the way he was singing it. He made my prized possession into something old and corny, like that shit my grandmother likes to listen to. This guy couldn't even pronounce the "Y's" in Yes Yes Y'all, he pronounced it with a fucking Jay... Jes Jes J'all! What kind of shit is that? Why on earth would you steal a song you can't even pronounce? Stupid fuck!

My song was made to Rap over a drum beat, and this guy was trying to sing it over a piano. I could hear him trying out the hook in different keys. He was singing the verses, totally fucking it all up. This dude was seriously trying to rewrite my shit.

I started to wonder if this guy was even in Manhattan. What if he was in another borough, and the music just traveled through the air making it sound like it was right here? The more I thought about it, the more I panicked.

As I turned another corner I spotted QUENEPA, trying to

hustle some other poor adult. He did a double take when he saw me, and then took off running. I thought about chasing him, but that could be a bad scene. I'll catch that little mother fucker one day, and if nobody's looking I swear I'm gonna slap those baby teeth right out of his fucking mouth.

And again, the music stopped!

CHAPTER 21

Mumble Jumble

"We might need to get a lawyer for this, Mijo, it's all mumble jumble to me," said Grams, as she and I stayed up late, sitting at the kitchen table trying our best to decipher the contract. Not even a steady flow of Bustelo and Gram's original Webster's Dictionary was helping. We defined most of the words individually, but when we placed them back into sentences, they still made no sense.

The only thing that I did understand was that this wasn't a recording contract. What I was signing on to was a production deal. No mention of any advance money, but there was a measly two cent royalty offered after all expenses were paid back.

Grams took off her glasses and looked up at me.

"What?" I asked. I could tell she wanted to tell me something.

"Reynaldo, listen to me sweetie." I placed the papers down on the table and sat up. "This is the contract you are being offered. It's for your talents. Would these people really want to screw with you if their success relied on your talents?" "Grams, they can tie me up for the rest of my life."

"It doesn't say that here, and even if it did, they can't *make* you be good, if you don't want to." I understood what she was getting at.

"It's just there are so many horror stories when it comes to the music business." "So why even do it?" She asked.

"It's all I ever think about."

"And all these horrible stories, do you know these people?" "No."

"Then how do you know they're true? And if they are true, how do you know that it wasn't them who were not cooperating?"

"So you think I should sign this?"

"Let's face it, Mijo, as much as I would love to help you make the best decision possible, I can't. Not only do I not have the money for a lawyer, I don't know anything about this business. So all you have right now, is what God gave you… a gut!

"A gut?" I asked.

"Yes." She nodded. "That inner voice that talks to us, you need to listen to it, and once it tells you what to do, you can't second guess it, because that's where most of us make mistakes. Believe me, I know.

Grams washed and put away the few dishes that were out, then walked up to me and said. "The only thing that's worse than a mistake, is a regret!" She then kissed me on the top of my head and went to her room.

"Goodnight Mijo" "Goodnight Grams."

I watched as her door closed and then gathered the contract and took it over to the couch. The clock read ten minutes to two, and I was wide awake. Grams was right, I had to go with my gut. Sort out my pros and cons, and in all honesty, the only con was the way I was currently living. Eighteen years old, living with my Grandmother, no job, no girl, no life. Anything else at this point would be a pro.

I didn't own anything, so nothing could be taken away. I risk my songs, but I could always write more, and like Grams said, they can't *make* me write anything I don't want to.

I was clear on the fact that they weren't a record company, but neither were the people who signed Nemesis. Production companies were the ones who would put everything together and then shop the deal, and they deserved to be compensated for their wok, maybe even more than me, so that too I can accept.

I looked down at the stack of pages in my hand. Eight in total, and thought, this could be the beginning of something great... or something horrible!

CHAPTER 22

But It's Rey... El Rey!

Roller Girl skated around Mr. D's office filling everyone's glass with Champagne. There had to be at least twenty people in attendance. I had no idea this many people even worked there. Roller Girl skated up to me and filled my glass and then turned and filled Mr. D's who was standing beside me facing his staff.

"Three years!" He began, loud and commanding, as everyone quickly quieted down. "For three years we've searched the *The One!* And today, ladies and gentlemen, we found him!" Everyone cheered. I couldn't believe what I was hearing. It was so strange that I swore he wasn't even talking about me. But he was.

"Rap music is the new Rock and Roll, and this here folks is the new Elvis, or should I say... The King!" A Funky Junky toast to our new artists... The King!

"The King!" Everyone repeated before gulping down their Champagne. I sort of glanced toward Mr. D and whispered to him that my name was El Rey. He smiled and patted me on the back as he and I looked out at the staff who were all still applauding.

"Speech!" Someone yelled out from the back. I had hoped that Mr. D didn't hear it, but then someone else seconded it from the other side of the room. Mr. D looked their way and smiled, then turned and looked at me.

"Why don't you say a few words?" He asked. "Oh, I don't know Mr. D, I'm not really…"

"Speech, speech, speech! Mr. D began to chant along with a simultaneous foot stomp. Everyone followed. Finally, after a moment they all quieted down. The place was absolutely silent, and every eye was on me. I could feel my ears burning up, and my mouth becoming dry. I looked at Roller Girl and held out my glass, she filled it again and I took a sip.

"Wow." I said, trying to buy a little time to clear my throat, and figure out what I was going to say. "This is… um, something!" I said, looking around at everyone nodding and smiling, though I hadn't said shit yet. Not only was this all happening so fast, it didn't feel real at all. My mind had gone blank, and the forty plus eyes staring at me didn't help. And though Grams wasn't here, I could sort of hear her telling me, "Say something, pendejo" So I did!

"There isn't a big demand for Puerto Rican Rappers these days, trust me, I know!" That was a great ice-breaker as everyone including Mr. D began to laugh. "Many times I thought about just giving up, maybe just writing, but every morning I would wake up and say to myself, today is *the* day, the day that some lucky person will discover me." I turned to Mr. D and smiled. He threw up his hands as if he was guilty, and smiled. Everyone applauded, though it wasn't clear whether it was for me, or for him. "Thank you, Mr. D, for this great opportunity, I promise, I won't let you down. To everyone else here… I didn't even realize this many people worked here." Again they all laughed. "I look forward to getting to know each and every one of you, and um… Thank you, thank you!" The applause was so loud that the room shook. Roller Girl popped open another bottle of bubbly and rolled around topping off glasses.

Mr. D walked over to his Boom Box and put up the volume. It was the first time I ever seen a box that lit up in colorful lights as it played. He then walked over to the wall and dimmed all the lights. His office looked even more spectacular in the dark, as colored fluorescents and glowing velvet posters set off the coolest vibe ever.

Mr. D and I sat at the bar off the side of the room looking out at everyone having a good time. I noticed a coupled standing in the corner passing a small piece of aluminum back and forth scooping out a white substance with a pen cap and bringing it up to their nose. I glanced at Mr. D and realized he was well aware of what was going on. The smell of marijuana filled the room and Roller Girl switched from pouring Champagne to pouring Hennessey. More people began pulling out their own personal supply of Cocaine. Roller Girl rolled up and handed Mr. D a small wax envelope. He pulled her close and gave her a tap kiss on the lips. She rolled away as he reached into his pocket and pulled out what looked like a tiny golden straw. Mr. D poured about six small piles of coke onto his black Formica counter, and with the straw sniffed up two of the piles. He then passed the straw to me and gestured for me to take a hit. I declined politely. Mr. D smiled and took back the straw, finishing off the other four piles left on the counter.

I took another sip of my Champagne which was now warm and flat, which really didn't matter because I didn't like to drink. Looking out at his people as they celebrated, Mr. D. Leaned towards me, and with his eyes still on the crowd, whispered.

"Had you taken any of that, your deal would've ended right here." "I guess that doesn't apply to anyone else?" I said, gesturing toward the crazy fucking scene playing out in front of us.

"I'm not investing a fortune into any of them. They can do whatever the fuck they want, so long as it doesn't affect their job."

"And if it does?"

"Every single one of them is replaceable. Shit, I can get interns to do what they do absolutely free."

Mr. D then turned to me and placed his hand on my shoulder.

"I have big plans for you, King, big plans!"

"But my name is Rey... El Rey!"

CHAPTER 23

Real Men Wear Skirts

Everyone had off for the weekend, but Monday morning, the office was in full swing. I walked down the long corridor, everyone who passed me, wished me a good morning, many using the name King, which I was still trying to get used to. I got to Mr. D's office and knocked.

Immediately he called out for me to come in. He was pacing the floor while on the phone. He gestured toward one of the Bean Bags. I pulled up the bar stool instead.

"Okay, perfect. You won't regret this!" He said into the phone and then hung up and turned to me.

"My man, King, How was your weekend, buddy?" He said as we shook hands. "I pretty much took it easy!" I replied.

"Great, that's exactly what I wanted you to do, in fact, whenever you have down time, get yourself some rest, 'cause trust me, you're gonna need it!" Mr. D walked over to his desk and pressed the button on the intercom. "Send in Antonio please, and tell him to bring everything."

"Right away Mr. D." The voice on the other end replied.

"Who's Antonio?" I asked.

"He's the one handling your wardrobe."

"Wardrobe?"

"King, you're gonna love this guy. Antonio is the fashion industries best kept secret, and you know what?"

I looked at Mr. D.

"I own the secret!"

Just then the door flew open and in rolled an entire clothes rack pushed by a tall, skinny, and flamboyantly gay fella.

"Antonio, this is King, our new Star!" Antonio gave me a big smile and held out his limp hand. I wasn't sure if I was supposed to shake it or kiss it. I went with shaking, though I think I hurt him.

"Show him what you got." Mr. D said, his enthusiasm way over the top.

"Keep in mind," Antonio began, "these are only samples. The originals will be tailored to fit you perfectly." I nodded, watching as he pulled the first one off the rack. Mr. D stood beside him with this huge child-like smile.

"You've seen these already?" I asked Mr. D. "Oh yeah, I saw them all, they're fuckin' magical!"

I turned back to Antonio as he held up what looked like a purple and silver waiter's uniform, except it had baggy pants. At the bottom of the rack were all the footwear and other accessories, from where Antonio reached in and pulled out a silver pair of boots. I looked at Antonio who's thinly shaped eyebrows arched high on his forehead. He smiled at me, his eyes looking for my approval, however, *my* eyebrows arched only in confusion.

Mr. D on the other hand, didn't seem to even care what *I* thought. He didn't even look at me, but rather at the clothes, as if he was seeing them for the first time. It was quickly becoming obvious... my opinions may never matter.

"Show him another." He told Antonio, who put that one back and pulled out another. This one was a gold and green jump suit, which he held up in one hand, and a pair of green on gold Adidas held in the other.

"Is this guy amazing or what?" Mr. D said. "Keep on." He commanded Antonio.

Antonio kept glancing my way, and he could tell, I hadn't anticipated any of this.

He dug into the rack a bit further, as if he was looking for something in particular.

Maybe something that he thought I might actually like. He grabbed hold of something, and then hesitated for a moment before finally removing it from the rack. It was a burgundy sweater. It was a bit glittery when you looked at it in the light, but so far it was only piece that I showed any type of interest.

"And what about the pants?" I asked.

"Well, because of its subtleness, many styles of pants would work...

"No no no!" Mr. D, so rudely interrupted. We went over

this already, subtleness will never work! Show him your original idea!" Antonio looked at me a bit hesitant, then looked at Mr. D who's eyes demanded he hurry.

"Wait till you see this!" Mr. D said to me smacking my thigh with the back of his hands, and at that very moment, from within the stacks of outfits, Antonio pulled out what looked like a fuckin' skirt! I looked at Antonio, whose face remained expressionless. I stepped forward to touch it, because I thought my eyes were deceiving me.

"Looks like a skirt." I said.

"Looks like genius to me!" Mr. D replied.

"So, it *is* a skirt?"

"It's a Kilt." Antonio replied with his thick Italian accent. I looked at Antonio, whose eyes turned toward the floor. Mr. D though was all smiles.

"You're joking right?"

Mr. D's smile faded.

"One thing you're going to learn about me, King. Is that when it comes to any of this shit... I don't joke. I don't have time, and the little time I do have, is very expensive.

"But it's a skirt."

"It's a skirt when women wear it. A Kilt when it's for men!"

"I can sew a pair shorts inside it, if that would make you more comfortable." Antonio added. I didn't see the difference, besides it didn't matter because Mr. D quickly crushed that idea too.

"Is it supposed to have shorts sewn inside?" He asked Antonio.

"Well… No but…"

"… But nothing! If we're going to wear this, we're going to wear it the way it supposed to be worn!" Not with fucking shorts inside."

"Come on man." I began pleading. "I'm a Rapper. This isn't what Rappers wear.

Mr. D turned around and walked up to me standing about eight inches from my face. He bent down a bit so that we were eye to eye and asked.

"What is your problem?' He said in a low stern voice. I have to admit, he was a bit intimidating but shit I had to speak up or else this dude's gonna dress me like I'm some fucking Barbie Doll.

"My problem is I not only wanna be a Rapper, I'd like to look like one too."

"You promised me that you would do as I ask."

"Yeah, but, come man… a skirt? And to be honest, I'm not feelin' any of that shit!"

Antonio started putting everything back on the rack. Mr. D looked at me, not at all happy.

"Okay King. So you tell me. What do you think you should be wearing?" I gave it a minute and then stepped back and gestured for him to take a look at what I had on.

"What's wrong with this?"

"Do you know how much money I plan on investing into

your career? We're talking recordings, videos, tour support the list goes on, King. And that's what you want to wear?" Pointing as if what I was wearing was bullshit.

"This is what's in. You want the kids to relate, this is what they can relate to, not me in a fucking skirt!"

"A Kilt!" Antonio corrected.

"Whatever!"

"King, listen to me."

"This is bullshit Mr. D. You're trying to humiliate me."

"Calm down and listen."

I took a couple of deep breaths, and then looked at him. He nodded to Antonio to leave and we watched as he struggled to roll out his rack.

"Sit down." Mr. D said as he gestured to the bar stool and slid over a glass of that nasty ass wheat Grass.

"I'm good," I replied as I pushed it back toward him and sat down.

"One of the first things I asked of you when we met was what?"

I thought for a moment, and then answered, "to trust you."

"That's right, to trust me. That's it!"

"But Mr. D, please, this shit's gonna embarrass me.

"You know why it's going to embarrass you?" He asked. "Because you follow trends."

"What are you talking about?".

"You believe that a Rapper has to wear a Kangol and Cazals."

"Well, yeah, that's what they wear." I replied.

"But who made that rule?" He asked.

I gave it some thought, and all I could come up with was,

"Run DMC!"

"Exactly!" Mr. D said. "And you're even wearing Addias. But you see, King. That isn't what Rappers wear, that's what Run DMC wears, but they're so good at what they do, that they have everyone following them."

"So what's wrong with that?" I asked.

"Nothing," he replied, "If you're just a fan, but if you're trying to do your own thing, unless you find a look of your own you're only gonna be a copy of them."

Mr. D was making a lot of sense, and I was starting to agree.

"But why *those* outfits?" I asked.

"Because new Rappers are popping up every day, and every one of them have the same beliefs that you do, which means that before you know it, the entire Rapp industry is going to be saturated by Run DMC look-a-likes. So if you want to stand out, and instead of following, Setting new trends, then you have to listen and do what I say.

CHAPTER 24

Cut Once

Mr. D hit the button on the intercom. "Send Antonio back in will you please!" I stood there, and for a person who was about to be made into a Star, I watched as Antonio re-entered the office. He looked directly at Mr. D whose eyes told him all was good now. Antonio seemed relieved, but when he looked at me his smile vanished. Following behind were two other people. A younger man named Marcus who was Antonio's assistant, and Marisol, his Seamstress an older Spanish woman, who sort of reminded me of a lighter version of my grandmother.

Marcus placed a small wooden box on the floor and invited me to step up. I watched as Mr. D. kicked back behind his desk to watch. As for me, well, I wasn't thrilled, but damn, no one else was knocking on my door.

Immediately, Marisol began taking my measurements. She measured absolutely every part of my body, from the top of my head, to the bottom of my feet, and everything in between, and I mean *everything!* Oh and not only did she measure the width of my ass, but her knuckles pushed deep inside as she also measure each cheek individually. I was however thankful, that the job wasn't assigned to Marcus or Antonio, and just when I thought it was over … She measured again!

"Measure twice, cut once!" Antonio said when he saw my concerned look.

After all the measurements were confirmed, Antonio and his crew packed up and rolled out. As I was about to put on my sneakers, I watched as Mr. D pressed the intercom again.

"Send in Doc." He said. I looked on, hoping that it was just somebody's name, but my hopes were smashed when in walked an actual doctor. An older white haired man with one of those black medical bags that I didn't even know still existed.

"Doc" Mr. D said as he got up and greeted him.

"How are you Donnie?" He replied. It was obvious that they've known each other for quite some time. I wouldn't be surprised if that was the doctor who delivered him, I mean, he was *that* old!

"So what do we have here?" The Doc said as he turned and smiled at me.

"This here's King, Doc, he's our new artist. This guy is going to be bigger than the Beatles, Doc. You watch!"

"Oh Donnie," said the Doctor, "you and that mind of yours!" He then he turned to me and continued. "Ever since he was a little boy, his dreams were bigger than life! You know, I'm the one who delivered this little rascal!"

"Really?" I replied.

"Oh yeah, cute baby, but a little guy... with this huge dick!" Doc added describing its length with his hands, as they both laughed. I however, didn't know how to react.

"So Doc, we just want to give him a basic physical."

"Physical?" I jumped in. The two of them looked toward me. "What do I need a physical for? I'm healthy!"

"Yeah, healthy from what we can see, but we never know what might be lurking inside." The Doctor replied.

"Look King," Mr. D began as he walked up and placed his arm over my shoulder. "When we see artist up on stage, or in music videos, they look happy, and content, as if their world is just perfect, and for the most part, it is! However, it took a lot of work to get them there, work that only other artists could understand. We're talking about round the clock studio sessions, rehearsals, video productions, meet and greets, and of course, touring. Do you think that someone who has any ailments could endure that type of lifestyle?" I stood there, my eyes focused on the floor, but listening. "Before we go any further I need to know that your body can handle this. I know your mind can, you've proved that to me, but your body, King. That's important."

"I don't have any kind of medical coverage. Once I hit eighteen, Grams had to take me off of her plan."

"Don't worry about that now, I got you, so let's get you checked out so we can move on to the next step.

I turned and caught the Doctor just as he was pulling on his latex gloves. I turned back to Mr. D. He let off a slight laugh, and then patted me on the back as to say, everything will be fine. I thought he was going to leave but instead he sat back down at his desk… and watched!

CHAPTER 25

Run!

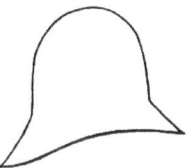

As I walked toward the subway to go home, I swear I could still feel the Doctor's finger in my ass. He may have been Mr. D's family Physician, but he wasn't mine, and I wasn't happy about Mr. D choosing to stay and watch. I'll tell you, I didn't grow up around many white boys, but the ones I did… they were fuckin' weird. All of them!

On the brighter side, I did get a clean bill of health, which meant we could move forward, and for that, I was excited.

As I was approaching the subway, I spotted that fuckin' Quenepa kid crossing the street. He didn't see me, so I ducked behind a mailbox until he passed.

I started off with a fast walk, and then into a jog. Though I would like my five dollars back, I could bet that he no longer had it, but he *does* know where the music is coming from. As I turned the corner, I came upon him arguing with the owner of a Bodega. Quenepa was trying to convince the guy to let him go in and buy something, but the owner didn't want him in his store, nor was he interested in any of his business.

He turned and looked at me. It took a second to register as I'm sure I wasn't the only sucker he suckered.

Once he realized who I was, Quenepa turned and took off running. I went after him. This kid was fast, even though his legs were probably only half as long as mine. My run was more like the gallop of a horse, his more like a rat. He made quick turns in between parked cars trying to throw me off, but I played that game too when I was a kid and was able to keep up.

People walking the street simply stepped to the side, as if this was a normal occurrence. A couple of them even smiled, probably hoping that I'd catch him, and bust his little ass.

Quenepa got to a school and dashed into a small hole in the gate that led into the yard. I followed, struggling a bit through the hole. I wasn't far behind and was hoping that his little tarred lungs would slow him down, but it didn't.

We ran across the large empty concrete yard just to exit out the other end. I had to hand it to him, this was a great escape route, and it was obvious he's used it many times before.

As we exited the yard, Quenepa made a right and began ascending a steep hill lined with tenements. I was beginning to feel it now, my legs were becoming numb. He managed to accumulate several more feet between us and I watched as he turned left behind one of the buildings.

This was the first time he was out of my sight since we began, and I could only hope that he didn't ditch into one of the buildings.

I made it to the top of the hill and then a quick left, stopping dead in my tracks as I spotted Quenepa standing among a gang of about fifteen guys and a handful of girls, all more or less around my age. I looked at them, my eyes visiting each one's individual craziness. They were all decked out in jean outfits, pants as well as jackets, painted with graffiti, logos and names. The smell of weed was so strong, it'd be impossible for anyone walking by not to get a buzz.

"That's him!" Quenepa yelled out in a sort of crybaby kind of way, pointing directly at me. I saw the first guy step forward and at that point I knew what I had to do… *Run!*

I didn't have to look back as I could clearly hear the stampede of sneakers and boots, along with the jangle of iron chains which they used to decorate their outfits, or so it seemed. Yelling and cursing as if they were on a witch hunt. A 40 ounce bottle of Ballentine Ale exploded on the ground beneath me, which only made me run faster. I had no idea where I was going, but for sure I wouldn't be trying to run through that yard, that would be like running through a lion's den.

I saw ahead of me a very busy street and decided to go in that direction, I figured, if I'm gonna get my ass kicked, let it be where someone might be able to help. Another bottle exploded ahead of me, missing my head by mere inches. As I got to the corner I couldn't believe my luck as a Police car drove passed. The gang slowed down and were about to stop, until they saw the Police car keep going, so, so did they!

I decided to make a right in the direction of the Police car, but when I did… they were gone! This wasn't good, and the gang continued to chase me. It was obvious, they weren't gonna to stop, and I could imagine what they would do if they caught me.

I ran so fast, and for so long that I couldn't even feel my arms and legs moving. It was as if I was in a daze. I started thinking about my Grandmother, coming to visit me at the hospital, the doctor telling her that I would be a vegetable, and her breaking down. I thought about Mr. D and staff bringing flowers to my funeral, and then signing Nemesis to The Funky Junky, dressing him up in the weird outfits that Antonio put together. A brick crashed into the ground beside me, a piece of hit striking my ankle. I turned another corner, and there, waiting for me was the Police car.

I stopped and looked back, the gang also had just turned the corner, and upon seeing the cops, they too stopped. Two officers stepped out of their vehicle and walked over to me, as they eyed the gang in the distance. They knew exactly what was up.

"You're not from around here." Officer Lopez asked. I shook my head, my eyes bounce from the cops to the gang and back. "I live in the Bronx."

"Okay, assholes. Playtime's over. Get the fuck outta here!" The older black cop said as he walked toward the gang, mumbling among themselves, as they turned back in the direction that they came from.

"Wanna come down to the station? File a report?" Asked Officer Lopez, as his partner got back into the car.

"Nah, I'm good." I replied, my eyes locked on the gang as

they disappeared in the distance.

"What's your name?" Lopez asked.

"Reynaldo"

"Gotta a last name Reynaldo?"

"Rosario."

"Reynaldo Rosario. So, you live in The Bronx?" I nodded. "What are you doing around here?

"I work over on 54th."

"54th? That's quite a ways from here!"

"I felt like walking home."

"Come on man, you're from the Bronx." Officer Lopez said. "You know better than walking through unfamiliar neighborhoods."

"Yeah, you're right, It's just that something really cool happen today, and I was excited, and felt like walking!"

"Well, I have to ask then. What the hell was so exciting, that it'll make you wanna walk from Manhattan to The Bronx?"

I hesitated for a moment, not sure if he would even understand. But he was waiting, and so I answered.

"I just got signed a production deal with a company called The Funky Junky."

"A deal? To do what?" The Officer asked.

Well... to Rap!"

Officer Lopez looked at me for a long moment, removing his shades and slightly tilting his head.

"A Puerto Rican Rapper?'

I didn't say anything, but gave him a sort of weird and hesitant nod. His stare was making me uncomfortable, and so I looked away.

"That's pretty fucking cool!" Lopez suddenly blurted out. My eyes immediately shot up to his.

"You think so?" I asked, baffled that he even knew what Rap was. Not that he was old, but older than me.

"Well, congratulations!"

"Thanks." I replied, again baffled.

"I see a lot of shit out in these streets. So whenever I see a young Latino doing something positive, it's only right I give praise."

The streets teach you to never trust the cops, but in this case, I couldn't agree. I liked this cop, I thought he was cool.

"Look, kid, here's my card. That there's the number to my precinct, and that's my name, you find yourself in another one of these predicaments, give me a call, I know all these assholes. I'm from the neighborhood too." Just as I grabbed hold of the card, a car drove by, and when I turned, I noticed a few of the kids that were chasing me, as well as Quenepa sitting in the back.

"There they go!" Lopez said as he nodded in their direction watching them as they pass. "Assholes!" He said, looking right at them.

Once they were out of sight, Lopez turned back to me and offered me a ride to the train station.

"I think I'll be alright, but thanks anyway."

"You sure? I mean, these guys can get pretty stupid."

Lopez was right, but I was already caught taking his card. Last thing I needed was to be caught getting out his squad car. Lopez knew what was up. He placed his hand on my shoulder and gave me a nod, and then settled into the passenger seat.

"Watch your back!" He said from the opened window. "And don't trust any of these mother fuckers."

I stood there and watched as the Officers drove offer, and just as I was about to walk off Yes Yes Y'all began playing.

CHAPTER 26

Ordinary Just Won't Do

Each time I stepped into the Office of The Funky Junky, I was introduced to a new room in which I had no idea even existed. This one was the Photo Studio, and that it was! I had never been in a place like this, but have seen them many times on TV, Movies and Magazines. It was huge, with a white paper backdrop that had to be at least thirty feet wide as it covered the entire back wall. Lights were everywhere, on stands, hanging from the ceiling, on the walls. The butterflies in my stomach felt like Humming Birds. This was great!

A photographer was testing the light up against the back drop as a couple of Gaffers adjusted the lights according to his direction.

Marcus was taking notes as Antonio fingered his way through the clothing rack, so that they can match the color of the outfits with the backdrops. Marisol sat in the corner on a sewing machine, putting final touches on a few of the outfits. To the far right was what looked like a small set up for hair and makeup.

"King my man!" yelled Mr. D from across the room. He waved me over as he sat in a small lounging area in the corner of the huge open space. I noticed that there were two other people sitting with him. Everyone stopped what they were doing and just stared as I made my way across the long wooden floor. All was silent, except for my footsteps. My cool bop was becoming awkward under the pressure of everyone's eyes, and now I was more focused on not tripping. I wish there was at least some music playing, I could at least then follow the beat. I was just half way across, and by now my cool ass walk had transitioned back into my original duck walk, the one I supposedly got from my father.

I don't know if it was all in my mind, but it seemed as if everyone's smile had suddenly turned into that of a question. Was this my walk of faith? Is this when Mr. D. Finally realized that he fucked up, and signed some cornball? Who are these two people sitting with him? They looked like members of a parole board, the woman, mid to late thirties, hair up in a bun, thick glasses and a skirt that reached her ankles. The guy was a complete nerd, a male version of his female partner.

Finally, I made it, as Mr. D and another gentleman stood to greet me. Sudden smiles put me back at ease, as Mr. D put his hand on my shoulder and introduced me to the fella beside him.

" King, I'd like you to meet Cire O' Dacrem." I reached out and shook his hand. Not only was Cire's voice monotone, so was his whole fucking being. Nothing moved when he spoke... only his lips, and he sustained each of his words as he spoke'm. A conversation with this dude would put me the fuck to sleep, and at times I couldn't even understand what the hell he was saying. The last name sounded Irish, but his accent was more English, or maybe even Australian, I couldn't figure it out.

"Cire, here is your Publicist."

"Publicist?" I asked.

"Yes! Everything you do King, has to be important. It has to be of interest to the masses, and Cire's job is to make sure of that. We don't want people to have their own impression as to who you are, but rather the impression that we create! He's here to immortalize you, to turn you into a Superhero. As far as the public's concerned, you're perfect, flawless. You don't sleep, you don't eat, you don't even shit, because that's ordinary, and that's not you! You're extraordinary; because that's what people want, and that's what we're going to give them!"

I looked at Cire, and would think, that after that presentation, that he would show some sort of expression, or at the very least…Some sort of Life! But he didn't! This publicist needed his own mother fuckin' publicist!

"Now, we have a long day ahead of us, King." Mr. D said as he guided me over to the grooming area and into the barber's chair. He removed my hat, and my fro popped out like a Jack In The Box, maintaining the shape of my Kangol. A short muscular guy suddenly appeared out of nowhere, and draped a Barber Cape around my neck.

"This here is Dominico." Mr. D introduced. "I found him

cutting hair in a little old shack in the Dominican Republic a few years back. This guy was using fucking rocks! He's considered an Urban Legend out there. To some, even a myth!"

He was a good looking kid, with the most perfect fade and trimmed beard and mustache. I've never seen *him* cut before so of course I was a little uncomfortable. Kind of wished I knew who *his* barber was, 'cause his shit was fresh!

"Dominico's a fucking artist, King." Mr. D said. "He even cuts his own hair!" I exhaled, and smiled.

"I've been thinking about going with a Cesar." I said to Dominico. "You know, something different!" Dominico didn't respond, but instead looked up at Mr. D.

"Just do what we talked about." Mr. D told Dominico, who then proceeded. I glanced first at Dominico who was already at it, then at Mr. D before finally asking "So... what did you talk about?" I really wanted to know, because after seeing the wardrobe Mr. D chose for me, Lord knows anything was possible.

"King, come on man. You got to let go already. My eyes glanced over at Dominico who refused to look at either of us.

"Mr. D, all due respect bro, but we're talking about my hair. I've been working on this Afro for years."

"Yes, your hair." Mr. D began. "Your hair is what pulls it all together. Your entire look is going to be based off of this style.

"But you already chose the wardrobe, how would you...?" and at that very moment I realized, Mr. D had chosen the style way before the wardrobe. I looked at him, as he knew then that I understood, and so he smiled.

Dominico was deep into his work, dancing around me like an Ice Sculptor. I realized then that they didn't even put up mirrors, so I couldn't tell what exactly he was doing.

Mr. D. stepped forward and spoke softly into my ear.

"King. You have to trust me, you have to let me to do what I need to do, in order to get you to where you want to be. It's the only way this will work.

"But I'm starting to feel like a Barbie Doll."

"That's good start, now all we have to do is get you up to Barbie Doll status." and as strange as that sounded, it made a whole lot of sense.

"And what about the music? I mean, we haven't even spoken about the music, the songs, studio time…"

"Believe it or not, King, that's the easy part. What takes time is everything else, and if we record, and then start doing all of this, by the time you're ready to get out there, your music will be outdated. We have to get everyone to the starting gate so that when we release the song, everything else is ready to go."

Mr. D. was a bowl full of logic, I just had to learn to eat from it. And though I would be his first artist, he definitely did his homework, and was preparing for a mighty onslaught. What I had to do was learn to leave him alone, and let him lead. He's promising me the one thing I always dreamed of, and that was fame and fortune, and unless I allow him to steer this ship, I will never know whether or not, he was telling me the truth. I looked at him, and then at his crew, and with a tight smile... I nodded.

"No more questions?" He asked, and though it took a moment for me to answer, I agreed. "No more questioning!"

Dominico had been working on my hair over two hours, and I hadn't a clue to what he did. I wanted so bad to see, or at least touch. But every time I attempted, my hand was smacked down.

Antonio and crew, dressed me, but with the stern supervision of Dominico, who made sure my hair stay intact. A cape was placed tight around my neck to then protect my costume, while the makeup people stepped in to do their part.

It seemed like by the time we were done, the entire Funky Junky organization had come down to the room. The Makeup people removed the cape from around my neck, and I was finally able to stand. Antonio came up to me, and placed on me a pair of glasses. It was done so quick that I wasn't even able to see what they looked like.

Dozens of eyes surrounded me... staring. I tried to read a few of them, but for some reason, I couldn't.

Mr. D stepped forward, eyeing me up and down, he too was expressionless.

As Mr. D continued circling me, everyone else looked on in silence. All I could hear was his footsteps, echoing throughout the wide open space.

I've only known Mr. D for a very short while, but for this guy to scrap everything we just did, and start all over, wouldn't be out of his ordinary. His level of perfectionism had no definition, because it was beyond what anyone has ever experienced, evident of course by the organization he created.

From the people he chose to work for him, to the art that hung throughout his establishment, you can tell, he had a hand in it, and obviously, the main hand!

And for those things, and people that might've fallen short of perfection, it was only because we didn't understand them, or they were still works in progress, for example… me, and maybe even Roller Girl, whose skating abilities were far from perfect.

Mr. D stopped directly in front of me. His eyes pierced mine as if he was reading my mind, when suddenly he broke out in applause. No one hesitated in following, and before I knew it, the room roared. I scanned the sea of people that stood in a half circle in front of me, until my confused looked turned into a smile.

I hadn't noticed the huge wooden framed mirror that was rolled out and placed behind me, until Mr. D gestured for me to turn around. When I did, it was like I suddenly became paralyzed. The thunderous sound of applause suddenly became muffled, and everything in my peripheral vision became blurred. My physical body couldn't move, but my outta body stepped forward and stood just a foot from the mirror, inspecting every inch of the stranger that stood in front of me.

CHAPTER 27

King's Crown

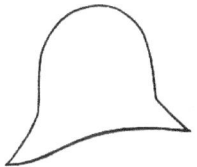

I looked like a fucking clown, and it wasn't even the outfit. It was my hair! What did they do? This had to be a joke, some kind of cruel prank, a possible conspiracy among my haters, lead my none other than my arch enemy, Nemesis.

My eyes glanced over the shoulder of my reflection at Mr. D and company, as they looked on with these dumb-ass smiles, each one looking dumber than the next.

My face was doused in makeup. I *thought* it felt like they were putting too much, but I gave them the benefit, and look, I was right! What did they do? What the fuck were they thinking?

I turned around and looked at everyone. My breathing was fast and shallow, and I couldn't speak. I searched everyone's eyes for some kind of sensibility, but there was none! I felt like a complete stranger, not just to everyone in the room, but to myself. The person who stood in that mirror was someone I had never before seen in my life, and he scared me!

The sides of my head were faded light, with decorated

lines cut in. From there it made its way up to where my afro once lived, but was now cut into this weird shape, almost like a…. Oh my God!!! These mother fuckers shaped my hair into a crown!!! King! Crown! Now I get it! They even dyed it gold!

I looked like an absolute fool, and felt even more so. I remained quiet, because I knew if I'd open my mouth to say anything it wasn't going to be nice. And so as to not fuck up this opportunity, I gave it a minute to think.

"Now if that isn't a King… I don't know what is!" Mr. D said "Now, let's keep it going, we have a lot to do today." And upon those words, the room quickly cleared out.

Mr. D walked up to me with his annoying smile. It was obvious that I wasn't happy. He put his hand on my shoulder, leaned into me, and again said, "Trust me."

Except for the photo booth at the movie theater, I had never taken a professional photo in my life, and though I've dreamt of this many times, never in my dreams have I ever looked like this!

"Give me a little toughness please!" Said Aldo, the very old German photographer, who I'm sure was also discovered by Mr. D.

"Toughness?" I asked, unable to dilute the sarcasm that kept seeping out of my mouth. But let's face it, no matter how tough I try to act, mother fuckers are still gonna take one look at me and laugh. Shit, every time I looked in the mirror, I laughed!

"King!" Mr. D said from his seat in the corner, "Come on man, just do what he says, he knows what he's doing, Aldo's the best in the world, trust me!"

"I'm dressed in a skirt!"

"You're a new kind of tough, King. Soon, kids all across the world are gonna be dressing like you."

"They already do… they're called little girls! I shot back. Mr. D looked away so I wouldn't see him laugh, but he shook it off quickly and turned back to me.

"Give us a few minutes!" Mr. D told Aldo, who then placed his camera down and walked off set. Mr. D walked over to me and guided me off to the side for another one of his pep talks.

"King," He began, shaking his head. "My man, please, you have to work with us."

"I'm trying." but I swear I feel like I'm on fuckin Candid Camera. Like my grandmother's 'bout to pop out of that garbage can and yell Got'cha!"

King if that were to really happen, then none of this would be real, including the promises I made to you. That's not what's happening, this is your dream and its coming true, it might not be exactly the way you've envisioned it, but it's happening, so except it."

'My dreams never looked anything like this."

"Because they weren't real, King! *This* Is real. This is the reality of your dream." He said, gesturing to the massive room we stood in and the dozens of people running around. "Look around, man. Tell me, what do you see?" I did as he said and allowed my eyes to scan the entire room and everyone in it. I watched as they all worked busily in their own areas.

"I see a huge room, photography studio, hair and makeup station…"

"What about the people, King?"

"The people?"

"Yeah, all these people in here, what do you think of them?" "Well, I don't really know them."

"That's right, and guess what?" I looked at him, his eyes as serious as ever. "They don't know you either, but I'm paying them. I'm paying *them* to help *me* fulfill, not just *your* dream… But mine too!"

I looked out at everyone again. Antonio was pulling outfits from the rack while Marcus and Marisol took inventory.

"Antonio didn't just pull those outfits out of his closet. Those outfits were thought of, designed, and made by Antonio and his crew, especially for you. He'd call me three o' clock in the morning with an idea, because he couldn't sleep, or eat, or even shit without you on his mind. That's something money can't buy. I can't pay for that, King. Nobody can.

"Look at Dominico." All I did was tell him your name and he came back to me with this!" Mr. D pointed to my crown-like do. He had sketched out the idea while he was still in DR, and then mailed it to me. "That was mother fucking genius. He could've come to me with anything, and I bet I would've loved it, but he came to me with this, a goddamn masterpiece!" I glanced down at my shadow, and for sure, it looked like a crown.

"Look over there, at Cire." I turned and saw him sitting at a table, writing. "What do you think he's writing?" Mr D asked, but I had no idea, so I just shrugged.

"Neither do I," said Mr. D. "But I can bet you this… It has something to do with you!

"Yeah King, money talks, but you see, trust… Trust yells! It yells loud, and clear." My eyes kept scanning the room as Mr. D continued.

"Nobody here is working for free. I'll tell you that. But, there's something that each and every one of them brings to the table that I could never afford, and that's trust!"

They trust me, I trust them, and we all trust you. Now all *you* have to do… is trust us!

Mr. D patted me on the back, and then turned and walked off, clapping his hands to summon everyone back to work. I watched as everyone gathered around Mr. D with their new ideas and enthusiasm, and I was feeling horrible as these people were putting everything they had into me, and all I did was complain like a spoiled child.

I started to wonder how Nemesis would've handled this situation. I bet he would've gone along with it all, without a complaint. If Mr. D trusted all these people, and they all trusted him, then who was I to doubt anyone. These people didn't have jobs, they had careers, and according to Mr. D, they were the best at what they did, which meant only one thing. They were smart, and made good decisions. Look at me, I wasn't much younger than any of them. In fact, Dominico had to be about my age. What did I have? Nothing! I was broke as shit and lived with my grandmother in a two bedroom apartment. Shit I couldn't even take the train here if it wasn't for her giving me money every day.

Mr. D chose all of these people because he felt they were the very best at what they did, and though they made me look crazy, I have to admit, they truly were incredible, and then I thought about it... Mr. D also chose me! Why was I questioning him? I had no reason. He obviously had more faith in me, than I had even in myself. It was like I was sabotaging my career before it even started. I heard about people like me... Just never thought I'd be one of them!

Like I was afraid of the success that I knew he was going to create for me.

I turned and looked back into the mirror, and stared hard. I wanted to see what they were seeing because to me, I looked like mother fuckin' Jack Frost. I allowed my eyes to absorb my entire image, from the point of my golden do, down to my custom Adidas of the same color. As crazy as the Kilt looked, at the same time, it looked expensive, and thank God for a decent pair of legs.

I couldn't rely on Mr. D's pep talks anymore. If I wanted this success, I had to be able to pep my own self, as well as those around me. Without me even realizing it, I had become a major investment. So far I had to cost Mr. D several thousand dollars, and we haven't even begun the music part of it. Through the mirror I could see Mr. D watching me from the other side of the room, as if he knew what I was doing, what I was thinking. He sensed a transformation happening at that very moment, and waited for it to complete.

I began seeing what he was trying to do, and it all started

to make sense. I continued to stare at my image, but only this time, I wasn't forcing it. In fact, I found myself being drawn to it, like some sort of magnet. Everything he's been telling me was suddenly making sense, and my music now seemed so unimportant compared to my image. This was the key all along and I couldn't see it.

My eyes glanced again, over my image's shoulder and I watched as Mr. D smiled assured now that my transformation has completed. He nodded at me, and I returned the same, and then he turned around and started talking with Cire.

I turned back to the mirror, and for the first time ever, I got to finally see him ... King!

CHAPTER 28

Thirteen Fifty Nine

I stepped out from behind the changing curtain and handed Antonio the final outfit. "Thank you, Antonio." I said with a smile. It caught him off guard, but he stopped, turned to me and smiled back.

"You're welcome," he replied, standing there staring at me trying to figure out what happened. He snapped out of it when Marcus walked up and placed the last outfit on the rack and rolled it away.

Everyone had left, except Mr. D who was sitting at a table writing in a notebook. I walked up and plopped down into the big cushiony chair across from him. Mr. D looked up from his writing and smiled at me.

"How you feel?" He asked, placing down his pen to give me his full attention.

"Pretty incredible," I replied, as I laid back a bit and stared up at the high ceiling. Mr. D just sat there. I looked at him, "Thank you." and he smiled.

"Don't thank me King, you know what I want."

"Yeah, I know…" I replied with a nod.

"It's all I'm ever gonna ask of you, and as for hard work? You got that, I'm not even worried.

Today, you proved that."

"Why are you doing all this for me?"

Mr. D stood up and walked in front of the table.

"Let me teach you something," he began. "Don't ever think that people are doing shit just for you."

"Wha'cha mean?" I asked, sitting up.

"There's always something in it for the next person, and it's important that you not only understand that, but that you also allow it."

"Why?" I asked.

"Because it will keep you from being selfish and thinking it's all about you, because it really isn't." I looked at Mr. D for more.

"Look at everyone here, running around, making sure that you're good, making sure that you *look* good. Do you really think they're doing that because they love you? They don't even know you. Nobody does. But you see, there's something in it for them too.

"Pay?" I asked.

"Among other things," he added. "Human beings are selfish by nature, and there's nothing wrong with that."

"I don't know Mr. D, I mean I look at my grandmother and…"

"She's selfish too!" I looked at him. "No disrespect, everything she does for you, is so that you have a better life."

"Exactly! Where is that selfish?" I asked.

"Well." He began. "Think about it. Why does she want you to have a better life?"

"I don't know… Because I'm her grandson? Because she loves me?"

"That! But also because she wants to make sure that you are good before she checks out… She wants to go in peace! That's her trade off. You see, she's giving something in hopes of receiving something back. There's nothing wrong with that, that's life, and when you fail to realize this, that's when you become disappointed."

I stood up, allowing Mr. D's words to really penetrate.

"Take for example, our situation. Do you really believe that this is all about you? Do you think, that if there wasn't something in it for me that would be doing all of this?"

I have to admit. Mr. D dropped some serious gems. Shit that I never thought of, and probably never would've.

"I do have one concern, though." I said, turning toward the huge mirror that had been rolled up against the wall. Mr. D didn't say anything, but rather waited for me to share.

"I'm gonna attract quite a bit of attention on my way home." I told him, gesturing to my new fancy do. Mr. D busted out laughing.

"I don't think the Kangol's gonna fit.

"No, no Kangol, please." Mr. D replied still laughing.

After about a minute of us both laughter hysterical, I looked at Mr. D, and this time with a very serious look, and said. "Serious man, what do I do?"

Mr. D simmered down, letting out a few leftover laughs.

"When you get down stairs, there will be car waiting for you. I didn't want to send a limo, because that would attract too much attention in your neighborhood. It will be a black Sedan, with a great driver. His name is Salvatore. You're gonna love him. 3rd degree black belt and he's well-armed, so you'll be good."

"Oh man, you didn't have to do all of that, a simple Taxi would've been fine" I replied, as I grabbed my things and followed Mr. D to the elevator.

"Remember what we just spoke about? That shit isn't always just about you?" I looked at Mr. D, and understood.

"And if you need to stop at the store or something, just let him know."

The elevator door opened, and I stepped inside.

"Oh, and he'll be outside your building by 7:am, tomorrow morning, so please, don't keep him waiting."

"Tomorrow morning?"

"Actually... every morning," Mr. D replied as the doors closed between us.

I stepped out of the building, and immediately spotted the black Sedan. A couple walked pass me and gave me a strange look, at first I didn't get it, but then the reflection in the car window reminded me.

I rushed over to the passenger side door, but it was locked. A tall older looking fella stepped out from the driver's side. He had thinning white hair comb back, and a tiny mustache of the same color. He had no wrinkles, which made his age questionable. He wore a black suit that fit his athletic build to a tee, and the white shirt and narrow black tie made him really look the part.

"Mr. King?" He asked walking around the car. I nodded. "He opened the back door, and held out his hand giving me a pleasant smile.

"Salvatore?" I asked, even though it was obviously him.

Please, call me Sal." He replied, gesturing me into the back seat. He guided me lower than I thought was necessary, but it was to make sure my hair clears the doorway, as if he was instructed to do so.

"Cool enough for you?" He asked, settling into the driver's seat.

"Umm, yeah, it's fine. Thanks." Sal then reached over to a small cooler that sat on the floor of the passenger side and flipped open its lid.

"I got 7Up, Pepsi, and this Orange stuff." He said, holding the last one up for me to see. I was a bit thirsty, but I had only seventy-five cents on me. I dug into my pocket and pulled out the change.

"I'll take a Pepsi." Sal dug deep inside the cooler and pulled out the frosty can. He watched me through his mirror as I counted my change.

"How much?" I asked, about to hand him everything I

had.

"For you, five dollars!" He said as he pulled out the can and held it up.

"Oh, um okay," I said, trying to buy some time while I thought of some kind of lie I could tell to ease the embarrassment. I could feel Sal staring at me through the mirror, as I reached into my empty pockets searching for money that I knew I would never find, when suddenly, out of nowhere, he started laughing. I looked up at the mirror and he was hysterical. Immediately I thought this guy was nuts, and uncomfortable knowing that he was armed.

"I'm sorry, Mr. King, I was just busting your balls."

I squinted in confusion.

"It's free, man, here." He said handing me the soda. I was just messing with you."

Half of me was relieved and couldn't wait to gulp down that Pepsi, though the other half wanted to slap this mother fucker in the back of his long narrow head.

"Enjoy." He then placed the car into gear and drove off.

"1359 Plim..." I started to say, when he once again interrupted me.

"...I have everything, Mr. King. You just sit back and enjoy the ride, would you like to hear some music?"

"Um, it doesn't matter." I said, sitting back and glancing out the window.

"What would you like to hear?" He asked as he turned on the radio and began twiddling around with the knobs.

"Anything is fine." I told him, certain, that I'd soon be regretting my answer, and sure enough, I did! For the entire trip this guy pumped some fucking Opera shit. I swore this was just another joke, but my mind quickly changed once he started singing along.

"I turned back to the window, sipping on my nice cold can of Pepsi. This was pretty nice, hell of a lot nicer than that dreaded train, but I was sure it was all just temporary. My whole life I traveled by train and bus, shit, I think I've only been in a Taxi maybe two or three times, and that was with my grandmother. There was no way this could continue. I couldn't imagine this car waiting outside my building every morning, and then taking me back home at night. If you asked me, it was a complete waste of time. It would've probably been a much better idea to just let me wear a hat, and have Dominico touch me up when I got in. Would definitely be cheaper! Well for however long it last, I'll just try and enjoy it.

"So, you do that Rap thing, huh?" Sal asked as we drove along the highway. "Excuse me?"

"Rap, that's what you do right?"

"Yeah." I replied. We both became quiet again. I noticed he kept looking at me through the mirror.

"Where are you from?" He asked. "Born and raised in The Bronx."

"No, I mean like from where. Like what country?"

"Oh, Puerto Rico. That's where my family's from. But yeah, I'm Puerto Rican. "

"Puertorriqueño?" He replied back. I laughed and

nodded.

"De que parte Puerto Rico eses?" He then asked, obviously showing off. I looked at him through the mirror, and exhaled a subtle laugh. I had to deal with not knowing Spanish my whole life, and It was always embarrassing to admit, and now I have this white dude testing me.

"I don't speak Spanish." I told him. He gave me, a bit of a smirk.

"Are you Spanish?" I asked, hoping to retarget the conversation. "Nope, I'm a white boy!" He said, proudly.

I have to admit though, I *was* impressed, or maybe just disappointed that this guy knew my language better than I did.

"I speak five languages," he then said. "English, Italian, Spanish, German, Japanese, and I'm studying a little Arabic now."

"Wow, so what made you want to learn those languages?"

"Well, I've driven for so many people from all over the world, that I found it to be a big plus to learn their languages. People seem to appreciate the fact that I find their language important enough for me to learn, and it's actually paid off in the long run, because whenever they would come to town, I would personally be requested, and of course, the tips!

"The tips?"

"Oh yeah!"

And there it was, the word I was hoping not to hear. *Tip!* I heard that drivers, just like waiters and waitresses relied on tips for their livelihood. Sal was here talking, or should I say, hinting about tips, and all I had on me was some change. I wondered what would be worst, tipping him with this measly change, or stiffing him all together? I should've thrown on my damn Kangol, and taken the fucking train.

My neighborhood wasn't used to seeing cars this nice drive through, unless they belonged to the local drug dealer. The windows were smoked, which added to the mystery of who was in this car. Had it not been for my hair, I would've had my head out the window yelling out at everyone to check me out.

As we approached my building I looked around and noticed practically everyone had stopped what they were doing, waiting to see who was going to step out this car. Boy, are they going to be disappointed when they see it's just me.

People had already started walking toward us, and before I could tell Sal anything, he had already made his way around to my door, and held it open. It seemed like the entire block was standing around just waiting. I heard many familiar voices talking among each other, trying to guess who it was. Not one mentioned my name.

Sal stuck his head in and saw my face. He looked around at all the people then back at me.

"Maybe you should drop me off somewhere else?" I asked sitting back so that those trying to peek in wouldn't see me.

"As much as I would love to, I'd probably lose my job. What's the problem? Don't these people know you?"

"They know Rey... They don't know King."

"Well maybe it's time we introduce you?" I looked at Sal, my heart beating so hard I could hear it.

"Want me to walk you to your apartment?" I considered that for a second, but realized that would be really stupid. Once these people see it's just me, they're gonna get a good laugh, and then go about their business.

"I'll be okay." I told Sal, then took a deep breath, and stepped out.

CHAPTER 29

Light Lit Bright

I kept my head down as I exited the car, terrified to look up. I always thought it was cool that my building was the only one with a street light right in front, even though most of the time, it didn't work. But tonight, out of all nights, this street light lit bright, brighter than it's ever lit before!

The gathered crowd mumbled in question until finally, I looked up. Gasp, and huhs filled the air as it became clear, that it was just me!

I tried hard not to look at anyone in particular, but rather glance at everyone as a whole. One thing I did notice was that there were people standing around the car that I had never even seen before. I never realized that this many people even lived on this block. Aside from the few whispered *oh shits*, and *What the fuck*s, everyone else was silent.

I heard one little girl ask her mother, *what's wrong with his hair?* But all she got back was a quick tug of her arm and told to hush.

I wanted so bad to get inside, but my legs weren't

cooperating with my thoughts, and Sal seemed to notice.

"You want me to walk you up?" He asked. I didn't say anything, just shook my head. I allowed my eyes to latch on to the few people that I knew, and were cool with. Like my boy George. He lived in my building. We don't hang out like we use to, but we still say what's up when we see each other. *He* didn't say anything, but his eyes did. He was proud of me. Not that he knew what was happening, because he didn't. Nobody did. But the scene spoke pretty loud, and it looked like a good thing!

My block had a pretty even mixture of Black and Puerto Rican, sprinkled with a few elderly white people, left over from back in the days, or as they would say, the good old days!

Standing next to George, was his younger sister, Emery. Now if anyone would've had jokes, it would've been her, but even she just stood there and stared. Her forehead crinkled as if trying to figure it out.

My eyes bounced around, sitting a bit longer with those I knew. My Spanish is horrible, but I did understand when Mimi, the old lady who owned the only single family house of the block called me Loco.

I looked at Sal who by now was probably questioning who the fuck he got involved with.

The crowd started moving in, and though I knew they were all harmless, it was getting scary.

Sal jumped in front of me and told me to hold on to him. I ended up grabbing the back of his jacket, and moved forward.

He held his arms out in front, blocking anyone who came too close. Damn, I felt like a little bitch. When we got to the steps, Sal turned around and just stared at the mob as I got out my key and made my way inside.

I thought everyone was gonna rush the building, but when he turned around, they all stopped. It was pretty incredible, and I have no idea how he did it. But it gave me enough time to get upstairs to my apartment. One thing I was happy about was that Gram's windows were all in the back, because had she seen this commotion, her nosy self would've been down here too.

It was kind of late, and I was really hoping my Grandmother would already be in bed. I just didn't feel like explaining anything tonight. I was exhausted, I didn't even wanna eat. I placed my ear on the door, and didn't hear anything, so I figured the coast was clear. Gently, I slid my key into the door, and turned till I heard the click, then gave it a moment before opening.

The door didn't creak anymore since I oiled it for Grams the other day. But I couldn't do much about the floor. I did however know the areas that made the most noise and did my best to avoid them. The entrance to the apartment began with a long narrow hallway that led straight into the kitchen, and to the left, just before that led to the rest of the apartment.

I took short high steps down the hall, which felt longer than ever. The moon lit up most of the kitchen, with some leakage into the hall. I stared straight ahead and just focused on each step as I came closer, when suddenly out from behind the wall jumped my Grandmother. She had something in her hand. She started yelling at the top of her lungs as she raced toward me. The moonlight behind her formed her silhouette, and I watched as she raised her hand high above her head and then come down with such a force missing me by a mere inch. Again, she raised her hand up high and that's when I finally yelled.

"Grandma!"

Immediately, she stopped. I was close enough to realize that she had her eyes closed all along, and opened them only when she heard me.

"It's me," I said through my raised arms

She looked confused, and shaken. She reached over to the wall beside her and flicked on the light.

"Reynaldo?

I reached down and took the pink furry chancleta from her hand.

CHAPTER 30

Ducks In Water

I stood in front of the mirror and started brushing my teeth. I usually get up pretty early, but 6:00 am was something I had to get used to. Last night was the worst though, as I tossed and turned all night long, not because I have so much on my mind, but because I didn't want to mess up my hair.

My royal-do had shifted a bit while I slept, and now sat a bit off to the side of my head. It was impossible to reshape with my hands, and that secret Hair Spray Dominico claims to have been made in DR, was no joke. It smelled like piss, but when it dried, it was so hard, that I could probably stab someone with one of its points.

After showering and getting dressed, I stood in front of the mirror trying to figure out what to do about my hair. I kept my eye on the clock because I knew Sal would be here in just a few minutes.

I walked into the kitchen, the smell of Bustelo filled the air, and Grams was already on her second cup.

"Good morning." I said, her eyes dashing straight to my

hair. "Oh, my God"

"Don't worry about it," I told her as she came over for a closer look." "Pero, It's like a rock!" She said, carefully touching one of its points.

"Yeah I know."

"And you're going out like that?"

"I have no choice, besides they'll fix it when I get to the office."

"What if the car doesn't come to get you?" She asked.

"It'll be here." I replied, waving off the thought, but then I looked up at the clock and it was already three minutes to seven, and no sign of Sal.

"I really wish we had windows in the front." I told her, and then leaned over and kissed Grams on the cheek, before heading for the door.

"You don't want to eat anything?" She called out as I made my way down the hall. "No, the car should be here any minute."

"Wait!" She yelled out, and then hurried toward me. When I turned around, she grabbed my hand and placed in it a five dollar bill.

"I don't need this, Grams, they're driving me home, and they feed us over there."

"A man should never walk around with empty pockets, even if it's just five dollars."

"But Grams..." I began, but she hushed me, turned me around toward the door, and sent me on my way, exactly how she did when I was in school.

As I was approaching the exit I could already see Sal outside talking to a few of the neighborhood kids. *What the fuck were they doing up so early?* I thought. I was really hoping they'd be no one outside. I turned to my right where the old lobby mirror hung, and sucked my teeth when I again looked at my hair. Damn! Now even my fucked up do was fucked up!

Another woman from across the street came out and was also talking to Sal.

As I exited the building everyone suddenly went quiet and watched me as I made my way down the stoop. Sal rushed to open the car door as I nodded at everyone standing around when I heard a young voice call out.

"Hi Rey!" I turned and noticed the two kids heading toward us on bikes. One of them I knew from the block, his name was Junior. He couldn't be more than nine or ten years old, his parents both died from drug overdoses so he lived with his older sister who was pretty popular with the guys. She would send Junior outside for hours at a time while she entertained guest.

Rolling along with Junior was this little chubby kid around the same age.

"Hey, what's up Junior?" I said, slapping him five. His chubby friend rolled up, obviously wanting to do the same... So I did, and then he asked. "What happened to your head?" I tried to hold in the laugh.

"I'm going to go get it touched up right now." I said to

him.

"Rey! What's happening?" Rudy, a guy I use to hang out with popped out of nowhere. We too slapped five, "Wadup Rudy?"

"What's up with the Do, yo?"

"Man, long story," I told him.

"I ain't got shit to do today!" Rudy replied, making himself comfortable up against the car.

"Well, we do!" Sal interrupted, moving Rudy from up against his car, and wiping off whatever residue he might've left behind.

"Gotta go, guys," I said as Sal guided me into the back seat and shut the door. I watched as the tiny crowd moved closer to the window, trying to see in, and though they couldn't due to the thick smoked window between us... I waved anyway.

Sal got into the driver's seat and pulled off. I looked out the back window and watched as more neighbors gathered.

We remained quiet until we hit the highway. Sal then looked up at me through his mirror, and asked.

"You okay?"

I nodded. He looked back to the road, then through the mirror, back at me, but this time with arched eyebrows.

"How can I sleep with this?" I said pointing at my head.

Sal tried not to laugh, but couldn't help it. It bothered me at first, but then I joined in.

"I just think this was a really dumb idea."

"I wouldn't underestimate him if I were you." Sal said. I looked up at him, not sure what he was talking about.

"I've been around him his whole life. I use to drive his father, and trust me, that apple didn't fall far from the tree."

"What did *he* do?"

"His father?" He asked letting out a sinister-like chuckle. "Let's just say, a little bit of this, a little bit of that!"

"Donald Senior was an opportunist, his son is the same, if there's an opportunity to do something big and make a lot of money, they're on it.

His father invested in everything from dogs to diamonds, Rocks to Real Estate, Donny's the same way.

"Donny?"

"Mr. D!" Sal clarified.

Trust me when I tell you, he didn't go into this Rap thing blind. He did his homework. Always does, and believe me… He'll pull it off!"

"You really think so?" I asked, looking for a confirmation.

"Oh, I know so!" He replied with a confident laugh.

"Always remember King, though ducks may seem cool and calm above water, they're paddling hard beneath it!"

…and so there it was. The confirmation!

CHAPTER 31

Walk of Shame

As I entered the Funky Junky offices, Roller Girl skated up to me showing off her new spin, nothing close to graceful, and thank God I was there to catch her.

"I'll get the hang of it," she laughed.

"I'm sure you will," I replied, though I was sure it wouldn't be anytime soon.

Once she regained her balance, she looked at me, and immediately, her face distorted.

"Oh my!" She said, sounding like Dorothy from the Wizard Of Oz.

"I know, I have to learn how to sleep standing up."

She reached up and gently touched it, surprised at how hard it was.

"Mr. D in?" I asked, "Of course, he's in his office," Roller Girl said, as she turned and proceeded in that direction. I caught up to her, as we continued side by side, down through what I would forever refer to as the Walk Of Shame.

Offices lined both sides of the hallway. Every door was open and everyone looked up and gave me a sort of awkward smile from whatever they were doing when I passed.

"So where are you from?" she asked, using the wall to help keep her balance.

"The Bronx."

"Hey King!" One of the employees greeted from the doorway of his office, his head flinching back when he noticed my hair.

"What about you?" I asked.

"I live in Long Island." She replied.

"Wow, do you skate here?" I joked, and she laughed.

"No, I take the train in."

Roller Girl loses her balance momentarily, but I catch her.

"I've saved your life twice within the last three minutes, what do you do when I'm not around?"

"Fall!" She said, and we both started laughing.

"Good morning." A woman said from her doorway, her eyes too latched on to my do.

"Good morning."

"That's quite a trip!" Roller Girl nodded in agreement. "Hope he's paying you well?"

"Paying me?" She laughed. I looked at her, curious. "This is an internship."

"What do you mean?"

"I don't get paid."

"Hold up. You mean to tell me that you come all the way from Long Island, work all day, and risk your life on these skates, all for free?" She nodded as though it didn't bother her one bit.

"Hey, good morning King," greeted another as he held the phone to his chest. "Dominico will be in shortly." He said, referring to my hair.

"Thanks." I replied, embarrassed of course.

"So why would anyone want to make that kind of trip to work for free?"

"Well, I'm in college, and I get credit for doing this, so it's like being in school. Besides, I love the atmosphere, the music, the people here are all great. Mr. D is really cool and really smart, and I get to meet people, like you. Plus it's cool to be able to say "I work here." Roller Girl stopped as we approached Mr. D's office.

"I'll see you later, King." She said as she awkwardly spun around, and skated off.

I was never really into white girls, but this one was kind of cute, and I couldn't seem to take my eyes off her as she rolled her way down the hall.

"Come in, King!" Mr. D yelled, snapping me from my trance. Shit, I didn't even have to knock. I opened the door and stepped in. Mr. D got up from behind his desk and rushed over to me.

"Oh shit!" He said, inspecting my hair.

Sorry Mr. D, I tried to be careful, but..." He put up his hand, and I stopped mid-sentence. Fuck, I think I'm in trouble. Mr. D circled me in silence. His eyes locked onto my hair. I didn't move. When he got back in front of me, I looked at him, awaiting his wrath, but instead … He busted out laughing!

I didn't know what to say, or if I should say anything at all. He threw himself onto one of the extra-large beanbags and rolled around on it hysterical. I continued to stand there, looking at him with a forced smile. His laughter went on for at least a good minute, until finally he simmered down. It sounded like he was trying to tell me something, so I waited until he was quiet. He took another look at me, and again, lost it.

CHAPTER 32

Dominico The Great

And there I was again, standing in the middle of Mr. D's office, as he circled me, inspecting my hair after Dominico spent about thirty minutes fixing the disaster that I woke up with this morning.

"We should start calling him Dominico The Great, because he's a fucking magician!" I couldn't agree more. "Pull up a bag." Mr. D said, gesturing to one of the bean bags at the side of the room. I grabbed one and slid it in front of Mr. D's desk, plopping myself down into it. I sunk so low that I couldn't even see him. I struggled to reposition myself, but Mr. D instead, made his way around to the front of his desk and sat on it. "Stay there." He said.

"So... King, How you feel man?" I looked at him strangely, and then replied,

"I feel fine, a little sleepy, but I'm good!"

"No no no, I mean about this whole situation?" I looked at him and thought for a moment.

"To be quite honest, it's all been happening so fast that I

haven't really had any time to let it sink in."

"Okay," he nodded, looking at me as he stroked his chin. "So, what I need you to do right now, is take a minute, and do that."

"Do what?" I asked.

"Let it sink in."

"Huh?" I asked, but he paid me no mind.

Ready?" He asked.

"Ready for what?" I asked back, and still, no mind.

"And… go!" Mr. D looked down at his watch, and remained there. I realized what he was doing, and so I went along with it. I looked past him and onto the blank wall, where I began to… let it sink in!

I thought about this whole situation, from my name change, my hair, to the clothes that were chosen for me. I thought about Mr. D, Roller Girl, Sal, Dominico, Antonio, and everyone else who I've come across at the Funky Junky. I thought about where I was not that long ago. About Nemesis, my short lived job at the restaurant, that little asshole, Quenepa, and of course, my Grams. What she means to me, and if I ever want to do right by her, well, I better hurry…

"And… Times up!" Announce Mr. D.

I looked up at him, he looked back and asked,

"so… what do you think?"

I gave it another minute, just to try and put my thoughts into words.

"Well." I began, a bit nervous and hesitant. "I feel that the opportunity I have right now is much bigger than I can ever possibly understand, and that it can end as quickly as it began!"

"And you're absolutely right, King. It's much bigger than what *any* of us can understand. I told you before, this is my dream too, and I dream pretty big."

"I have to admit though." I cut in. "I mean, the name change, the clothing, the *hair*! It's all totally out there. I personally would never have dreamt up any of it, but I think I'm starting to get it."

"I'm glad to hear that," Mr. D replied with a huge smile, "and I promise you, do exactly what I say, and you'll have no regrets." I looked at him for a long moment, as that was a pretty ballsy promise to make. Not to mention the subliminal ultimatum thrown in. All I could really do was nod, and as far as Mr. D was concerned… That was good enough.

"Cool! So now that we got all of that out the way, let's move on to the next step!" I looked at Mr. D, both worried and excited to find out just what that might be. And there it was. What I had been waiting for all this time."

"Let's talk about the song!"

CHAPTER 33

The Song

His words put my hair on ends, as this was what I've been waiting for. My whole reason for ever wanting to do this was to be able to put out my own raps, and with *me* rapping them.

I immediately got up from the bean bag, but this time I didn't struggle. For some reason, I raised like a phoenix.

I unzipped the old knapsack that I found in my closet to replace the one I lost, and pulled out my latest notebook.

"You have no idea what I've been through with these." I said, handing him the notebook. "I was able to rewrite most of them. And to be honest, I think they're better now than before!"

Mr. D opened up the notebook and flipped through the pages of chaos, some written in pencil, others in pen. Multiple eraser marks and rips, as well as crossed out words.

I stood there, like a proud daddy, trying to read Mr. D's reactions, though he didn't give me much to work with.

"Let me know if you want me to Rap any of them." Mr. D didn't say anything, instead he got up from the edge of the desk and took the notebook with him back around to his seat. I stood there watching as he flipped randomly through the pages in no particular order. In fact, I sort of got the impression that he wasn't actually reading, but rather thinking.

I became a bit worried, I mean, I've never had a problem with my raps before, shit, everyone wanted my raps. They just didn't want me! Mr. D has in his hands the pick of the litter, a couple of dozen hits just in that one notebook alone, raps that others were willing to pay me for. I couldn't wait to hear which one he wanted to start with, and if he asked me? Well, of course it'll be Yes Yes Y'all… My version!

For a second I could've sworn I saw him nod.

"If you want me to rap something, just let me know." He didn't answer, nor did he look at me, and after flipping through a few more pages, he closed the book and adjusted it perfectly on his desk.

This guy was killing me. My heart was pounding a mile a minute and I just wanted to fuckin' yell! He looked up at me, and gave it a few more seconds.

"You got some good stuff here," he told me, but the way he said it, was weird.

"There's more." I assured him, my confidence now beginning to crumble.

"What I like is the fact that you tell actual stories." And for that moment, it was as if a surge of energy suddenly swooped down upon me.

"Exactly! I confirmed, feeling as if shit was about to turn for the best. "People wanna hear stories, they don't wanna about hear how great you are, or what you had for dinner, they wanna be entertained."

"That one you have here about school is pretty funny." Mr D said. I smiled, as I honestly thought that he hadn't read any of it.

"What about the spaceman one?" I asked.

"Genius!" He replied "They're all great, King. You're an incredible talent, with a whole lot to offer, so glad we're on the same team.

I was smiling now from ear to ear, and felt bad for ever doubting him.

"Your songs are…" He continued. "What's the word?"

Mr. D closed his eyes tight and tapped his fingers on my notebook.

"Relatable?" I said, snapping him out of his thought.

"Boom!" He said, mimicking the actual sound of an explosion. "That's it! People who go to school can relate, people who have cars, wear clothes, astronauts, shit even fucking cavemen can relate to this!"

Mr. D was getting very excited, and so was I. He understood me, and my raps, and that's all I needed to hear to start churning out these hits. I could spit these types of songs out like nothing, all Mr. D had to do was get me in the studio. We would be an incredible force, a mother fuckin' dynamic dual. My mind was on turbo and my thoughts so loud that I couldn't hear anything on the outside.

Through puddled eyes, I could see his lips moving, but I was too caught in my own zone to hear what he was saying, until his eyes sort of shifted. His bright blues and arched back brows suddenly went dark and squinty.

My brain detected a problem, and immediately, my hearing cleared, and caught the tail end of what to me made no sense.

"What did you say?" I asked, the universe suddenly going silent as I waited for him to answer. He realized that I hadn't been listening, and now had to repeat it all, so he gave me the short version.

"I already know the first song."

"Okay," I replied, a bit of hope still hanging on, "Which is it?"

Mr. D let off a light and nervous laugh.

"Well, it's actually one, I wrote!"

I was about to take a seat, because the room started spinning, but I didn't want to fuck with the bean bag.

"You okay?" He asked as he stood up from behind his desk.

"What do you mean?" I asked.

"Songs come a dime a dozen, King. Come on man, that's why you had such a hard time getting a deal. The image is the key, and that's what we did with you, we molded your image for success, as for the songs, honestly at this point we can probably do any song and it will still be a hit.

"So then why not do one of mine?"

Mr. D looked at me for a long while, then sat back down and gave it a little more thought before answering.

"King, I want to be open and honest with you, and I need you to listen and try and understand, now sit down." He gestured toward the beanbag, and with a shake of my head I declined his offer. And so he shrugged and proceeded to explain.

"What I am about to do for you, and your career, I can honestly do for anybody. I have the money, I have the resources, and most of all, I have the balls! I told you in the beginning that this wasn't just *your* dream, that it was mine too. You see, you dream the big picture, King. The fame and fortune, going to the studio, performing at concerts, signing autographs and making a lot of money, and there's nothing wrong with that, in fact, that's great! That's the dream of an artist, which you are without doubt, one. Me on the other hand, I dream in detail, as you can plainly see by the image I've created" He said, snapping both of his hands at me like a magician.

"You dream of performing, I dream of how your performance will look. You dream of signing autographs, I dream of the name you will actually sign. You dream of making money, I dream of how much you make!"

"But what does that have to do with the song?" I asked.

"You dream of recording, I dream of what songs you'll actually record."

"Something just doesn't feel right about that."

"And that's okay for *you* to feel that way, King. The problem only occurs once *I* start feeling that way." He threatened, disguising it though as a concern.

"Look, King, we're not too deep in yet, I'm willing to release you from the contract, if that's what you really want. However, it would be nice if you could maybe help me out with some of the expenses I've already laid out." I looked at him, and he really didn't seem like he was trying to be spiteful or anything like that. He honestly looked like he was beginning to doubt our working relationship.

"I know you're not working, so we can defer payments, and it won't be for everything, obviously I'll eat some of it, like the drivers, hair, the publicist. But Antonio's work was custom, if we can agree on some type of payment arrangement with that?"

"How much would that be?" I asked. Mr. D picked up his phone, and got Antonio on the line.

"Hello, Antonio? Yes. I need a favor please, for the King project, I need a price on labor and material… Yes. Okay, I'll hold." Mr. D looked up at me and held up a finger. I nodded and a moment later, Antonio came back on the line. "Yes… Just give me the total, and I'll get the break down from you later." Mr. D listened as he wrote on a piece of paper. "Okay, thank you." He hung up, smiled and slid the paper across his desk. I stepped forward and picked it up.

"You just have to tell me how long you would need and we'll divide that price accordingly."

"This says $23,000," I said as I stared at the paper. Mr. D nodded.

"Everything's imported, King, even the designer, so if we did a thousand dollars a month, you could have that paid off in just under two years. Of course I am not charging you any interest." Not looking to make a profit, man, but Antonio's work is exclusive, and I did sign an agreement that I have to honor.

"So I guess this is how you became rich, huh?" I asked, a bit sarcastically. "Oh no, not at all," he replied in his cool, nonchalant way. "But it is how I keep from being poor!"

CHAPTER 34

Too Good To Be True

I could hear Mr. D calling me back, as I dashed out the door. But it didn't matter, I was out. I made my way downstairs and out the door where Sal was leaning against his car reading the paper. He saw me coming and quickly opened the car door for me, but I just kept walking.

I should've known it was too good to be true, were my thoughts as I headed my way back uptown. I felt so damn stupid, and the image that reflected from the parked car windows as I passed, said I *looked* stupid too. "God, why did I let them mess with my hair?" I thought out loud, and those who overheard me as I walked by, stopped and stared.

I couldn't afford twenty-three *dollars*, let alone twenty-three *thousand.* In an instant I found myself hating this man, despising his very existence. No wonder he was so damn rich, he was a crook, a fucking con artist, and I got caught up. I signed a contract that I didn't understand, because I couldn't afford a lawyer. Grams told me to follow my heart. But my heart was wrong, and my already fucked up life is now fucked up even more!

I walked past a grocery store, and stared at Nemesis' ugly-ass face as it graced the cover of yet another popular teen magazine. His annoying smile began looking more like a smirk, and his eyes latched on to mine. He was mocking me, laughing, though he had no idea of how close he was to losing his spotlight. In my opinion, he was wack, everything about him was wack. He only got that spot 'cause he was black, and even *his* particular shade of black was wack.

I continued walking and turned onto one of the side streets because there were too many people staring at me. As I made my way up a little past the halfway mark of the block, I saw a large crowd of teens suddenly turn the corner. I stopped and stared until their images came into focus, and there he was, among them, that little fuckin'. Rodent, Quenepa!

"That's him!" Quenepa yelled as he pointed at me. I snapped out of my trance and took off in the opposite direction. I was pretty fast, but so were they, my only advantage being that I had already a half block head start, my disadvantage? Well… I had no idea to where the hell I was running!

I kept looking back, praying that they'd just leave me alone, but they wouldn't, and were determined to catch me, and when they did? Lord only knew!

Gangs were notorious in these areas, and their violence made the daily papers. For me to stop running was simply suicide, and thinking about my grandmother having to identify my body was enough to keep me from getting caught.

People around here made sure to mind their own business. They wouldn't even look my way, let alone try and help. They assumed the younger generation was up to no good, and if a gang was after someone, they probably deserved it.

The sweat that accumulated beneath my 'do began to drip into my eyes, burning the fuck out of them. I couldn't see, so instead of continuing down the well populated street the way I should've, my dumb ass made a "White Woman" left turn down a deserted alleyway.

The mistake didn't quite register until I heard one of them yell, *We got him now!* And though I had no idea where this would lead me, I just kept going.

It was a disgusting back alley, to where tenants of two buildings back to back tossed their garbage from out the windows. Broken bottles and hypodermic needles covered the ground, and a wave of rats scurried off just as I entered.

The smell of rotting flesh from curious pets made me gag, as I carefully tiptoed my way through the rubble. This was not the place to get caught, and I can hear the gang approaching.

Though the sun was out, the alley remained dark, damp and cool. The gang got to the alley just as I made my way to the end, but they must've done this before, because they moved across it much faster than I had. A loud cry echoed in the distance. I looked back and noticed it was Quenepa. Leaning against the building, inspecting his shoe, I assumed something must've pierced his foot.

Ahead of me was a wide open lot, this one filled with

bricks, cinder blocks, pipes, and even more rats.

I made my way to the other side, but only to realize, that the only way out from there is to scale the very high gate with the tiny holes. I could fit my fingers in it, but not my feet. I would have to climb this thing with nothing more than just my fingers, and looking up at the thirty foot gate, I thought, *damn this kid might be right … They got me!*

With no other options, I looked toward the top of the gate, and then jumped as high as I possibly could. Grabbing hold of the gate, my fingers barely making it through the tiny diamond shaped holes, I began to scale. I tried placing the pointiest part of my sneaker into one of the holes for leverage, but it was no use. I slipped, dangling painfully by my fingers.

I looked back, and when I saw that they were rolling up quickly, my adrenaline kicked in, getting me up and over the gate.

I considered jumping from the top, to add a little more space between us, but the chances of a bad fall was too high to risk. Halfway down, and through the gate I came face to face with one of the members. He started yelling and shaking the gate violently in hopes of me losing my grip, but I was holding on for dear life. He unlaced the fingers of one of his hands so that he can pound one of mine, but lost his balance and fell so hard that I heard a snap, and when I looked his foot was twisted in some weird way. His cry bounced off the buildings, sounding how I would imagine a hurt moose would sound like.

I finally got low enough to jump to safety, but when I did, mid-air, I felt a sharp pain in my ribs, that sent me tumbling to the ground. When I looked up, I noticed another one of the members standing there, holding a broken broom stick, while others were scaling the gate.

I took off running, every step, delivering a sharp pain to my ribs. I looked back and saw a few of the members making their way over. Looking ahead I could see another gate. This was the main one that secured the entire lot, and though it wasn't as high as the last, this one was topped with a coil of barbed wire.

When I got to the gate, I ran along the length of it, hoping to spot a gap in the barbed wire, but instead, I found a slit at the bottom, I only hoped that I could fit through it. I looked back and can see them catching up.

I grabbed hold of the two sides of the opening, and with my body turned sideways, I placed my right leg and shoulder through the slit first, when suddenly, a huge rat took off from under the dumpster that sat on the other side of the gate. It scared the fuck out of me, and when I jolted back, my hair got caught.

They could tell I was stuck, and picked up their pace. This was it. Not only would they catch me, they gate would hold me down while they pulverized me.

Just as the first guy got to me, I broke free, leaving a lock of hair, dangling from the gate. I was about to take off, when I noticed that this guy was a bit too big to get through the slit, but the guys behind him were not.

I went over to the dumpster that sat just a few feet to the side of the slit, and pushed it with everything I had. At first it didn't budge, but on my second try, it did, and I was able to push it right in front of the slit, and had dude not pull his arm back, he probably would've lost it.

I turned and ran off just as the rest of the gang made it to the gate. I can hear their curses and threats echo as I continued to make my way through the back lots of an entire block of abandoned buildings. I remained alert, sure that I would run into these guys again.

My nerves now had me jumping at the slightest sound or movement. Each attributed to those nasty bastards that infested these back lots. Even though I was practically raised around them, I still could never get use to them. Even the images posted on those Beware of Poison signs creeped me out.

Other than being in Manhattan, I had no idea where I was. These hidden back ways were like a maze and threw off what little sense of direction I might've possessed. As I carefully stepped over the low cement divider that separated the yards I heard voices that made me freeze in my tracks. Unless this was some magical place where rats spoke, I was sure there was someone else back here. I reached down and picked up an old corroded mop handle, and held it in front of me as I made my way in the direction of where the voices were coming.

The voices became louder and echoey, but still difficult to pinpoint, or even understand. I turned toward a passageway that looked as it could possibly lead to some sort of civilization. I stepped directly in front of it, and there I spotted two of the oldest looking crackheads I'd ever seen, playing tug of war with a burnt and broken crack pipe. They both froze, and stared at me, like a couple of deer caught in the headlights of a car.

"How do I get out of here?" I asked calmly. It took them a moment to answer, until finally one, pointing behind them simply said.

"That way!"

I stuck my head out from the cement passageway that led to the street, reuniting once again with civilization. The day was much brighter than my eyes had grown accustomed, as those back alleys, forever blocked from the sun, sat dark and dreary.

People passing by looked at me with disgust, as if I was just another one of them crackheads invading their block. And why shouldn't they? I popped out, paranoid as fuck, looking as if I just took a blast.

The filth on my face from the constant wiping of sweat with my dirty hands, left on it, tribal-like streaks, and my already confusing hair-do now made absolutely no fuckin' sense at all!

I stepped out of the walk-way, and jogged cautiously toward the corner, my head turning nervously in every direction, when suddenly, something smashed into my face, making my legs give out from under me. The second strike is what made me realize that the first one was actually a fist, and just as I had been imagining all along. The gang, standing over me as I lay helpless on the ground… began!

Like a fly trapped in a web I couldn't move, let alone escape, as a fury of fist and feet explored my head and body.

Fighting back wasn't even an option, as it would leave me open to even more blows, including the one that might eventually kill me. I decided to simply cover my head and face with my hands and arms, and ball into a fetal position, allowing my body to absorb the punishment, because the only defense I had at that moment, was prayer.

The violent strikes to my back and ribs were making it hard to breath, and I was becoming lightheaded. The sounds around me sounded echoey and in slow motion, as pins and needles began working their way up from my toes to my head. It was at this point that I knew I was in serious trouble. It was also at this point… that I blacked out!

CHAPTER 35

Jesus Was White

The image in front of me was too blurry to make out, and the bright sky and clouds behind it, hinted that I might've made it to heaven. As the face became clearer, my first thought was that Grams was right all along, Jesus *was* white!

I tried to sit up, to apologize to the Lord and Savior for all the jokes, but he guided me back down, and told me to take it easy. The Messiah's voice threw me off though, because he sounded a bit like Sarge from the Pizzeria, when suddenly I realized, it wasn't Sarge at all, nor was it even Jesus. It was Sal from the Funky Junky!

"You okay?" Sal asked, kneeling beside me, inspecting my face.

"Let me get up." I said. Sal helped me. I was dizzy as hell, and when I finally looked up, I jumped as the entire gang stood in front of me.

"What the fuck!" I told him, as I quickly stepped back.

"King. Please, don't worry." He assured me.

I looked at him, confused.

At least two dozen eyes watched me as I tried to make sense of what I was seeing, and then I spotted him. That little fuckin' rodent. At this point I didn't care how old he was, I wanted to fuck him up!

Sal turned from me, and looked at the gang. Some were standing, others sitting or leaning on a parked car.

"What the fuck is wrong with you?" He blurted out. They all looked at him, then at each other, before dropping their eyes in shame. I looked up, in awe of what I was seeing.

"Man Sal, dude was fucking with Q." One of the guys protested.

"He stole my money!" I yelled back pointing at Quenepa and trying to act at least a little tough. Sal raised his hand for me to be quite.

"He wanted me to tell him where some corny ass music was coming from, and I did."

"No you didn't!"

"What?" Quenepa yelled back stepping forward with his arms spread.

"Hold the fuck up!" Sal commanded, stepping between the two of us.

"How much?" Sal asked. I gave it a moment before answering.

"Five dollars," I mumbled. Sal leaned in and asked again. I took a deep breath and repeated it within my exhale. Sal stared into space for a moment, then reached into his wallet and pulled out a ten and held it out toward me.

"You got five on you?" He asked. but Shamefully, I shook my head.

"Anybody got change for a ten?" At first hesitant, Quenepa stepped forward and pulled out a fat-ass roll of bills. Flipping through it he pulled two fives and handed them to Sal.

"Here," Sal said as he handed me one of the fives.

"But…" I tried to say, but I was interrupted when he pushed the money into my chest and gave me a stern shush!

Shamefully, I took the bill and just held it in my hand embarrassed to even put it in my pocket.

"Okay, I'm gonna tell you kids this one time, so you better listen." He said as each of the gang members stared at him attentively. Sal had this commanding aura about him. His charisma was truly extraordinary.

"His name," he began, pointing at me, "is King!"

"King?" Quenepa responded with a flinch and a smirk.

"Shut the fuck up, and listen!" Sal demanded, and right away, Quenepa lost his smirk and paid attention.

"I… work for *him*!" Upon hearing this, the small crowd suddenly became uneasy, and started whispering among themselves. I couldn't help but notice Quenepa, looking toward the ground, he wasn't saying anything, but he was shaking his head.

"I'm not done!" Sal blurted out, silencing them all once again. "Not only do *I* work for him… So do all of you!"

"I don't know about all that." I began saying to Sal shaking my head and smiling as if this was all one big fucking joke. Sal raised his hand in front of me, silencing me once again.

"Am I clear?" He continued, his eyes had this weird ability to look at everyone at the same time. Everyone nodded. With a few, *Sure Sal's* in the background.

"Now get your dumb asses over here and introduce yourselves" I looked at Sal, as if he was going a bit too far with this. I had no interest in getting to know any of these guys, I just didn't want them fucking with me every time I came through this neighborhood.

One by one, the gang members stepped forward, introducing themselves as they either shook my hand, or gave me one of those thug hugs. It was a pretty diverse group of fellas, though Puerto Ricans made the majority, including Quenepa, who I still found way too young to be a part of any of this. I was surprised however to see one white boy in the gang, though he looked the craziest of them all.

Speaking of crazy, their names seemed to be straight out of the encyclopedia of gangs.

Spider, Snake, Blood, Crush… you get the idea! I also got a chance to look at their jackets. Typical denim with the cut sleeves, and military patches covering the front. On the back, in large letters it said LOS PERROS with a vicious looking Doberman Pinscher in the center.

Quenepa was the last to approach me. He wore a wise-ass smirk, but got rid of it when he glanced up at Sal who was staring right at him. With a tight grip, he took my hand. I was pretty surprised at how strong this little mother fucker was.

"Now," Sal said as he stepped between me and the gang. "I want all you mother fuckers to get the hell out my face." They all sort of huffed and puffed, taking their time to disperse. Sal tried to be patient until Quenepa really play himself. He sucked his teeth, and said something stupid under his breath. It didn't matter whether or not Sal actually heard him, the gesture alone had Sal pick his little ass up high into the air, and then bash his head through the windshield of the car they were all just leaning against. I jumped back.

'Oh shit!" I gasped.

"Now mother fuckers," He yelled out, like the psycho I was learning he was, his voice, bouncing off the buildings, and echoing as if it was God himself. Quenepa, pried himself from the windshield, blood dripping from his hairline, staggered off with the rest of them, I just stood there, trying to process what the fuck I just saw.

"Let's go, kid." Sal commanded, snapping his head to the side as a gesture to follow. I hadn't noticed that his car was right behind us. Sal opened the back door and I got in.

Sal and I remained quiet for the first ten minutes of the drive to my house.

"Where's that kid's parent's?" I asked.

"Quenepa's?"

"Yeah, that kid's always out in the streets, I swear, he keeps it up he'll be dead before he hits his teens!"

Sal began to laugh. I looked at him through his mirror

and he saw I was serious.

"Hold, up! How old do you think that kid is?" Sal asked.

"He can't be more than nine or ten years old." I replied.

Sal laughed some more.

"What?"

"King, now do you really think I'd throw a ten year old through a windshield?"

I didn't know if that was a trick question, so I just shrugged my shoulders, and watched Sal shake his head and laugh.

"Oh, my God, is that the impression I give you?"

"Well, no, that's why I was so surprised."

"Wasn't like you tried to stop me of anything."

"It was too late. By the time I realized what was happening, he was picking glass out his forehead."

Our conversation continued for the entire ride. The more we spoke about it, the funnier it became, even to me.

"King, if you never listen to me about anything else, that's fine. But this one thing, you have to." I watched Sal through his review mirror and waited to hear what that one thing was.

"Mr. D's a good guy." He said, his eyes meeting mine through the mirror. "He's a businessman. A good one I might add, and he's not going to take a loss. But at the same time, he will never take anything that's not his, and every penny he makes, he earns! Believe me." I glanced out my window watching the ghetto zoom by.

"I have never seen him this excited about a project, like he is about this one he's doing with you. And when he's excited, there isn't anything he wouldn't do to make it successful. Kid, you are extremely fortunate right now. You're about to live a life most can only dream of. Okay, fine, he's going to put you in some funny clothes and give you a weird haircut, but I've been around him long enough to know, that if you allow him that, and simply follow his lead, he's going to make you the Super Star he promised. You have to trust him!"

I gave it a second, before speaking, because I wanted what Sal was telling me to sink in.

"It's just that everything's happening too fast."

"Too fast?" Sal laughed. "People bust their asses for years, invest everything they own, and pray to every fuckin' god in the universe just to get where you are right now. Some will give an arm and a leg just for a shot, and you're complaining that shit's happening too fast?"

Sal was right, I needed to wake the fuck. Nemesis already swiped up one of my opportunities, and now here I am, complaining about another.

"You're right Sal, but it might be too late. I might've messed this one up already. I mean, I said some real craziness before I ran out." Sal pulled up in front of my building and threw the car into park. He then turned all the way around and looked at me.

"Don't worry about that, I'll take care of it, you just be ready by 7am tomorrow morning." I stared at Sal for a moment, and then nodded. He smiled and then got out the car and rushed over to my door and opened it. I stepped out once again to a crowd of nosey neighbors.

"Hey Rey, what's up with the door to door service, man?" One of the kids from the block asked.

"Yeah, and that new 'Do looks a bit jacked up, yo!." Another said. I turned and looked at my reflection, and sighed.

"You need me to walk you in?" Sal asked.

"Nah, I'll be alright." I nodded at everyone as I rushed by them and into my building. I looked back and watched Sal get into his car and drive off.

CHAPTER 36

Not Quite Hollywood

It was only 8:00 a.m. and the Funky Junky was already in full swing. I stood at the door of Mr. D's office, not sure of what I would say. The way I insulted him and his team, and stormed out like a little bitch, I wouldn't blame him if he sent me to hell.

Come in!" He called out after my knock. I opened the door, and there he was, as usual, on the phone looking out the window. I tried to catch a bit of his conversation, praying that he wasn't speaking to my replacement.

Mr. D turned, and upon seeing me, gave me the biggest smile and waved me in, gesturing for me to take a seat. I've been trying to stay off these beanbags, but I truly owed him this, and dropped down into the biggest and brightest one he had.

"Well, he just walked into my office." Mr. D said to who ever it was he was speaking with over the phone. "I don't know, let me ask him." Mr. D cupped the phone with his hand then looked at me. "Hey King, do you have a Green

Card?" I looked at him, confused.

"I'm American!" I replied. Mr. D smiled, as if what I had just said was the cutest thing, and then turned back to the phone.

"No, he doesn't!" He said into the phone. "Okay, I'll take care of it. Talk soon."

Mr. D hung up the phone and looked back at me. I wanted to apologize for my behavior yesterday, but he seemed to have forgotten all about it.

"Do you know who I was just speaking with?" Mr. D asked me. I shook my head. He looked at me, and proudly replied. "Domingo!" As if *everyone* should know who this guy is.

"Sorry, don't know who that is." I replied. Mr. D's face remained proud and unaffected by lack of knowledge.

"Well, good thing for him, because had you known, he would've lost the job!"

"I'm sorry, you lost me."

"Domingo is one of the world's greatest directors."

"From Hollywood?" I asked.

"No, better… from Mexico!

"I still don't get it."

"Okay, let me break it down a bit. In your opinion, what is the biggest thing to happen to the music business just recently?"

I thought hard, but then shrugged my shoulders when I didn't know the answer.

"Music videos," Mr. D answered, excitedly. "You see, King. Music isn't just for the ears anymore. A whole other sense now contributes to the record buying process, and because of these Music Videos, records are now flying off the shelves.

"I heard they're pretty expensive to make."

"Very expensive," he corrected, "which is why they aren't for everyone. Anyhow, Domingo has agreed to film *your* music video!" And in an instant, we were back on that fast track again.

"But we haven't even picked a song, yet."

"I have, King, and you came back because you trust me, am I right?" I gave it a second before nodding.

"But why *that* director? Why not someone from like, Hollywood?"

"Well if we want to stand out, we have to be different. We want people to see your video and say, *Wow that was fucking awesome! I don't know why... But it was!*"

As off the wall as Mr. D's ideas could be, I couldn't deny the fact that within them there was pure genius. Everything he did was well thought out. He didn't run off instinct, everything he did was a part of a plan, and every plan a part of a master plan.

"When was the last time you were on an airplane?" Mr. D asked.

"Never," I replied.

"Well, that's about to change... Drastically!" he laughed, and so did I, except, mine was more from nervousness.

"Mr. D, please, no more riddles, man. I wanna see what it is you see. Right now, it's like I'm holding your hand while you guide me through the dark. And yes, I do trust you, but I just think I would enjoy this journey a bit more if I could only see where it was we were going."

Mr. D, placed both his hands on my shoulders and looked directly into my eyes.

"King, the boat hasn't even left the dock yet. But when it does, I promise, you will have the best seat on the ship, and will be able to see everything!"

CHAPTER 37

I See Red

I followed Mr. D down the spiral staircase where we had gone for the photo shoot. We walked the long corridor, way to the back. Every day I am more impressed at just how big this place is. We came upon three doors, one that said Studio A, the other Studio B, and the third said Editing. We stepped into Studio A. This place was huge. I had only seen places like this in magazines and movies. We stepped into the control room where a short and chubby redheaded white guy stood over the engineer, the two of them fiddling around with the knobs on the huge mixing board.

Upon spotting us, the redheaded dude rushed over.

"Wadup Mr. D!" He said, displaying a bit of swag, and slapping Mr. D a hard five.

"How are you, Red?"

"Large and in charge, know what I'm saying?" Red replied, his hands accentuating his every word. I did my best not to laugh, as this bird did not match his chirp.

"Red, this is here's King." Mr. D said as his hand guided

me by my shoulder.

"Oh shit, wadup my nigga!" Red said as he pulled me into his thug hug, and then stepped back to inspect me. I couldn't tell if he was checking me out, or sizing me up, but either way, it felt weird.

"Yes, I see it, yo!" He yelled out to Mr. D, making it obvious that I was the subject of a conversation

"I told you, right?" Mr. D. Replied, though I wish I knew what they were talking about.

I just looked straight out into nowhere, as he continued his inspection, circling me like I was a new car.

"I'm lovin' the fuckin 'do, yo!" He said, though it was weird that he was complimenting Mr. D for my hair. "*And you named this mother fucker, King?* Mr. D Smiled and nodded, "Fuckin' genius!"

I was kind of hoping that Mr. D would at least explain the origin of my name, like, how it came about, but he didn't, and so I just kept quiet.

"King, Red here is a one of the greatest producers to ever walk this earth!" I looked at Red, expecting to see at least a hint of humbleness, but never did. He stood there, with a confident smirk, chest out, nodding in agreement with every compliment Mr. D dished out.

I on the other hand was trying to at least recollect the name, but it was no use, I ain't never heard of this mother fucker in my life.

"King, this here is Joe, our engineer. This guy's got golden ears," Joe spun around in his seat and shook my hand, then spun back to his console, and continued whatever it was he was doing.

"So, Red, you ready? Mr. D asked.

"Hell the fuck yeah!" Red sang out.

"These dudes spoke in code, and I could never figure out what they were talking about. Red smacked his hands together and then rubbed them together like some sort of mad scientist. He gestured for us to sit, and once settled, another gesture to Joe, had him start the music.

The song began with what sounded like a thousand trumpets, the kind you hear upon the entrance of a King. I honestly thought this was some type of joke, and I was waiting for Allen Funt to pop out and tell me to *Smile!* But that never happened. What did happen was a voice. A powerful man's voice with a thick English accent, announce, *All Hail The King!* The final word fading in an echo, till suddenly in drops a beat, loud and piercing *Kick-Snare- Kick Kick- Snare!* Repeating itself over and over. The sound was enormous, filling every square inch of the room. I have to admit, I was definitely feeling it and when those bells came in with a cool swing like flow, light and airy? My hairs stood on ends!

Everyone was sort of in their own zone, bopping to the beat, I started rapping in my head, my lips slightly moving. It fit perfectly to Yes Yes Y'all and I was just about to give them a taste, when suddenly, out of nowhere, Red began to Rap!

It caught me off guard, and took me a moment to refocus, but I have to admit, once I started listening, there was no doubt, this shit wasn't bad. In fact, it was pretty good, maybe even genius.

The storyline was oddly relatable, not just to me, and the challenges I faced seeking success, but to anyone experiencing any struggles in life, whether it be drug abuse, homelessness, or even racism.

The undertone referenced everything royal, from royal colors to knights in shining armor. I glanced over at Mr. D, and caught him mouthing every word.

Joe had turned back to the console, tweaking the knobs every time he caught something that he didn't like, and we couldn't hear. Mr. D stared at me, not seeking approval, but rather transmitting it. Red however *was* seeking approval, as he was obviously the one who wrote it.

He went into the Hook that sang out I AM KING, while Joe and Mr. D sang along. By the second pass, I found myself also joining in.

During the instrumental break, Red changed up his voice to sound almost like one of those Lollipop Kids from the Wizard of Oz, and in that voice he improvised the idea of talking to an audience, hyping them up. He referred to himself as The Court Jester. I laughed, and not for any other reason except that I thought the idea was incredible. Cool, weird, and of course different! Just the way Mr. D intended.

"Not sure exactly what I wanna to do with that, but that's the idea." Red told us both. "Well." I began to say. "Maybe you could…"

"…I love it." Mr. D rudely interrupted. I think we should find someone to not just record it, but maybe even make them part of the act. That might be interesting."

I didn't really like that idea, however, Red played the perfect kiss-ass.

Joe slid down the faders, ending the song like a real record. The room went silent, and everyone just eyeballed everyone else. Until Mr. D stood up and lead the applause.

Red and Mr. D looked at me, but didn't say a word. They didn't have to, I just couldn't fake it. As corny as this song might've been, it was obvious… It was a mother fuckin' hit!

CHAPTER 38

Cheers

Red and I worked late that night, and the next day we were back at the Funky Junky bright and early.

Roller Girl greeted me at the door and rolled beside me as we headed down the hall to the back stairs. She gave me the rundown of what the day would consist of and then stopped at the top of the stairs as I made my way down.

"Good luck!" She called out as I got to the bottom step, but when I looked back to say thanks, she had already skated off. I walked over to Studio A, and opened the door. Immediately I thought I was in the wrong place, giving the sign above the door a double take.

"King," I heard someone yell out, recognizing it as Mr. D, and sure enough, from the midst of the crowd, out he stepped.

"Come on in!" He waved. My eyes sort for at least one other familiar face as I entered, but found none.

"What's all this?" I asked. Mr. D laughed and guided me toward the crowd of people bunched together in the middle of the control room.

"Everybody, listen up." Mr. D ordered, and immediately the crowd silenced. Red spun around in his chair and gave me a peace sign. I was glad to see him and returned a corny smile and thumbs up. This white boy was so cool that he made me look like a nerd. I noticed everyone had a glass of what I would image was Champagne. Time of day didn't matter. Mr. D toasted everything.

"Take a good look around, King. Mr. D said as my eyes did as they were told, giving each person in the room a smile and a subtle nod, and when I was done, I turned back to Mr. D.

"You'll probably never see any of these people ever again!"

That was a weird thing to say out loud, I thought, but everyone else seemed to be fine with it.

"I love to work in first person," he continued, his eyes bouncing from me to them, and then back to me. "I love working with the artist," his hand gesturing toward me, "the producers, the writers, musicians, editors, anyone who plays some kind of role in any of my projects, I'm down with, because without you guys... I have nothing!"

He got quiet for a moment, and glanced into the air, his eyes began to gloss over, and so he continued.

"But in order to bring those talents to life, in order to be able to share them with the world, I need a whole other group of people, with a whole other set of talents. Like the blood that runs through our veins, we don't see them, or hear them.

They're rarely credited for their hard work and dedication, sometimes, not even thanked." Mr. D then looks at the crowd in front of him. "You are the blood of this organization. Without you, our heart stops." He then raises his glass.

"This is to you, all of you… Cheers!"

At that moment, everyone, including myself, raised our glasses high and cheered.

"Now, let's go make some hits!"

Surprisingly, Roller Girl skated out from within the crowd, holding the tray on which everyone placed the empty glass. *Who's idea was that?* I wondered, wishing those glasses had been made of plastic.

Everyone went up to Mr. D to say goodbye before leaving the room. That entire crowd was a total mystery. Who were these people?

After everyone had left, all that remained were myself, Mr. D, Red, Roller Girl, and the engineer.

Mr. D walked up to me after locking the door. "You're ready to do this?"

"Who were those people?" I asked.

Mr. D gave it a thought, and then smiled.

"Important people, from important places," he said, squeezing my shoulder. "Now let's get to work!"

CHAPTER 39

Can You Hear Me?

I had never been in a professional recording studio, and now, here I was, standing in the booth of a state of the art facility, with headphones on and about to record for the first time ever. I was so nervous that my mouth kept drying up. I was embarrassed to keep asking for water, but Red assured me it was normal and that I would get used to it.

I looked out through the glass as Red and Joe sat behind the console. Mr. D stood behind them with his arms crossed. He looked excited, and I hoped not to let him down.

"You ready, King?" Red said as he pressed a button somewhere on the console. His voiced sounded as if it came from the sky. I looked up and around, never having experienced the sound of professional headphones. They all laughed.

I looked at Red, who gave me a thumbs up, and the moment I returned it, he nodded to Joe.

The trumpets that opened the song scared the shit out of me, sending everyone into hysterics. I took my headphones off and looked their way. Their lips were moving, but I couldn't hear anything. Red pressed the button and when I didn't respond, he stuck his head into the booth.

"King, leave the headphones on, man. So you can hear me." I apologized, and then quickly did as he said.

"Can you hear me?" He asked, his voice echoing as if he was God. I looked at him, and again nodded. Red and Mr. D smiled, and again, the music started.

I could see Red and Mr. D, bopping to the music through the glass, so I followed. Holding the lyrics in my hand, I watched Red, and just as we had rehearsed it last night, he counted me in with his fingers. One! Two! Three! and there was my cue.

My mouth suddenly felt like it was filled with rocks as I made a complete mess of the very first line. Frustrated, I stopped and pulled off my headphones. Red stopped the music and then hit the intercom to communicate, but I couldn't hear him, until Mr. D made a motion for me to put back on my headset.

"King, my man, check it out." Red began, "whatever you do, don't stop rapping."

"But I messed up!" I said, hearing myself loud and echoey in my headphones, so again I took them off.

"Can you hear me?" I yelled out loud at the window. They flinched back and laughed.

Red, made the motion again for me to put the phones back on.

"King, check it out homes, quickly, a few things we spoke

about last night. Number one, keep your headphones on at all times. You can't hear anything I say if you take them off. I know it sounds strange, but you'll get used to it, I promise. Number two, you see that microphone in front of you?" I nodded. "That shit cost over three thousand dollars, it's the best that money can buy, so you don't have to yell. In fact, that shit is so powerful that we can hear your stomach rumble when you're hungry."

"Okay!" I yelled again into the mic, everyone jumped back. "I'm sorry."

"And number three," Red continued. "never… and I mean, never stop rapping until *I* tell you to."

"But what if I mess up?"

"Let me decide that, okay?"

I nodded, agreed, and apologized once again. Red looked at Joe, and signaled him to hit record.

It took a while for me to catch on to the whole recording process, let alone all the rules, which I still kept messing up on. But what I did admire about Red, besides the fact that he knew his shit, I admired the extreme patience this man displayed. Shit, *I* would've thrown my ass out already.

Mr. D also played his role like a pro. He just sat back on the couch, and let Red do his thing. I learned so much just watching Mr. D do absolutely nothing!

When he hired someone, he hired them because he trusted them, and believed in what they did, so when you worked for him, he let you do what he hired you to do… Period!

We had already burned through about three hours, and though I didn't see much progress, Red and Mr. D felt different.

Normally I would think he was just fluffing my pillow, but after working with him for a while, I realized that Red was a straight shooter, a real pro. He sort perfection in all he did, and he understood that perfection took time, so that... he gave it!

We had started out with just the first verse, continuing only when I got it right, and was comfortable doing it. He then added the hook, the next two verses, the bridge, and then the closing hook, and when I was finally on a roll... he called it quits for the night!

"Man, I was just getting it!" I said excitedly into the microphone, but he didn't hear me, he had already turned off the monitors. I took my headphones off and went into the control room where he and Mr. D were talking. Mr. D seemed very pleased and the two turned to me. Red stepped up and gave me another thug hug.

"You did so good today my brother," he said in the sincerest way. "You really did, King. This is no doubt your calling," Mr. D added. "So are we gonna finish, today?" I asked.

"We're done for today." Red replied, go home, get some sleep, and tomorrow we'll finish.

"Time flies when you're having fun, huh King?" Mr. D said with a pleased smile. "Wow, yes, that was incredible!"

"Well, I'm glad you're enjoying it." Red added. "Because

by the time we're done with this album, you and that mic are gonna become best friends."

"I could see that." I replied.

"So check it." Red began. "You're gonna get home, if you're gonna eat, make it very light, we don't need no farts doing your backgrounds." I laughed, he didn't. "Stay away from all diary." "Dairy?"

"Yeah, you know, milk, cheese, eggs, ice cream."

"Why's that?"

It creates Phlegm and will give you that gargling sound. It's nasty, son. And you'll feel like shit." I never heard of that before, but it made sense, and I nodded.

"Also, sugar."

"Sugar?" I asked.

Yeah, that shit scratches your voice, make you sound like Fred Sanford."

"Anything else" I asked.

"Oh, and nothing cold, that freezes your vocal cords. If anything, you wanna keep'em warm, so they work properly.

"So in other words, don't eat shit when I get home?"

"No, you can eat shit," Mr. D joked, "just nothing else!" We all laughed

"And most important, get your ass to bed as soon as possible. Don't stay up."

"Yes, very important!" Mr. D added.

"What time do I need to be here tomorrow?"

"Don't set no alarm," Red advised, "let your body wake up naturally, we need you rested, but once your eyes open, don't roll over, get your ass up!

"What about, Sal?" I asked.

"Don't worry about him, he'll be downstairs, waiting."

"Imma grab the lyrics, bring'em home with me." I said, but just as I was about to go grab them from the booth, Red stopped me.

"No King!" I stopped and turned. "No lyrics, man."

"It's just that I …"

"…Trust me homes, you'll be okay. Your body needs rest, and so does your brain, so chill for the night, and we'll see you tomorrow." Red and I shook hands, and I said goodnight to Joe. The thing I noticed about Joe was, he never really looks up from his work, nor does he say much.

"Come on, I'll walk you out." Said Mr. D

We left the studio and ascended the spiral staircase up to the main floor. It was after ten, and except for a few late nighters, everyone else had gone home. The floor seemed very strange, very quiet, as if the Funky Junky itself was resting, getting ready for the next day. No music, no telephone rings, no roller skate wheels humming across the wooden floors. It was Strange!

"So how do you feel?" Mr. D asked as we strolled down the long corridor.

"I feel great!" I said with a smile and a nod.

"And the song?" I remained looking forward, and smiled.

"It's fresh." I confirmed. Mr. D smiled back.

"So I was right? You like it!" He asked.

"Actually, you were wrong." I replied. I could feel Mr. D looking at me, so I stayed looking ahead.

"I love it!" I then turned and smiled at him, and he laughed and gave me a light playful shove.

"And once we get radio on it, so will everyone else." Mr. D. added.

"So you really think radio will play this?" I asked.

"They'll have no choice." Mr. D replied with a confident smile. He then stopped and turned to me and said..

"King, turning this record into a hit, is the easy part. Turning *you* into a hit is where the work is. When we release this record you need to be ready to hit the road to support it. If the record is selling a hundred thousand units in any particular market, a performance in that same market will triple it." We stopped by the elevator.

"You have a ton of work ahead of you my friend, and me pulling you in really didn't have much to do with your talent. It was your drive that sold me. You have no idea King, just how big I plan on making you, and all you have to do, is listen to me, follow my directions, and of course..."

"Trust you!" I added.

He looked at me, smiled, and then pressed the elevator button.

CHAPTER 40

Dream Big

1:00 p.m. was perfect, had an earlier session been scheduled, I would've felt like shit as the excitement kept me woke most of the night.

Roller Girl skated beside me as I walked through the busy Funky Junky. I was never really into white girls, but this one was starting to grow on me. She loved wearing those tiny Basket Ball shorts, and today they were red with two white stripes on the side. Her tight Funky Junky tee shirt flaunted her perfect breast, and I loved how her blonde curls bounced just above her shoulders.

Blue eyes weren't that common where I came from, unless you were a cop, but even theirs were nothing like Roller Girl's. Hers were much lighter than usual, sort of Ice Bluish, yet still warm and friendly.

"So you guys worked pretty late last night?" Roller Girl asked. "Yeah sort of, and today we start the actual recording."

"That's so cool!" She said.

"Yeah, it is."

"I'm so happy for you, King. You seem like a really nice guy, I wish you lots of luck." Roller Girl stopped when we got to the stairs, and sent me down with a smile.

I stepped into studio A, as Red and Mr. D were giving the music another listen. Mr. D waved me in as Red stopped the playback.

"Wadup King," Red said as he slapped me five.

"How'd you sleep?" Mr. D asked.

"Man, I was wired, but I'm ready to do this."

"Just be careful," Red replied, "this shit will catch up to you after a while, so you need to put yourself on a schedule."

"At least while you still can." Mr. D added.

"The two times you never want to record." Red said as he looked over Joe's shoulder, zeroing out the board, " is when you're tired, or at night."

"Why not at night?" I asked, "I mean, I thought that's when people usually recorded."

"They only do that, to save money on studio time." Mr. D explained. "Those off-peak times are cheaper, but you get what you paid for."

"Not to mention, like the rest of our body, the ears also get tired, and therefore, what you hear while recording isn't always accurate, and you usually don't realize that until the next day, after a good night's sleep."

I have to admit, hanging around these two will make me a music expert in no time. The things I've learned in just a few days, is more than I learned my whole life.

"So did you eat?" Mr. D asked.

"Nah, I wasn't hungry. Speaking of which, my Grandmother made us some lunch."

"Word?" Red asked.

"Bless her heart!" Mr. D said, as they both watched me pull from my knapsack a bunch of sandwiches, each one wrapped in its own tin foil.

"What is it?" Red asked.

'Peanut Butter. I replied. Mr. D walked over picked one up. "How many did she send?" He asked, looking at the huge pile.

"That depends. It's sixteen sandwiches, cut in half."

"So technically, thirty-two Peanut Butter sandwiches, no jelly!" I looked at Red and nodded. "She said these are not dairy, and that this brand has no sugar."

"Well, she was right about that" Red said. "However, this shit will literally glue your mouth shut."

"Oh, damn, so we can't eat them?"

"You can't," Red replied. "but we can, he said with a smile, sorting them between himself, Mr. D and Joe.

I stepped into the booth and positioned myself back behind the mic. I took the headphones that hung from the stand and placed them around my neck so as not to mess up my hair.

"Hey Red," I said into the mic and watched as he pressed the intercom.

"Wadup?"

"Have you seen the lyrics? I left them here last night."

"Yeah, but you don't need them, you got this, bro!" He replied. But I wasn't so sure. I removed my headphones and popped my head into the control room.

"I'm not a hundred percent with the lyrics, yet." I told him, my eyes bouncing between him and Mr. D.

"You'll be fine, King, trust me." Red assured.

I was already a nervous wreck, and not having the lyrics really did me in. "Relax, King, you're gonna be fine, brother, trust me."

This place shouldn't be called the Funky Junky, it should be called the trust me, company, because that's all everyone fucking says around here.

"Just like yesterday," Red said into the intercom. "We're going to leave out the intro and go right into the first verse, cool?"

I nodded, though I couldn't even remember what that first verse was, when all of a sudden, the music began. I looked into the control room and watched as Red counted me in with his fingers. But it was no use, I couldn't even remember the first word, let alone the first line, my mind had gone completely blank.

Joe stopped the music, and Red looked at me.

"I'm sorry, man. I said into the mic, clumsily bumping my face into it.

"It's cool, King. Chill out bro!" I shook out my arms and shoulders, and gave Red a nod to begin. He gestured for Joe to start. Again, Red counted me in, and again I went blank.

Joe again stopped the music, and Red hit the intercom.

"You okay?" He asked. I was afraid to say it, but it was obvious.

"I can't remember the first line." I thought he might be upset, but he waved it off as not a big deal. He grabbed the lyric sheet that was lying on top of the console and read the first line. It all suddenly came back to me, so I stopped him and told him to let's try again, and that we did.

Red cued me in, and it was as if the vault had suddenly been blown wide open. The words flowed from me, as if they had a mind of their own. I couldn't believe it, and as soon as I got through the first verse, I broke one of Red's most important rules… I stopped!

Before I could even begin to apologize, Red and Mr. D broke out in applause.

"But I stopped?" I pleaded.

"That's okay, but you did it!" Red said excitedly through the intercom, as Mr. D nodded proudly behind him.

"Now let's do it again, except this time…"

"…I know I know…Don't stop!" I told him. Red gave me a thumbs up, and then we continued.

Today's session worked similar to yesterday's except this one seemed more like work.

Every time he stopped my performance, I noticed he wrote something down in a little notebook. Smiles I received yesterday for my efforts had now become squints, as if I was this puzzle Red was putting together, and when a piece didn't fit, he'd study it for a moment, and then try it another way.

"Okay, King." Red said after about three intensive hours of recording. "Take five."

I removed my phones and hung'em up, then stepped out into the control room. Mr. D was over at the table fixing himself a cup of coffee. It looked and smelled great, but before I could even think of having a cup, Red stepped up beside me.

"Tea with warm water, not too hot, and no sugar!"

"Tea?" I said looking around at the variety available on the table. Mr. D. Reached into one of the small baskets and pulled out a teabag and handed it to me.

After we both prepared our beverages, I followed Mr. D out into the hall and through a door that led to a balcony that I had never noticed was there. Never in my life have I ever seen New York City from such an incredible angle.

The sun was starting to set, and an amazing orange and red glow sat just behind the skyline.

"You know, I'm in this pretty deep now," said Mr. D. I turned and looked at him, watched as he stared out into the sky.

"I know you are, and I really appreciate everything you're doing."

"Not just financially," he continued. "you see, I don't just *want* you to succeed, King." I looked at him and tilted my head like a puppy. "I *need* you to succeed! There is no choice," he clarified. I turned back to the skyline.

"I understand," Was all I could really think of saying.

"That's not exactly what I was hoping to hear." He said. I turned to Mr. D, still staring out at the city, and sipping his coffee.

"I'm gonna do this, Mr. D. I promise you!" He still didn't look at me. But he heard me, and he smiled.

"You know, ever since I was a little kid, I use to dream of owning it?" He said, changing the subject.

"The city?"

Mr. D nodded.

"That's a pretty big dream."

"What's the point of dreaming if it isn't going to be big?"

It seemed like every time Mr. D. opened his mouth, gems would just topple out.

"We're ready." Red said, sticking his head out onto the balcony. Mr. D. And I finished up our drinks and on our way back into the studio he placed his hand on my shoulder and reminded me. "Dream big, King... Dream big!"

CHAPTER 41

Compliments of The Funky Junky

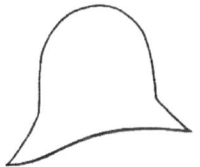

"Just put it on the table." I told Sal as he helped me with a shit load of groceries, compliments of The Funky Junky, of course. I've been working long hours and coming home late, so Mr. D wanted to make sure Grams had everything she needed and didn't have to go out for anything. I wasn't into taking handouts, but Mr. D assured me that I earned this, and more.

"Reynaldo!" Grams, barked as she stepped out from her bedroom tightening her robe. "Uh oh!" Sal said as he froze halfway down our hall.

"Hi Grams. I'm sorry I tried not to wake you."

"Well, Mijo you didn't do such a good job." She then looked up at Sal, and asked me. "So, what's going on here? Who's this?"

"Grams, I'll like you to meet Sal, the driver I told you about."

Sal tried to shake Gram's hand but was having difficulty with all the bags in his hands. Grams grabbed one of the bags and placed it on the table, making room for Sal to place the other.

"So what did you do, rob the Food Bank?" She asked in a tone that made Sal think she was serious. But I knew better, and laughed.

"These are groceries, Grams, compliments of Mr. D and The Funky Junky."

"I never even met the man, and he's buying me groceries? Hmm, I don't know about this."

"I've been putting in a lot of hours, and Mr. D just wanted to make sure we didn't need anything." Grams looked at all the bags on the table and then looked at Sal.

"Mr. You have to excuse me, but I wake up to find my grandson with a strange man bringing what looks like about two hundred dollars in groceries into my home at two o'clock in the morning…"

"I understand perfectly Ms. Reyes, and please call me Sal. I've worked with the Duck family for many years, even before Mr. D was born. They're great people, and this is in no way a hand out. King here…"

"…King?" Grams asked. Interrupting Sal mid-sentence. He looked at me. "Grams, King is my stage name." I turned to Sal. "I never told her." "Ooops, sorry." Sal replied.

"Mr. Sal, first off, it's nice to finally meet you, Reynaldo has told me a lot about you, and I appreciate you driving him around, but please understand that this is all very strange to me, this here is my grandson, I've raised him since he was a baby, I worry about him all the time, and I don't want him getting caught up in any craziness.

"I understand, and I can only try and assure you that King, I mean, Rey is in great hands, I am his personal driver, and yours too if you ever need me."

"Well thank you." She replied. "But I've been taking the bus and train for over fifty years, so I'm okay with that, But thank you anyway.

"He's an incredible talent, and my boss knows talent when he sees it. Rey is destined for greatness.

"Greatness is wonderful, as long as it comes with happiness, because that's what *I* want for him."

"I understand. And we're going to do everything we can to help fulfill both of your wishes.

Grams got a good feeling from Sal, I could tell by the way her eyes suddenly relaxed.

She smiled and then turned to the groceries.

"So what do we have here?" She asked. Sal and I laughed, and began digging through the bags.

We sat at the table eating steak and eggs that Grams had prepared for us. She didn't like eating that late, but she sat and kept us company. It was during this time that I got to know Sal a little better, as all other times I spent speaking to the back of his head while he drove.

We really clicked, and though he was a bit older than me, I felt like I found a new friend.

He told us so many stories. From his childhood growing up in Brooklyn, to his time in the Military, baffled to learn that he had been a Green Beret. We heard how he started working as a personal bodyguard for Mr. D's father, and then for Mr. D by the time he was eight years old.

Mr. D didn't feel a need for a bodyguard once he got older, and felt it more as an intrusion of his privacy, but Sal was on payroll for life, worked into the will of Mr. D Senior, with the promise that he would stay close by and keep an eye on his only son.

After eating, Sal thanked Grams for everything and they hugged each other. I learned that he and Grams were pretty close in age. Grams had him by just a few years. But Sal was in excellent shape, and looked much younger than he actually was. For a second I imagined them as a couple, but quickly shook the thought from my mind as it was way too creepy.

"Thank you for everything, Ms. Reyes."

"Oh no, we are practically the same age, you call me, Dora!"

"Okay, Dora," Sal replied with a smile, and then held up the to-go cup had Grams prepared for him. "And thank you for the um...?"

"Bus-tel-lo!" Grams said, accentuating each syllable.

"Yes, Bustelo... This is some good shit!" He said, and then apologized for cursing!"

"Oh please, don't apologize, I drink that shit too!"

We all laughed as I walked Sal to the door. He reminded me that he'd be back to pick me up around 7:00 am.

"Try and get some rest." He said placing his hand on my

shoulder. I smile and nodded.

I locked the door and walked back to the kitchen where Grams was washing the dishes. I had to stand there for a second and just look at her.

"He's a very nice man," She said, focused on the dishes.

"Yeah. He is."

"But what's with the gun?" She asked.

"The gun?"

"Yeah, the one under his arm."

I'd been hanging out with Sal for a while now, and I never once noticed a gun. Grams however, caught it right away.

Grams, he's an ex-Military guy, I guess if you have the right to carry a gun, then maybe you should! Besides, he's on my side, so that should make you feel a little comfortable."

"Guns will never make me feel comfortable." She replied.

"But how do you feel about this whole situation?" I asked as I grabbed the kitchen towel and gave her a hand.

"Well, at least I'm not totally in the dark anymore, however, how are we so sure Mr. *Sal* is telling us the truth?" Grams didn't look at me when she asked that, but she knew I heard her, loud and clear, but no matter what, Grams will always question anyone who has anything to do with me.

"I'm gonna jump in the shower and then hit the sack for a couple of hours."

"Okay, Mijo." She said, putting the dishes up in the cabinets. I stepped behind her and wrapped my arms around her body, giving her a gentle squeeze and a kiss on the side of her face.

CHAPTER 42

Pow

After my shower I laid in my bed, pondering over everything that's been happening to me. It was like my mind had hit the replay button, and every part of this experience was playing back. From the auditions that rejected me, to my meeting at The Funky Junk. Each person I met became crystal clear, including Roller Girl, rolling around with her ass wrapped in a tight pair of metallic shorts.

Looking at my new haircut in the mirror, I couldn't help but feel it was a bit exaggerated, the wardrobe even more so. I relived the photo session, except the twenty people who watched, now seemed more like two hundred, and each of flashes triggered by the photographer were like bolts of lightning.

From my recording sessions with Red whose hair was now a bed of fiery flames, vibrantly redder than ever before, to the inspiring talks with Mr. D. My mind just wouldn't stop.

I heard the doorbell ring, and looked at the time. It was four in the morning. Who the fuck could that be? I got up and rushed across the apartment hoping they didn't wake Grams.

As I walked down the hall, I could see shadowy movement underneath the door, confirming that there was indeed someone there.

I looked through the peep hole and to my surprise, it was Sal! I hurried and unlocked the door, hoping that everything was okay.

"King I'm so sorry!"

"What happened?"

"Fucking car won't start."

"Oh damn, come in. Just try and keep it down, don't wanna wake Grams, she'll fucking wanna start cooking and shit."

Sal nodded as he tiptoed inside.

"Is there anything I can do? I mean, I don't know much about cars but…"

"No, I tried everything. I just need to use your phone?

"Oh yeah, sure, go 'head." I said as I gestured to the phone hanging on the wall. "You want anything? Soda? Snack? Steak and eggs?" Sal shook his head and laughed.

Sal picked up the phone and began to dial. I plopped down on the couch, and just watched as he began pacing the floor, stretching the cord, just the way Grams hated. I just hoped she wouldn't walk in.

"Don? It's Sal! Sorry to wake you." He said into the phone, as he continued stretching the cord.

"Yeah yeah, I know, I'm here at King's. No, I left earlier,

just came back up to make this call, the car ain't starting, can't figure it out. Yeah, I checked everything. Yep, I even let it sit for a couple of hours… Nothing!"

I peeked over at Gram's door hoping she wouldn't wake. Sal saw me look, and apologized with his hand, lowering his voice as he and Mr. D continued talking. I got up and grabbed the Yellow Pages from the shelf and sat back down to search under mechanics. I found an entire section. I held it up for Sal to see, and he nodded, and gave me a thumbs up.

I started noticing that Mr. D was speaking pretty loud. In fact, it sounded like he was yelling. I pretended to read, but was instead trying to tune into their conversation.

"Even if I stayed with the car, D, what's going to happen tomorrow if you can't get a hold of him?"

The yelling on the other end of the phone became louder, and for the first time, Sal seemed scared, timid. This couldn't have been the guy who I saw step to an entire New York City street gang.

I looked up at Sal, and was thrown off a bit, as his age suddenly started to show. In fact, the more I stared at him, the older he seemed to be getting, and the hair that I could've sworn was that sophisticated silver most people love, now looked gray and dull.

The smooth, tanned skin that made him look so young, now looked wrinkly and pale. Was it the cheap light bulbs that Grams got from the discount store? Or did I just imagine a whole different Sal?

I watched him as he continued to pace my living room. His steps were slow, and he had a slight limp that I hadn't noticed before. I got up and slid a chair his way, but he shook his head and turned away from it.

"Well, his Grandmother made us something to eat, I couldn't say no, bless her heart."

I took it now that Sal was being scolded for staying for dinner. I guess had he left when he was supposed to, the car wouldn't have broken down.

"Yes, he's right here." Sal said looking toward me.

Cupping my mouth, I called out in a loud whisper. "Hey Mr. D!" But I don't think either of them heard me.

Sal moved over to a corner, and began whispering into the phone. I would've gone into my room to give him privacy but too much walking around would've definitely woke Grams.

"But I don't understand why we gotta do that?" Sal asked. I could hear Mr. D on the other end but couldn't make it out even one word.

"We really don't have to do that, I can fix this," and then suddenly, I was able to make one word coming over the line.

"Now!"

It was thin and tinny over the phone, but still pretty clear.

"Now!" He said it again. I looked at Sal and his eyes were watery, all I could imagine was Mr. D demanding for him to walk home... Now.

"Now!" There it was again. Shit, if I have to, I'm gonna walk with him, 'cause it'll be impossible to catch a cab at this time, especially in this neighborhood. Earlier today he seemed like he would've been able to handle these streets, but right now, Sal seriously looked like an old man.

"Now!" Mr. D again commanded, his voice sounding as if was standing right here in the living room, and at that very moment, Sal turned to me, with the phone still held to his ear, the other reached under his arm, he pulled out his gun and… *Pow! This mother fucker, shot me!*

CHAPTER 43

Pins and Needles

I tried to open my eyes, but couldn't. It was as if they were glued shut. I tried moving, but it was no use, it was as though something heavy was holding me down. I tried to yell, but all that came out was air. I didn't feel any pain. In fact, I couldn't feel anything. I couldn't tell whether I was standing, sitting or lying down. I wasn't cold, nor was I hot. I couldn't even tell whether I still had limbs or not.

I listened closely to try and figure out where I might be, and hearing neither harps nor flames, I figured I was somewhere in between. A faint tone rang constant, low and far. Anxiety was already kicking my ass, and Just the thought of this becoming my eternity was torturous.

The only thing that I seemed to be able to do was fill my lungs with air. So I pulled in as much as I possibly could, and then, adding a hum to it, I pushed it out with everything I had left. The result was this loud and eerie cry that just echoed in my head. Whether it was God or the devil himself, I didn't care who heard me, so long as someone did. I would've taken any other punishment besides this one, and I could feel a tear drop slip out from the corner of my eye and run down the side of my face. I gathered more air into my lungs, and again let it out, louder and longer than before.

Pins and needles covered my entire face, and I knew that if I wasn't dead yet... Then I was definitely dying!

The tone in my head rang louder, and with a bubbling effect that made it sound like I was underwater. I continued to squirm, giving it everything I had, but all I was doing was draining my own self of the little strength I had left. The pins and needles that dug deep, felt as if they were being pushed now through the bones in my face.

I couldn't take it any longer, and would gladly have confessed my darkest sins just to make it end. In one final attempt, I opened my mouth as wide as I possibly could, and with the last bit of air I had left, I let out the eeriest sound ever. I sustained the note until my breath ran out, when suddenly, it broke free, and turned into the loudest yell. As if whatever was holding me down suddenly let go. I quickly sat up, trying to catch my breath when I noticed Grams standing over me.

I couldn't speak, and I began inspecting my chest for bullet holes. But there was none.

"Reynaldo!" Grams yelled out, her voice echoey and distant. I just looked at her, still unable to speak, when suddenly she smacked the shit out of me, making those pins and needles disappear.

I froze!

"Are you okay?" She asked. I took a deep breath, trying

to lower my heart rate which seemed to be pumping a mile a minute. The pins and needles were now gone, but the left side of my face was on fire.

Everything went silent, and my eyes scanned the room, until finally, Grams spoke.

"You scared the hell out of me." I couldn't think straight, so I didn't know what she was taking about.

"Where's Sal?" I asked.

"Isn't he supposed to pick you up at seven?" I nodded. "It's only five." She said.

"But he was here last night."

"Yes, and we ate." Grams looked at me, really concerned. "Are you okay? Did I hit you too hard?" Grams reached out to check my face.

"I mean, did he come back?"

Gram's looked at me as to say that she had no idea what the hell I was talking about, and at that moment I figured it out.

"It was dream." I said to myself and with an exhale.

I stood up, and walked over to the mirror on my dresser. A red imprint of four of Gram's fingers decorated the side of my face.

As the cold shower beat down on my head, my Do, protected by a plastic shopping bag, I couldn't help thinking about the horrible experience I just had.

Was it because of the heavy meal I had just before bed, or was this actually a sign, warning me of something terrible to come?

I could still feel everything I was feeling just moments ago, the anxiety that made me wish I was dead. The struggle to cry out, the stinging of my swollen cheek, and of course, the pain in my chest from the bullet hole, I could've sworn pierced it!

CHAPTER 44

Paranoia

I peeked out the lobby window, and there was Sal, as usual, leaning against his car reading the Newspaper. I kept replaying the part of my dream where Mr. D yells out *Now!* and Sal turns and shoots me in the chest. I knew he was more than capable of doing it, and the cannon he carried under his arm, gave him instant access.

I never said anything to Grams, because she would've pulled out her book of dreams, to try and interpret. I was obviously paranoid, and it sucked, because I had to get in his car.

Sal must've felt me staring at him, because he looked my way. Immediately I pulled back, and remained hidden off to the side. I stayed there, trying to decide what to do. It'll really suck if all I was experiencing was nothing more than a panic attack, because it was about to cost me an opportunity. But, I guess that's better than a sign from God, because *that* will in fact, cost me a life!

I leaned over to take another peek out, only to find Sal

standing right outside the window, our faces mere inches apart.

I felt like I didn't have a choice now, and stepped outside.

"You okay?" Sal asked. I nodded, and he smiled. He then took my bag and headed to the car. I was hesitant at first, but then followed behind.

The regular neighborhood crowd made room for Sal to open my door. I waved hi to a few, and slapped five with a few more. Those that asked questions, I promised to explain soon, and the rest just stared as if I were a part of a freak show.

I settled in as Sal closed the door and made his way over to the driver's side. I kept shifting in my seat, as it was impossible for me to get comfortable.

Once in, Sal adjusted his review mirror so that he can look at me, and then drove off.

"King, I just wanna thank you again for last night, and your Grandmother's an absolute doll." He stayed looking at me, waiting I guess for a response. But I had none.

"You alright?" he asked, but still, all I could do was nod. This dream was so real that I couldn't shake it. I kept visualizing him, turning around and putting one in my chest. It kept playing, over and over again!

Once we got into the city, we made a right down an unfamiliar street.

"What are you doing?" I asked, sitting up, my eyes wide and bouncing from window to window.

"It said Detour." Sal replied, but I never saw a sign. "You

sure you okay, King?" Sal asked again. "You seem a bit strange today, Buddy, too much of that Boos-ta-low, maybe?" I could feel him staring at me through the mirror.

"That's some strong-ass shit you people drink, that's probably why you all are such good dancers." Sal started laughing. I however, wasn't amused. I sat back and tried to think of reasons why Mr. D would want me dead. But I couldn't think of any.

I noticed that we were passing by the Library.

"Can you pull over for a minute?"

"Um, Mr. D, doesn't like me to make any stops once I have you in the car."

"We had to detour anyway. I just wanna say hi to someone, I'll be quick." Sal looked at me through the mirror and exhaled. Then pulled over and opened the door for me.

So far, no one saw me. I turned to the smoked windows of the car to make sure my hair was still intact, then rushed up the library steps skipping a few in the process.

The minute I entered, my eyes caught hold of her. I stood at the entrance a bit longer than I should've when her eyes glanced in my direction, and then back to what she was doing. I looked back through the doors and saw Sal just leaning on the car reading the paper, and then turned and started walking toward Charlotte. As I approached she looked up, her eyes immediately latching onto my hair, then down to my eyes.

"Oh, my god!" She gasped when she saw it was me. I smiled and waved, but she couldn't pull her eyes from my hair.

"How are you?" I asked.

"I'm good," she finally said. "What's up with that?" She asked, gesturing toward my hair with a weird twist to her smile.

"It's a long story, but I'd love to tell it to you, maybe over dinner?"

"Are you into Punk Rock or something?" I laughed and shook my head.

"I swear, I'll explain it all."

"Wow, I've just been so busy, you know, between work and school."

"I understand."

"Okay, sure." "How about…"

I was about to pick a day, when Charlotte's boss stepped up behind the counter.

"Can I help you with something, young man?" She asked as Charlotte immediately turned and walked off.

"No thank you, I was just asking if you were open on Sundays."

"Till one, and then we close."

"Okay, thank you." I said backing up, my eyes bouncing between her and Charlotte. I then turned around and rushed for the exit.

Before leaving though I looked outside, and of course, Sal was standing beside the door of his car waiting for me. I thought about leaving through another exit, but figured, if Sal let me out so easy, then, the paranoia was all in my head.

CHAPTER 45

Ugly Ass Worms

"Walk past Studio A, through the double doors, and straight down," said Roller Girl, from the top of the steps. "You'll see a sign over a door that says Rehearsal. Just go in there!" I looked up to say thank you, but as usual she was gone.

As I approached the door, I could already hear I AM KING playing over some loud yelling that I couldn't make out on the other side. I opened it slowly so as not to distract anyone, and was in awe of what I saw.

This room was huge gymnasium type. Large windows lined the back, and the front was covered with mirrors. A diverse mixture of kids, more or less my age, we're either sitting on one of the folding chairs lined beneath the windows, working one on one with one another, or on the floor stretching. It was obvious. They were all dancers, and this felt like a scene straight out of the TV show, FAME.

"King!" Mr. D called out waving me in from where he sat across the room. The music stopped, and everyone turned toward me. I stood there for a moment and just smiled at everyone. I wish they would've at least kept the music playing, as the place was now silent as fuck.

Even though I had a pretty cool walk, whenever I knew someone was watching, I would often go off-step, sometimes even trip, and I could already feel that this was going to be one of those times.

Every eyeball stared as I made my way across the huge open room. I tried to step in rhythm, going so far as playing a beat in my head, but it was no use. Even before I made it to the half-way mark, I was already walking like a fucking dork!

I focused down at the floor, my eyes glancing upwards every now and then, only to catch smirks and rude whispering that were obviously about me. Mr. D met up with me, and guided me to the front of the room. Before I turned around, I caught a glimpse of my reflection in the huge mirror in front. I hated what I saw. I not only looked stupid, I felt it. I couldn't believe that I was allowing them to do this to me, and now, to humiliate me in front of all these people.

"Everybody, I'll like you to meet, King." At this point, I had no choice, so I looked up and just as my eyes reached theirs, the entire room broke out in applause.

I knew the type of influence Mr. D had over everyone who worked here, but there was something different about this crowd. My body relaxed as they all got up onto their feet and continued clapping. It didn't seem fake, either that or they weren't just great dancers, but great actors too!

I turned to the gentlemen, who stood off to the side,

holding a pen and pad, not to mention, an expression unreadable, I knew at once that this was the head dude in charge.

He had to be in his seventies, and the little bit of hair he had left was totally gray, and sat neatly around his ears both of which dangled tiny gold hoops.

He was extremely tall, and just as skinny. The tight purple leotard he wore accentuated his bony legs, and his pink cut up sweatshirt matched the largest pair of ballet slippers I had ever seen.

"King, I'd like you to meet, Princess," and though his clothing said enough, his name answered any question I might've had.

"Princess is our choreographer, and the absolute best there is."

I extended my hand, and he met it with just three of his extremely fingers.

"Nice to meet you," I said, smiling, and hoping he'd smile back. But instead he leaned back and turned his head sideways, and from there looked at me from the far corner of his eye, after which he then turned to Mr. D and asked.

"Are you serious?"

I could already tell, this guy had no filter, and I was scared to hear what he had to say. Mr. D just laughed, I on the other hand refocused back to the floor.

"As serious as I was when I brought *you* on board." Mr. D replied. Princess sucked his teeth and rolled his eyes, then turned back to me, and threw his hand onto his hip.

I could feel his eyeballs exploring every inch of my being, while the entire room remained silent and still. I could hear my own heartbeat, hoping that no one else could.

I looked up until my eyes were caught by his, and I smiled. He gave off an annoyed exhaled, as if his mother had just ordered him to throw out the trash.

I followed his eyes over to Mr. D, who just smiled, as if to say, *tough luck!*

Back to me, Princess turned, and I continued smiling.

"Well aren't you a box of sunshine!" He said, shaking his head. "Okay, Sunshine, let's see what kind of shit I got stuck with."

I looked at Mr. D, and he nodded.

"Let's begin with your toes!"

"My toes?"

"Yes, your toes, now touch'em!"

I looked at Mr. D, and he gestured for me to do as I was told. I looked back at the class, and of course every single one of them looked on. Ever since I stepped in this room, it's been a constant string of humiliation.

I looked back at Princess, and he just stood there, his arms now crossed, waiting.

I bent down, touched my toes, and then quickly popped back up, then I turned to Princess and smiled, everyone except he and Mr. D fell into hysterics.

"Shut the fuck up!" Princess yelled out, with a clap of his hands and foot stomp, and again, the place went silent.

Princess turned back to me, and though I've known him now for just a few minutes, I felt I was the one he hated most in this world.

He walked up to me and turned his back to the class. He didn't look at me, but whispered from the side of his mouth.

"Let's hope you're really that stupid, and not purposely trying to fuck with me. Now try it again, but this time, don't bend your fuckin' knees."

I looked at Mr. D, and his eyes told me to just go ahead and do as I was told. So again, I bent over, struggling to keep my legs as straight as possible, but this time my hands barely made it past my knees. People were trying not to laugh, but doing a horrible job of it. I didn't fight it though, and the moment I felt that strain behind my legs, I gave up. I proceeded to stand upright, until Princess placed his long bony hand between my shoulder blades, and just held me there.

"Now, for all you got damn hyenas, I wanna know how many of you remember *not* being able to touch your crusty-ass toes?" I watched through the mirror as Princess was the first to raise his hand, until one by one, everyone else's hand was raised.

Princess remained with his hand on my back, gently applying a bit more pressure.

"You!" He said, pointing to one of the guys leaning against the wall. The guy stood straight.

"Yes?"

"Do you remember being like this?"

"I do, very well."

I was becoming very uncomfortable, and when I attempted to straighten up a bit, Princess again applied even more pressure.

"How long did it take you to finally be able to touch your crusties?"

"Um, I don't know maybe a year?" the guy answered.

"A year?"

"Yes sir."

The back of my thighs were now burning, and I could feel a slight shake coming on.

"What about you?" he asked, pointing to the Asian girl sitting in a split position. "How long did it take you to touch your fortune cookies?"

She seemed embarrassed by the racial comment he made.

"About ten months!" She replied, a bit shy.

"Ten months?" Princess replied, looking for a confirmation which she gave with a nod.

I wasn't sure if he was doing it on purpose or not, but he kept pushing down on me. I wasn't sure how long I could stay like this. I grabbed hold of my legs to help give me a little support.

"So, how many of you were able to touch your toes in eight months?" Five people raised their hand.

'Six months?" He asked his class, and three people raised their hand. I was starting to feel light-headed, and the burning sensation that attacked the back of my thighs was now burning my calves, so I started rubbing them.

"So, was anyone in here able to touch their toes in less than six months?"

A hand rose from a guy sitting closest to us. "Well, of course you did!" Princess said sarcastically to the guy who honestly looked like a black younger version of him.

"So tell us. How long did it take you to be able to touch those ugly-ass worms of yours? And trust me, I'm not saying this to insult you, they really do look like ugly-ass worms.

"It only took me a couple of weeks." He said, sucking his teeth, and raising his brows.

"Well, thank you for sharing that with us... you arrogant fuck!" The last word joined by another push down on my back. The pain was intense. And I couldn't imagine this shit being healthy.

Everyone sort of looked toward the floor, scared of making any type of eye contact with Princess. My legs were beginning to shake and I was feeling a spasm about to come on. I took a deep breath and tried to relax.

"Now, by a show of hands, how many of you sorry son of a bitches were able to touch your piglets within the first day of trying?" And not one hand went up! All was silent, as Princess just stood there. My legs were now beginning to shake, and my eyes flooded with tears. And this time... people noticed.

"Do you wanna know why it took you all so long, to be able to do the most basic, yet important exercise in dance?" Everyone looked at him, waiting for the answer, and so he said…

Because it wasn't me teaching you! He so proudly professed. At that moment, he let go of my back and gestured for everyone to look, and without even me realizing it, my hands were flat on my toes. Everyone began to clap.

Standing straight up was easier than I had expected. The class continued clapping as I turned to Mr. D whose look simply said. *I told you so!*

I looked at Princess, who wasn't at all smiling, but rather looking at me, as if he was proud, but not of me, but of himself.

"Go 'head." He said, pointing at me. I looked at him, clueless as to what he was asking.

"Touch your toes, just like you did. Remember, don't bend your knees."

I was so reluctant to do this because I felt like either I wouldn't be able to do it, or, if I did, I wouldn't be able to stand back up. I glanced at Mr. D, and he was just standing there, waiting to see this miracle, and so I did, and amazingly, I was able to touch my toes and more importantly, stand back straight. The class continued clapping, and I have to admit, I felt pretty good.

"Okay everyone, back to work!"

CHAPTER 46

Sunshine

Not only was this the hardest part of my transition into King. It was without doubt the most humiliating. I counted twelve dancers, me making it thirteen. Princess placed me way in the back center, so that I can watch everyone and *try* to follow along. I thought it was a great spot, but the random snickers among the dancers told me that not an awkward move I made went unnoticed.

These people have been doing this for years. Who was I to think that I could just step in and pick up from where *they* left off?

I looked to my left, and there was Mr. D, sitting on one of the folding chairs, just staring at me, his face void of any expression. Every so often, Princess would stroll through the ranks, each person he'd have something to say to.

"Look forward!" He'd tell one of them. "Act like you're enjoying it!" He'll tell another. "Keep your head straight! Stay with the group! What the fuck are you doing!!!" and so on.

We were doing a very simple two step, repeating it over

and over, when Princess walked up and stood directly in front of me. He crossed his arms, with his hand holding up his chin. His eyes seemed to have gone from my feet, up to my dick, and stayed there for a moment, before continuing up to my eyes, from which he stared hard. Remaining there until I would eventually lose the timing of my two step.

"Stop!" He commanded, and immediately everything was still and silent. For a tall lanky gay dude, Princess could be pretty intimidating. Everyone was looking my way, but I just stared out into space.

"What's the problem, Sunshine?" He asked.

"Um, nothing."

"Nothing?" Princess asked, looking at me with squinted eyes.

"Then why are you screwing up the steps?"

"Well, I kind of lost my timing a bit."

Someone laughed, and quickly, Princess turned around.

"Who was that?" he asked, his eyes tagging each person in the room, but no one said anything.

"I said, who was that?" and still, no one came forward, he then turned to Mr. D and asked.

"What's the deadline?"

"Um, maybe three weeks."

"Three weeks." He said to himself, scratching his chin while looking up into the air, and after a few moments, Princess turned back to the class.

"Everyone grab your shit, and get the fuck out of here!"

He ordered. The room filled with gasp, as no one understood what was going on.

"I need you to run that ad again in The Voice, and also in Backstage." Princess said to Mr. D, who didn't know what to say.

One girl walked up to Princess and asked him

"Me too?"

And from the top of his lungs he yelled dead in her face.

"Yes… you too!"

Mr. D got up and walked over to Princess.

"Is this necessary?" He asked.

"You said you will not get involved!" Princess replied in a stern angry tone.

"I'm not getting involved, it's just that, they've put in so much…"

"But what's the point?" Princess shouted, "Without loyalty, we have shit!"

"But they're being loyal to each other," Mr. D added.

"That loyalty means nothing! If it isn't to me, you, and the company, then what's the point? I have no need for that. If they rather be loyal to each other, then great, they can get their loyal asses up out of my studio, and together they can all go look for another job!"

Suddenly, a voice called out.

"It was me!"

Everyone went silent and turned to the girl standing

toward the back.

"I didn't mean anything by it, I'm sorry," the girl said, standing there in tears. I looked at Princess, and felt a bit of softness come through. In fact everyone looked at him. Princess just stood there, looking at the girl, and thinking.

After a couple of intense moments, he took a deep breath, and exhaled, as did everyone else.

"I'm sorry." again she said, tears rolling down her face. Princess gave her a slight smile and calmly crossed his arms in front of him.

"Now, grab your shit, and get the fuck out of my studio!" Everyone's jaw dropped. The poor girl started shaking her head and begging, but Princess didn't care and turned back to the class.

My heart broke as I watched the girl grab her things then run out the door.

"Let me make something clear here, the opportunity you guys all have, is in fact the opportunity of a lifetime. Loyalty to your dance mate is beautiful, and I respect that, but if that loyalty means choosing between them and me, well, you better think long and hard.

Princess then turned to me, and asked.

"What should we do?"

I didn't know what he was talking about, and looked around like an idiot.

"About what?" I asked.

"Should we keep these ass-holes, or should we dump

them for a better bunch?"

I hesitated. Not because I thought they should go, but because I didn't feel qualified to even be a part of that discussion.

"They should stay," I finally said, and could feel the tension in the room suddenly go lax.

"I also think the girl you kicked out should be able to come back."

"Well, I don't know about that one," Princess said.

"Please," I replied. Princess looked at me for a moment then asked the class.

"Who's in touch with her?" It took a minute for someone to finally raise their hand. "Make sure she's back here tomorrow morning, and tell her to leave her shits and giggles at home."

"Now does anyone else have tickly balls?" He asked, and this time, there wasn't a sound, or a movement, the place looked like a wax museum.

"Now, back to you Sunshine."

"If you don't mind, I prefer Rey."

"Not in here. In here, it's going to be Sunshine, and it will remain Sunshine until I feel you earned the name Rey, and then, you will remain Rey until you earn the name King, and the way it looks now, you are going to be Sunshine for a pretty long time, and for the rest of you assholes!" Princess continued, now turning to the class, "If I hear anyone call him by any other name but Sunshine, you will find yourself scouring the streets of Manhattan with a fucking backstage newspaper under your arm, looking for work. Is that clear?"

Everyone said yes and nodded, but that wasn't enough.

"I said… Is that clear?" He yelled again, and this time the class answered to his satisfaction. Princess turned back to me and eye balled me once again.

"Don't move," He said, and then turned and walked into a small office to the side of the studio. We all stood around like the assholes he said we were. I looked over at Mr. D and he gave me a wink and a smile as if I was handling this well, but little did he know, I wanted to get the fuck out of here.

A few moments later, Princess came out of the office with a few items in his hands. They were dance wear, complete with sweat shirt, leotards and ballet slippers.

"I'm pretty good at sizing men so these should fit you perfectly." I looked at everything and then back up at him, and Mr. D.

"I don't know about all this." I told them both.

"First off," Princess began. "When you are in *my* studio, you address *me*, not him!" he said, thumbing back at Mr. D.

"To everyone else, you may be King. But in here, I'm the mother fucking Queen. Now you take your little skinny ass, and get in that dressing room and put that shit on now!"

I dared not look back at Mr. D. I could feel everyone staring at me, and as I approached the curtain that led into the dressing room. I peeked inside and saw a bunch of lockers, benches and women's underclothes scattered about. Of course I assumed that this was for the women, and when I looked back at Princess, he said.

"We're one big happy family, Sunshine. Now go in there, grab a locker and change your clothes. You're holding us up."

He wasn't kidding, it was one dressing room for everyone, and it didn't even have a door.

"Oh, and Sunshine!" He called out. I stopped and looked back. "No underwear!" I looked at him, and then at the others, before continuing into the room.

I found the only unoccupied locker in the room, and looked at the poster of the naked man hanging on the inside of its door. I didn't know who it belonged to, so I left it, and then glanced at the curtain behind me hoping that no one would enter.

I should've opened the package that held the leotard before I took off my clothes, because now I stood butt naked wrestling to open it.

"There's a scissor in that little basket there." I heard Princess say as he stood in the entrance holding open the curtain. I jumped and quickly tried to cover up. I could clearly see some of the others that stood outside, which only meant that they could see me as well.

"Can you close the curtain please?" I asked.

"Sure." Replied Princess as he stepped in and let the curtain close behind him.

"I would really like a little privacy while I change if you don't mind?"

"Hmm. Sorry, privacy doesn't exist here, Sunshine. In order for me to get one hundred percent out of anyone here, they need to be one hundred percent comfortable. Now hurry up and change, I need to make sure everything fits properly."

I didn't know which would be better, should I face him, or have my back to him? I decided on the latter.

I reached over and grabbed the scissors from the little basket on top of the locker and cut open the bag. From the corner of my eye I could see Princess still standing there, watching.

I held up the leotards, and I swear, they looked like they'd fit a two year old.

"There's no way I could fit into this." I told him, and then regretted it when he started toward me.

He took the leotard from me and held them up in the air, then looked down at me, as I tried desperately to cover myself.

"Nope, this is your size." He confirmed. "They're supposed to be tight. They're called tights."

Princess handed them back to me and told me to put them on. I tried, but it was no use, not to mention embarrassing. After several attempts, he became frustrated and told me to give it to him before I ripped them. I did so gladly, and was relieved, hoping that now he would give me a pair that fits, or better yet, a pair of sweat pants.

I handed them to him and watched him rolled them up, sort of the way I remember Grams use to do to my socks before putting them on me.

"Sit down," said Princess. *He isn't really gonna do this is he?* I thought, and sure enough, he was. I wanted to just run out of there, but decided against it, as I was completely naked.

What possessed me to sit, I still can't figure it out, but I did, and watched as Princess knelt in front of me.

I covered myself as best as I could and looking toward the curtain, I prayed that no one would enter.

"Give me your foot." He told me, just like Grams used to. I held up one foot and watched as he placed the rolled up leotard over my ankle, and then did the same with the other.

"Stand up." He ordered.

"I could do the rest." I assured him.

"Stand up!" He yelled. I know everyone heard him. I glanced toward the curtain as Princess worked the leotard up past my knees and up my thighs where he stopped. I figured he'd let me take it from there, but when I tried to take over, he yelled and smacked my hand.

He reached around my waist and pulled the leotard up from behind me, his face a mere inch from my crotch.

Finally he got it up over my hips, pulling on a few areas inside my thigh to keep it taut. "There, what I tell you?" He said as he stepped back for a better look. Now finish getting dressed and meet us on the floor… and hurry!"

Princess turned and started walking toward the curtain when he grabbed a stick of deodorant and tossed it to me.

"Keep that in your locker and make sure you put plenty of it on. I don't like my studio smelling like a boxing gym."

I pushed the curtain to the side and stepped out of the dressing room. Immediately, Princess pressed the play button on the cassette player to the song "I'm Too Sexy" By Drop Dead Fred.

It was a pretty lengthy walk from the dressing room to where we were rehearsing.

Princess led the applause with a smile, everyone followed, even Mr. D. Gold leotards with a purple cut sweat shirt and black ballet slippers. I felt ridiculous, and the mirrors at the front of the class agreed.

"Okay, simmer down everyone." Princess said while still laughing. I watched as Mr. D gave me a thumbs up, before turning and exiting the studio. I stood there, staring at the door, like a child being left at school for the first time.

CHAPTER 47

Five Thousand Pieces

I was given the impression that dance class went up until 8:00 pm, but it was almost nine by the time we called it quits.

"Okay everyone." Princess announced as he clapped his hands above his head. "I'll see you all tomorrow morning, remember, if you think you're going to be late just stay your ass home, because you're fired!" Everyone got up and headed for the dressing room. I dreaded having to go in there, and sort of felt that if anything, I should at least have my own changing room.

"Sunshine, let me rap to you for a minute." Princess called out. I don't know which was worst, having to change in front of my entire dance class, or having Princess say he wants to rap to me.

I turned and walked toward him. He was straightening the music area, putting the cassettes back into their cases.

"Yes?" I asked as I approached him. He didn't even look at me, instead he continued straightening up.

"So what do you think?" He asked. I thought for a long

moment, careful with what I said.

"Umm, Think about what?"

"About everything, everything that's happening to you."

I gave it a moment, and then answered.

"Well, I still find it baffling."

"Baffling?"

"Yeah, you know, hard to believe."

Princess didn't respond, but rather squinted as he dusted off the boom box and the shelf it sat on.

"Does the being *hard* to believe have anything to do with your lack of talent?" Princess asked.

"I don't think Mr. D would've chose me if he didn't think I had talent."

"Is that what you think?" he asked, having yet to even look at me.

"I do!"

Princess grabbed the bottle of Windex and began spraying and wiping down the mirrors. "Do you know what a Triple Threat is?" Princess asked, his eyes focused on cleaning the many smudges.

"Isn't that when someone can do three things at once or something like that?"

"A triple threat is someone who has pretty much mastered the three art forms of song, dance, and drama."

I gave a simple shrug, as if to say, who gives a fuck?

"Now, do you think you can tell me, which medium of

entertainment relies on triple threat talent?"

I was exhausted, and really not in the mood to play trivial pursuit. I just wanted to change and get my ass home. I thought about it for a minute but couldn't come up with anything, so I just looked at him through the mirror, and shook my head. I watched a subtle smile grow across his face, before he gave me the answer.

"Theater!" he simply said.

"Theater?"

"Yes, and if you haven't noticed, New York City *is* the Theater capital of the world.

Which means what, Sunshine?"

I knew where he was going with it, but didn't give me a chance to answer, he then turned to me with this attitude that lived up to his name, and with one hand on his hip, and the other pointing directing at me, began to explain.

"It means that New York City is full of talented triple threat individuals who have dedicated their entire lives to perfecting their craft. Who sacrificed their relationships with friends, families, and lovers, all because their dreams meant everything to them! Those who would suck a dick dry, and give their ass to an entire team of producers, to do as they wish, for the incredible opportunity that is right now being placed in *your* lap!"

I watched through the mirror as students hurried out of the studio, leaving me alone with this bitter maniac who seemed to be confessing his own personal struggles. Princess suddenly dropped down to his knees, crying hysterically into his hands. He bent over, placing his head on the hard wooden floor and cried like a baby. I don't know if he was expecting a hug or some other type of consolation, but I wasn't getting next to that crazy fuck. Instead, I dashed back to the dressing room, grabbed my shit, and still dressed in my dance gear, I ran the fuck outta there.

As I hurried down the hall and up the spiral staircase, there of course was Roller Girl.

"So how'd it go?" She asked with her big bubbly smile. I looked at her about to say something, but didn't. I just started walking.

"What are you still doing here?" I asked.

She rolled up beside me and grabbed my arm. I stopped and turned to her. My face told her that something was wrong.

"What is it?" She asked.

I looked around to make sure no one was listening, and then asked her, "Why me?"

Roller Girl's face scrunched up a bit in question.

"Why you what?"

"We live in a city saturated by talent, lots of talent. Talent I could only dream of having, why did Mr. D pick me?"

Roller Girl looked at me, and then gave it some thought.

"I don't think it's about you, King, or even your talent."

"What do you mean?"

Roller Girl waved me to follow her into a room, and when the door closed behind us, we ended up in total darkness. Of course I assumed something was about to go down, but when she turned on the lights, though a bit disappointed, I was in total awe of what I was seeing.

The room turned out to be a full-sized roller rink, complete with DJ booth and concession stand.

"You gotta be kidding me," I said as I followed her to a counter where behind it were shelves filled with roller skates.

"What size are you?" She asked, but I just waved her off, as I hadn't skated in years.

"Nah, I'm..." Leaning over the counter she looks at my feet.

"You look like an eleven." She said and grabbed a pair, but then I corrected her.

"Twelve."

Her eyebrows arched and she smiled at me, placing a pair of size twelve roller skates on the counter.

"I don't know." I said to her shaking my head. "Come on, it's just us. It'll be fun."

I took the skates and put them on, while Roller Girl went behind the DJ booth and flipped a switch that made the lights dim, the strobes flash, and the music play.

She laughed when I tried to stand and nearly fell.

"It's been a while." I said as I tried rolling forward, again nearly falling. "A long while!"

Roller Girl then took me by my hand, and led me into the rink.

"I used to be pretty good at this," I tried to explain,

though by the way I was skating, you could never tell.

After a couple of laps, it pretty much all came back.

"It's about Mr. D, and *his* talent." Roller Girl said, continuing our conversation from before.

I looked at her, and was trying hard to understand. She turned and tried to skate backwards, nearly knocking us both down, so instead, I did it, and it came to me like it was just yesterday. I took her by both her hands and we continued around the rink.

"Do you remember when you were in first grade, and the teacher gave you puzzles to put together?" She asked me.

"Yeah."

"What do you remember about those puzzle pieces?" I thought for a second, and then answered.

That they were pretty big, and the whole puzzle consisted of maybe just four or five pieces."

"That's right. Basically, most of the puzzle was already put together, but as a child, when you put those four or five pieces together and saw that final product, how did you feel?"

"Great!"

"But if I would give you that same exact puzzle right now, and asked you to put it together, and you did. How would you feel?"

"I don't know, I probably wouldn't feel anything at all!"

"Exactly!"

I looked at her trying to understand where she was going with this.

"Mr. D doesn't want a puzzle that is practically completed, he wants one of those ten thousand piece landscape ones, that he can personally place each piece himself. He wants one of those puzzles, where even after five thousand pieces, you still can't figure out what it is?"

"But why me?"

"Because with you, he's at least sure, that all the pieces are in the box!"

I looked at her, and smiled. I understood, and though it felt like only a few minutes, Roller Girl and I had skated and talked for over an hour, when suddenly I realized.

"Oh shit, Sal!

"Don't worry about it," she replied, "he'll wait for you." We took another lap around, this time, holding hands.

"So how is it you know all this?"

"That isn't important, King. What *is* important is that I do... and now, so do you!"

I could've skated with Roller Girl all night, but I had to go. She escorted me through the lobby and to the door, and before leaving, I turned and looked at her. God knows how bad I wanted to kiss her, but decided not to, well, at least not tonight!

She looked on as I made my way down the hall and stopped at the elevator. Just before getting In, I turned to her and asked.

"Everybody here calls you Roller Girl. What's your real name?"

"It's Mary."

"That's pretty." I replied. "Can I call you that?"

"Sure, if I could call you Reynaldo?" I looked at her, and laughed.

"Goodnight, Roller Girl."

"Goodnight, King!"

CHAPTER 48

A Day Off

Mr. D gave me every Wednesday off. He preferred the middle of the week because weekends he assured me would eventually get busy. Wednesday was also good because it was the one day that I was sure Charlotte would be at the library.

I was watching TV in my room while I got dressed when Nemesis' new music video came on. I tried to put aside my hatred for the guy, because I knew that wasn't cool, so I sat at the foot of my bed and tried to watch his video with an open heart, or at least, an open mind. But it was no use.

From the way he looked, to the way he sounded, I cringed. I found every flaw that existed, and even made up a few that didn't.

To me, his lyrics made no sense, and his flow didn't flow at all. I dissected his entire track, laughing at the weird sounds that were chosen.

He tried to represent hip hop in dress, but to me, he looked like a bum. Even the girls he used in his video I had something to say about. Either they were too fat, too skinny, or just straight up ugly. I really hated this dude, I don't know why, I just did!

I couldn't take it anymore, and turned off the TV in a way that had Grams caught me, would've punched me dead in my head.

"Good morning Mijo." She said when I stepped out of my room, "what do you want to eat?"

"I'm not hungry, thanks." I said as I gave her a hug and a kiss. "You're going to the Flunky place?"

"Funky Junky, Grams, and no, I'm going to the city to see someone."

"A girl?" she asked, always being nosy.

"A friend."

"A *girl* friend?" she asked again. "No Grams, not a Girlfriend,

Just a girl I met at the Library."

"Is she Puerto Rican?"

"I don't know, I didn't ask."

"Is she black, or white?"

Grams wasn't letting up, she wanted to know everything.

"She's black!"

"So what, you can't find a nice Puerto Rican girl?"

"Who said she wasn't Puerto Rican?"

"You just said she's black!"

"So what, you're black!"

"I'm a different kind of black."

I just looked at her cute little racist face, and kissed her cheek.

"I promise, I'll let you know as soon as I know," and at that moment, I dashed out the door before she could say anything else.

Laughing hysterically as I raced down the staircase, I suddenly hear, echoing from above, "que dios te bendiga!"

This was my first day off since signing and I'm already spoiled. Since then, I've gone nowhere without Sal, and it already feels strange.

"Hi Rey!" called out a small voice from behind me. It was Junior, on his bike as usual. An odd looking bike in fact, obviously built from parts he must've found in the garbage. The only thing I noticed was missing, were brakes. I figured that out when he put his foot on the tire to slow it down as he pulled up to me.

His chubby friend pulled up beside him. His bike seemed to be a bit more intact, and at least had working breaks. However I did notice he needed some air, as both tires were a bit flat.

"What's up, Junior," I greeted as we slapped five," how come you're not in school?"

"Ah man, my sisters in the house asleep, and she won't open the door, so I couldn't put away my bike."

"Why were you out so early?"

"She had one of her friends over last night. He gave me a dollar to go out and get some candy. I saw my friend." He said gesturing to the chubby kid parked beside him "So we just rode around all night."

"All night?" I asked, and Junior nodded.

I knew about his sister, she was the biggest hoe on the block, but she was all Junior had.

It was surprising that he was such a good kid, considering his lack of parental guidance, or any type of supervision for that matter. I only hope he'd stay that way, though the odds were terribly against him.

I reached into my pocket and pulled out five singles, and handed Junior three of them. "Go up to Sarge's and get yourself a couple of slices." Junior gladly took the money and smiled, Chubby smiled even more.

'Wow, thanks Rey!' Junior said, before turning to his friend. "I told you he was cool."

"You guys be safe, alright?" I said as they both slapped me five before riding off. I stood there and watched them disappear around the building, heading toward the Pizzeria. I didn't have to ask, I knew they must've been hungry, besides, I really only needed a couple of dollars for the train.

CHAPTER 49

Crumble

As I stood at the corner waiting to cross the street, a car stopped at the light and from it I could hear Nemesis's song blasting from inside.

I looked at the driver as I crossed, and it was a woman, and from what I could see, she was fine. She seemed to be mouthing the words perfectly, and her head bopped in perfect time to the beat.

I couldn't help but try and imagine that same exact scenario, except this time it being *my* song. I couldn't help but to compare my song to the one that was playing, and I have to admit, Nemesis' song made mine sound like elevator music.

I shook my head and made my way up into the subway station. I immediately spotted the undercover cop pretending to be reading the paper, he probably would've not have brought attention to himself had he not do a double take of my hair. But that was fine, as I had no plans of sneaking through this time.

The train pulled up just as I got to the platform. It was

pretty crowded so I just stayed up against the door. With nothing much to do during the ride, my eyes usually bounced around the car looking at the different people. There was always something I could find interesting in a person just by watching them.

Whereas some people liked to read or listen to music, I liked to read people. Imagine what they were like, what kind of work they did. The chubby white guy sitting there asleep, his legs crossed under his seat, his fingers laced just above his round belly. I guess nobody ever told him that fat people shouldn't where horizontal stripes.

The woman, somewhere in her fifties, her hair perfect, and make up painted on thick. She had on a maroon blazer, black pants, and heels. The colors worked great as I'm sure she planned, though she did OD a bit on the perfume, as I could smell it from where I stood. But that's alright, as it sometimes it becomes our only defense against the inevitable bad breath and B.O. that will surely come aboard.

She was reading one of those corny novels with long haired Fabio on the cover, which I always thought was an indication that she was either single, or in a terrible marriage.

And there he was, that one crazy mother fucker that you found on every train, arguing with that invisible friend that sat beside him, the only open seat in the car that nobody dared sit in. He mumbled loud, and I still couldn't understand him. Shit! I wanted to know what the fuck he was talking about.

To my right was a young black girl, sitting down, reading an issue of Right On Magazine, she sensed me reading over her shoulder and repositioned herself from my view.

I've only read Right On a couple of times, and though sometimes I couldn't find it, most times, I couldn't afford it.

From the corner of my eye, I watched as she peeled open the centerfold, and when she did I didn't care anymore. I looked down and said to myself, "who in their right mind would put that ugly mother fucker in a centerfold."

The girl turned around and looked at me just as we approached her stop. She got up and just as she exited the train, she turned around and gave me the finger."

A few people caught that, and gave me dirty looks as they probably thought I was hitting on her. I decided to exit that car and walk through to the next.

I was in deep thought as I made my way through the crowd noticing even more kids were reading Right On.

A part of me wanted to get my own copy, but the other part of me, the jealous part, the hater, was in total denial that this guy was anything special. I had the opportunity to write for him, make money, and possibly become famous, even if it *was* only as a writer. But, of course, I threw it away. Maybe I shouldn't be hating on him and instead hate on myself. Maybe that's what's keeping my own career from going the way I'd like. Maybe cursing him has made me cursed, which is why I was signed to this crazy-ass company, where they gave me this ridiculous cut, dress me in a skirt, and make me record corny-ass songs, before handing me over to some old bitter queen to teach me how to move. The more I thought about it, the more I was convinced… I was fucked!

I got to my stop and made my way up and out of the station. I walked a couple of blocks, eyes from everywhere grabbing hold of my hair. I can even spot people from way across the street looking and pointing at me. I was getting used to it, and pretty much forgot how unusual I still looked to others.

"Love your hair!" One girl said as she passed. That caught me off guard as I was yet to have anyone compliment me. Shit, I didn't even say thank you.

As I approached the Library, a black convertible drove by me, and not only was it blasting Nemesis' song, I could've sworn that it was Nemesis himself. He must live around here because I keep seeing him in this area.

I jogged up the stairs to the Library, and upon entering, my eyes shot to the counter. Charlotte had this thing about her, a certain glow that made you wanna stare at her. She had a stack of books beside her, stamping each of the index cards inside, a Job that would've made me wanna hang myself, she did with the grace of a figure skater. Well, at least that's how *I* saw it.

"Can I help you?" She asked, not realizing that it was me standing in front of her.

"Yes, I'm looking for a book on how to ask out a Librarian?" Charlotte looked up, saw it was me, and started laughing.

"Sorry, totally unpopular topic, therefore, no books exist!"

"Well, hopefully one day *I* can write one."

"All you have to do is find yourself a Librarian." Charlotte said.

"You wouldn't happen to know any, would you?"

"Actually, I do." She replied, her shy smile pulling attention to her dimples, as she nodded a gesture toward her boss standing at the other end of the huge L-shaped counter.

I looked over at the woman, with the tight bun and cat eye reading glasses. She wore a dark skirt down to her calves with those dull skin tone stockings and shoes that look like they were prescribed by her doctor.

I looked at Charlotte, and shook my head. "I'm talking about you."

"Are you sure? I mean, she could really use a date... Really!"

We both started laughing, a bit louder than we should've which made her boss look our way.

"Uh oh!" Charlotte whispered, continuing what she was doing. I didn't know what to do, so I just pretended to be writing... There was just one problem...

"Are you writing on my counter?" The Librarian asked. Charlotte turned and walked away.

"Ah, no ma'am," I assured her, as she carefully inspected the counter.

"I could've sworn you were writing on my counter."

"No ma'am, I would never do that."

"So what is it you need?" I wanted so bad to answer that question, but wouldn't dare.

"I was wondering if you had any of the Village Voice's left?"

The Librarian turned and pointed to the rack where they usually are, staring into the air as if she had absolutely no more patience for this job

Charlotte was so right about her, except I felt she could use a bit more than just a date.

"I didn't even see them."

"Maybe you were a little distracted?" she replied, her eyes bouncing between mine and Charlotte's.

"Charlotte, go downstairs and find this book, would you?" She said, handing Charlotte a small piece of paper."

"Yes, Ms. Crumble."

Ms. Crumble? Wow, I couldn't think of a better name myself. Charlotte turned and disappeared through the door that led down to the basement.

The Librarian then turned to me as if to say, *why are you still here?*

I thanked her with a nod, grabbed a Voice from the rack and took a seat at one of the empty tables, making sure to face the counter. Ms. Crumble watched my every move, staring at me with the puss of all pusses.

I wondered if she was married. If I had to bet, I'd say no. but if she was, I'd bet she's a widow… a *Black* widow that is!

I gave Ms. Crumble a light friendly smile, figuring that since she's playing Charlotte's gatekeeper, the smart thing to do would be to get on her good side. Except, I don't think she had one. She just stood there, staring at me with her mouth half open, looking like she was about to throw up at any moment.

This week's Village Voice was the most sickening yet, as just about every other story in it found a reason to somehow someway, reference Nemesis. I glanced up at the clock and realized that an hour had already passed. I looked back at the counter, and there was Ms. Crumble, staring at me while stamping cards.

Charlotte was still in the basement, and I couldn't help but imagine, what that place must be like. I mean, basements in New York City, were never the place to be, and I began to wonder if she was to stay down there until I was gone.

I closed the paper and clumsily stood up, making sure to grab Ms. Crumble's attention by banging around the chair. I wanted to make sure she saw me leave, so that she can release poor Charlotte from that dark, rat infested dungeon.

I got outside and began to walk uptown when surprisingly I ran into Charlotte coming out of a store.

"What are you doing out here?' I asked.

"I'm just getting off lunch."

"But I thought you were in the basement all this time looking for some book?"

"No, I went to lunch, but I'm going back now to find that book."

"So, I guess you can't chill a bit?"

"No, I'm sorry, I only get an hour."

"So, can I call you? Maybe we can hang out some *other* time?"

"Hmm, that might not be such a good idea. I'm staying with my brother while I'm in school, and he could be a little, you know… Big brotherish!"

Damn, another obstacle? Getting with Charlotte was like trying to break into Fort Knox.

"But, why don't I call *you*?" Charlotte suggested. I looked up and smiled.

"That'll be great, maybe we can hook up for a movie or something?" I replied overly excited.

"Or we can hook up over the phone, you know, chit chat a bit?"

I got the hint, and replied.

"I'd like that."

"Look, I gotta get back." She said as she began to step backwards. "But, I'll call you!" My reply was nothing more than a smile. A big one, though.

I stood there and watched as she turned around and headed toward the Library.

Damn, she was so fine. I thought as I watched her ascend the Library steps.

I continued uptown, my regular way. I loved the City, the energy. I could walk for miles without a problem.

As I got around 41st street, I started hearing Yes Yes Y'all echoing above the noisy city streets. I stopped and listened closely, trying to figure out where the music was coming from. It seemed to have just risen out of nowhere, then exploding in every direction. People walked by, following my gaze into the sky. I already looked like a fuckin' maniac... This just made it worst!

I decided to just walk until the music either got louder, or faded away. I figured that might give me at least an idea, as from where it was coming.

Once again that sonofabitch started singing my shit. I cringed every time I heard him, and that obnoxious accent made me wanna rip his fuckin' tongue out.

It sounded Spanish, or even from one of those weird European countries. I clocked the time, the day, and even the weather, trying to figure out some sort of pattern. The clarity of the music told me his windows were open, and that was great. However, it also meant that once the weather changes, his windows might very well close, and therefore... I better hurry!

CHAPTER 50

Vanessa

I was last to enter the dressing room, trying to kill as much time as I could before having to go in there and change in front of all these strangers. My locker was in a corner, and everyone else coincidentally was behind me. The room was a bit musty due to the heavy sweat Princess made sure to generate among his students.

I kind of peeked a bit behind me and noticed everyone getting completely naked and drying themselves off before anything.

I didn't want to seem nasty, so I did the same. I could feel the stares on my white ass, when suddenly I heard someone say.

"Hello!" I turned, and in front of me stood a girl with a towel wrapped around her. Dark skinned and tall, her hair pulled tight into a bun. The sweat on her body accentuated the muscles in her arms, and her face invaded by acne, with thick glasses, and a mouthful of braces, contributed to the offset of her clearly natural beauty.

"I'm Vanessa." She smiled.

"I'm Rey" I replied, extending my hand.

"Don't let Princess hear you say that." We laughed. "You see guys, I told you he wasn't stuck up."

"Hi Sunshine, I'm Emerald." One of the male dancers rushed up. We too shook hands, his feeling a bit more feminine than even Vanessa's.

"They call him Emerald because of his eyes, aren't they beautiful?" She asked grabbing Emerald by the chin. I just nodded.

"I'm Jini" The tiny Asian girl said as she too walked up.

"Jenny?" I asked. Vanessa corrected.

"No Jini. Vanessa corrected, and then spelled out J-I-N-I."

"Nice to meet you."

"and I'm Lily!" Said the cute Latina I spotted the moment I entered the studio. I saw the way she was looking at me, and now we were formally introduced.

"Are you gay?" Lily asked, throwing me off a bit.

'No, sorry" I replied, with a smile.

"Sorry Emerald." Lily said. Emerald walked away acting like he was crying.

I was being asked so many questions, that I didn't have a chance to get dress, and by the time I noticed, I was the only one still naked.

Everyone waved a goodnight and left, Vanessa hung around and waited for me. In such a short time, I got a good feel for her, and could tell, she'll make a good friend.

"So how long have you been dancing for Princess?"

"Since he started teaching, I was about seven or eight years old, so figure, fifteen years?" "That's a pretty long time."

"He's the best, taught me everything I know."

"He's hard."

"He has to be hard, the competition is fierce out there."

"You ever thought about teaching yourself?" I asked Vanessa. "I was watching you, you're really good!"

"Thank you, and yes, one day I'd like to open up my own studio."

I sat down to put on my sneakers, Vanessa watched.

"So how long have you been a rapper?"

"That's a tricky question."

"Why's that?"

"I mean, I wanted to be a singer when I was a kid, but I wasn't that good."

"Said who?"

"Said me!" I replied laughing, but Vanessa didn't laugh.

"Well, no one, really, I just kind of knew it."

"Did you ever sing for your parents?"

"I was raised by my Grandmother, and no I never sang for her."

"So technically, you never really knew whether you were

good or not?"

"Technically, you might be right."

"and the Rapper? When did that come about?"

"The moment Rapping became popular, I knew it was for me."

"Did you ever Rap for your Grandmother?"

"Yeah, but she calls it poems!" I said laughing.

"That's cute." Vanessa agreed.

"She's so old fashion. But, to answer your question, this here is actually my first attempt of being a Rapper, like, for real!"

"Wow, so you're one of the lucky ones, huh?" Vanessa asked, as we got up and exited the dressing room.

"What do you mean?"

"Well, look at your situation, you woke up wanting to be a rapper one day, and voila, you're a Rapper!"

"Wait, hold up," I said stopping Vanessa right outside the studio door. "It wasn't all that easy."

"Hey, don't get me wrong," she replied, "I'm not hating on you. I think that's great. Look, you have an incredible opportunity here. Just the fact that Mr. D's got your back pretty much stamps your success. It's like being blessed by Jesus himself."

"How long have you known Mr. D?" I asked.

"Well, I don't really know him, but I do know Princess pretty well, and everything that Mr. D's done for him, believe me when I tell you, you're gonna be good... real good!"

"So, how long have you been with the Funky Junky?"

"Well, the truth is, I'm not."

"What do you mean?"

"The only two people in dance, who are a part of the Funky Junky, are you and Princess.

The rest of us, belong to Princess."

"In other words..."

"In other words, he has the say as to who stays and who goes, I don't worry about it though.

Going up the spiral staircase, I couldn't help but glance at her ass as she led the way, big ass indeed, but I wasn't interested in her that way.

We continued strolling along the corridor that cut through the entire floor, when Roller Girl popped out of one of the rooms.

"Oh hey King!" she greeted with her bubbly self.

"You're still here?"

"Yeah, you know me."

I looked at the two girls as they sort of smiled at one another.

"Oh, I'm sorry, you two don't know each other?"

"Well, I've seen her rolling around before." Vanessa replied.

"More like stumbling," Roller Girl laughed "Hi, they call me Roller Girl." She said with her hand extended and a big smile."

"Hi Roller Girl, I'm Vanessa, nice to finally meet you."

"Well listen, I gotta go, make my rounds before I leave. I'll see you tomorrow, King. It was nice to meet you, Vanessa."

"Same here."

Vanessa and I stepped to the side and allowed Roller Girl to skate off between us. We both turned and watched as she rolled awkwardly up the corridor and then disappeared into one of the rooms. Vanessa and I walked a bit in silence.

"She has the hots for you." Vanessa suddenly blurted out, looking forward with this big cheesy smile.

"Nah, we're just cool like that." I replied.

"No Sunshine, that girl's into you!"

"You can drop the Sunshine bullshit, we're not in class."

"Oh, hell no, when Princess drops it, then I'll drop it!"

We continued walking, and again I turned to her.

"I think you're reading her wrong." Vanessa laughed and shook her head.

"I'm not, and maybe you should go for yours, I mean, she is fine!"

I turned and looked at Vanessa, waiting for her to say it.

"Yes Sunshine," she confirmed. "I like girls!"

"So I guess I'll scratch *you* off my list."

"Good idea, but don't scratch off the white girl. In fact, you better hurry."

"Why, you think she might be…?"

"No… But that doesn't mean shit!"

Sal spotted us coming and quickly opened the back door to the car.

"Hey! How was your day?" Sal greeted.

"Interesting," I replied. "Sal, this here's Vanessa. Sal's my um…"

"…Driver!" he jumped in. "Nice to meet you, Vanessa." The two shook hands.

"Hey, can we give you a lift home?" I offered.

"Thanks Sunshine, but I have my car right there." She said thumbing toward the old lime green Pinto across the street. We stood and watched as she crossed the street heading to her car.

I noticed she got in through the passenger side and then shimmied her way behind the wheel. Though I didn't mean to, I could tell she was embarrassed. I just thought it was gentleman-like to at least wait till she drove off.

After a few attempts to start her car, it finally turned over. Sal and I both exhaled, and then waved goodbye as her car went Putt Putt down the street.

Sal and I went over to his car and got inside. But before driving off, he turned to me and asked.

"Sunshine?"

CHAPTER 51

Making Monsters

This was the first time Mr. D ever personally answered his door. He usually just calls out to come in, because he's either at his desk working, or on the phone.

"You wanted to see me?"

"King my man! What's up?" He greeted enthusiastically before stepping out into the corridor.

"Come with me," he said, waving for me to follow.

"I don't get to talk to you much anymore." He said as we walked.

"Yeah, after rehearsals all I wanna do is go home."

"I'm sure you do. Princess has that effect on people."

"I figured by this time the muscle pain would've went away."

"Oh, I'm sure it did." Mr. D added. "Now it's those other muscles you didn't know you had."

I listened carefully as Mr. D continued to explain. "You see, most physical activities are repetitive, so your body becomes immune to them. Your legs for example hold up your weight all day long, it's an exercise in itself. But your body has been programmed to handle it."

"Yeah, I read something about that. It's called memory something."

"Yes, muscle memory!" Mr. D confirmed. "Now, if you want to strengthen the legs even more, you have to reprogram them with more weight. This is the idea behind weight lifting, swimming, bike riding, and yes, dancing which, to me is probably one of the most difficult of them all, because dancing does not allow the body to become immune. Once it does, the moves change, therefore challenging other muscles. This is why some of the most physically fit people you'll ever meet, will be dancers!"

"I will never laugh at a dancer again." I said with a smile.

"It's still just the beginning, King. I promise you, it's going to get harder. But if you listen to Princess, and trust in me, it will all pay off.

"So how's the rest of the class treating you?" Mr. D asked.

"Everybody's really cool."

"Good dancers?"

"Oh my god…They're incredible!"

"Better than you?"

"Of course" I said with a laugh, assuming that he was just joking. But he wasn't!

Mr. D stopped and looked at me.

"Why?"

"Why what?"

"Why are they better than you?"

I looked at him, trying to figure out where he was going with this. The question was actually stupid, and I felt like I was now being picked on.

"Mr. D, these people have been doing this all their lives, this is all they know.

"And you feel, that's what makes them better than you?"

"Well… Yeah! Take for instance that girl, Vanessa." I figured if Mr. D didn't already know her, he would now.

"Which one is Vanessa?" He asked.

"The black girl." I replied.

"But there's two black girls isn't there?

"Yeah, um…."

"… So which one are you talking about? The pretty one, or the ugly one?"

I thought that comparison was kind of fucked up, and I needed to be careful how I answered.

"The one with the glasses," I replied. I watched as Mr. D looked up in the air as if recalling the images of the two girls.

"Okay, that's the ugly one! What about her?

Though I've only known Vanessa for just a short while, I couldn't help but take it personal. I didn't find her ugly at all, in fact, I thought she was quite beautiful!

"Well, she's been dancing since she was a toddler, and

has been working with Princess since she was like eight years old."

"And how old is she now?"

"Same age as me, but you gotta see her, she's amazing!"

"I'm sure she is, King. But let's be real, if she was in fact so great, then why would she be working for you?"

I didn't know what to say at this point, because no matter what, Mr. D would have an answer, a smart-ass one at that, so I just stayed quiet.

"King, listen to me. I don't care if they've been dancing for twenty years, and you just twenty hours. I expect you to catch up, surpass, and then lead them. That's the characteristics of a superstar, and that's you." You're a Superstar!

"Superstar is a pretty big role to fill," I said as we continued down the stairs.

"Yes it is, a very big role, but I chose you because I believe that you can fill it. I just need you to start believing the same."

We stopped, and Mr. D turned to me.

"While they're sleeping, you should be working. When they're eating, you should be working, and when they're working, you should be working harder! I would never give you a task that I thought was impossible, in fact, had I doubted your abilities in anyway, we wouldn't be here talking about it."

Mr. D opened yet another mystery door that I had never noticed, and when we stepped in…

"Holy shit!" was all I could say. Through this door was a state of the art work out facility, a massive one at that. It seemed to have every workout contraption you can think of, as well as a few I've never even seen before.

It wasn't one of those sissy gyms that you go to stay in shape, this place was like a factory, a factory that made monsters!

"I had this built just before you got here, no one's ever used it yet."

"This is incredible" I said walking through, admiring everything.

"I want you to break this place in." He said, as I grabbed a five pound dumbbell, and started curling it all fast and awkward.

"When would I find the time?" I asked, as I tried unsuccessfully to pick up one of the many medicine balls lying against the wall.

"Oh that's easy."

Mr. D turned and looked at me.

When everyone else is sleeping... and eating!"

I went over to one of the machines, not knowing what I was doing and just started messing with it, when suddenly I heard.

"Hey, get the fuck off that!"

I turned around, and as if the entire scene was staged, in walked this short muscular gentleman, dressed all in white. He sort of reminded me of a miniature Mr. Clean, complete with shiny bald head and earring.

"This is Jacq." Mr. D said, as Jacq hurried me off of the machine. "He's gonna teach you how to use all this stuff."

I watched as Jacq pulled a white rag from his back pocket and started dusting off one of the machines I tried.

"Nice to meet you," I said, extending my hand out to him, but instead of shaking it, he placed in it the rag, and gestured for me to wipe down the one I was just on.

"Do not touch anything in here without my permission." He ordered, though it sounded more like a warning.

For such a short guy, Jacq's German accent was deep and raspy. He stood completely still with his hand on his hips, jaw raised proud. Jacq had to be at least twice my age but with the body of a young athlete. Every muscle in his chest and shoulders could be seen through his tight white tee, tucked neatly into his white pants and separated by a black leather belt that matched his boots.

"Jacq's an incredible trainer, and will get you into the best shape of your life." Said Mr. D, as Jacq just stood there, sucking up all the praise.

I didn't mean to come across cold and uninterested; it's just that all I understood was more work, and the worst kind of work... Exercise!

Mr. D looked at me for some type of response, but I had nothing.

"You're okay?" He asked me.

"I think this is great." I replied to Mr. D, and then turned to Jacq. "And I really appreciate everything. But I'm feeling like this might be just a little too much." I looked at the two of them, and then continued. I mean, right now, they have me rehearsing six hours a day, five days a week. Don't you think that might be enough?

Mr. D didn't say anything, but instead looked at Jacq for his opinion.

"That all depends on the goal you're trying to achieve."

"He's definitely going to need the strength and stamina to go on the road." Mr. D said.

"Yeah, and I'd also like to look good in these outfits. There's a few that are going to be physically challenging" I added .

"Well for strength and stamina." Jacq began. Either of these will do the job. However, if you're concerned about looks, then you'd have to make a choice as to how you prefer to look. Like this?" Jacq busted out a bicep flexing pose, impressive as hell,

"Or would you prefer to look like Princess?"

"Jacq's going to put together an entire regimen for you, complete with a nutritional menu." Mr. D turned to Jacq who continued.

"Tomorrow morning I will need you here before rehearsal, you will need a complete physical…"

"Wait… But I already had a physical!"

"You'll have another. There are things I need to know before we begin on Monday. I don't need you dying all over my new machines.

Mr. D and I laughed. But Jacq was dead serious. We all shook hands and exited the gym. Mr. D walked me down to the dance studio, and just before I entered, I turned and asked.

"You don't think I might be doing a bit too much?"

"Extraordinary efforts bring extraordinary results!"

CHAPTER 52

Got Jokes

"One-Two-Three-Four-Five-Six-Seven-Eight and One-Two-Three-Four-Five-Six- Seven-Eight..." Princess counted off our every step, over and over until it was perfect, and once it was, he'd add in something new.

Princess had me do everything. The only indication that I was leading this group was the fact that he now had me at the front of the class. He didn't want me following anyone but him.

Our rehearsals were super intense, and those six hour days, quickly jumped to eight. In just three months I had finally become, acceptable.

But it took a lot of work. I did my part, exactly as I was told, and just as I had been promised, it was paying off. Princess's method of teaching was a combination old school stretching, and repetition, each time improving on the last.

The things that I was now able to do, I use to think were impossible for a straight guy, but what flexibility did for a dancer was remarkable. It made even the most difficult moves look graceful.

"Wake the fuck up!" Princess yelled, snapping me out of my trance. But it was only my eyes that gave me away, because the rest of me was seriously on point. I once asked him what type of Dance we were learning, expecting him to say something like, Modern, or Jazz.

"*My* Dance, he replied!" Was his answer, and that it was. In fact, the routines we were taught, according to Vanessa, who was trained in all aspects, were a combination of Modern, Jazz, Tap, Ballet, Country, African, and Latin, with bits and pieces of gymnastics that bridged together all the different styles.

I had already lost a bunch of weight, and was starting to get concerned, thanks to Jacq, and his constant slew of Princess jokes. But what I really noticed was going on, was a sort of competition between the two, with the million dollar question being, which one of them worked me harder?

And though he did everything he could to try and bulk me up, he was no match for Princess, who after each rehearsal had practically swimming in sweat.

Princess walked up to me and looked at my hands, then at the hands of everyone else. My legs, then at the legs of everyone else, and then finally at my feet, and that's where he saw the problem.

"Look at your goddamn feet!" He shouted. I was pretty immune to the shouting so it didn't have the same effect on me as it once did.

I looked down at my feet.

"I don't see anything!" I said, still standing in the exact position.

"What?" He asked, with his wise-ass grin. I shook my head. Princess gave me a look of annoyance.

"Don't move!! He commanded. "Don't anyone move!" He took off into his office and came out a moment later with this huge dildo.

"Shut the fuck up!" He yelled as some of us began to laugh. It was clear he wasn't playing so we all did as he said.

Lily was to my left and a step back. Princess walked over to her, holding the dildo like it was a club that he was about to beat her with. He bent down and placed the back part of the dildo against her left toe.

"This mirror is at twelve o'clock, Lily, at what time does your foot point to?" Lily looked down at her foot and then back at Princess.

"Ten o'clock?"

"Are you asking me, or telling me?"

She looked down again and then changed her question to an answer.

Princess went over to her and picked up the dildo, and walked over to my right where Emerald stood and placed the dildo at *his* foot.

"What time is your foot pointed to?"

"Ten o'clock!" He immediately said. Princess grabbed the dildo from in front of him and placed it now in front of me the same way. Up against my foot, pointed out.

"Mr. Sunshine. What time is your foot pointing to?"

I swallowed the huge knot in my throat as I could clearly see where I screwed up.

Princess had a way of highlighting your mistakes in a way that you would never again forget. His technique of humiliation, though a bit primitive, sure as hell worked!

"Eleven." I said, in a pretty low voice. Just then, Mr. D walked in and took a seat, Though a few of us turned to look, Princess didn't say anything, he was too interested in my answer.

"Excuse me?" He asked cupping his ear.

"Eleven o'clock!" I said again. I glanced at Mr. D from the corner of my eye as he sat back and folded his arms.

"Eleven O'clock?" He asked, and I nodded.

"Now, let me explain something, and it's important that you listen carefully." I nodded.

"I don't let any of these assholes fuck up like that." He began, pointing out at the rest of the class. "And most of the time, the audience isn't paying them much mind." My eyes glanced out at my classmates, as I could tell, that statement hurt a few of them. "Now, do you really think that I'm going to let *you* get away with it?"

I didn't say anything, just shook my head.

"Now, take this!" He said handing me the dildo. God, I didn't wanna touch this thing, but I did as I was told, grabbing it from the very edge.

"Now go in there, wash it good, dry it, and then put it

back on my desk where it belongs."

I looked over at Mr. D trying to read whether he approved of Princesses method or not. I got nothing!

As I headed toward the bathroom, Princess yelled out. "And that shit better not give me an infection!" I was sick.

I didn't hear any laughs or spot any smirks, so I figured this was how he did things. I wanted so bad to just throw this shit at his head and leave, but I was warned of his unorthodox ways, and promised Mr. D to abide. I just never expected this.

From inside the bathroom, I could hear him giving everyone instructions about tomorrow's rehearsal.

I dropped the dildo into the sink, and ran hot water over it while I tried to think of the best way of cleaning this thing.

I pumped soap on it from the dispenser, and with one finger, I spread the soap on it, until it was totally covered. I didn't want to spend too much time in here so I immediately began rinsing. But there was a problem. Damn soap wouldn't rinse off. In fact, it seemed to be lathering up even more. I went from one finger to two, then four, until finally I had to use my entire hand. I looked behind me and just like the dressing room there was no door, only a curtain.

I guess I wasn't supposed to use soap, I only wished someone would've told me, because now it wouldn't rinse.

I was getting frustrated and found myself practically jerking this thing off in an attempt to remove the soap. But the more I jerked, the more it lathered. I was getting really pissed when suddenly there was a flash, and when I looked back the entire class stood behind Princess as he took a picture of me with his Polaroid camera.

The place roared in laughter, and though it took a minute for it to sink in, I realized, I'd been pranked. Shit, even Princess was hysterical, something I had yet to see.

Vanessa walked up to me, and took the dildo from my hand.

"It's never gonna rinse," she said.

"What do you mean?"

"It's soap! The whole thing is made of soap!" I took a closer look, even went as far as smelling it, at which point everyone totally lost it. Even Mr. D was standing way in the back, shaking his head and smiling.

Vanessa handed me a paper towel to just wipe it dry. "You still have to put it back." She said.

I went over to Princess' office, first time I'd ever been in there, and stood it up on his desk. When I turned around to leave I caught him tacking one of the photos to a huge cork board. I went up to it and noticed that this was a regular prank he pulled on nearly every new student that came through. The only difference though... My picture caught me smelling it!

CHAPTER 53

I Got You

"So how was rehearsal?" Sal asked through the rear view mirror, watching me settle into my seat.

"Was okay, I guess," definitely not wanting to share the prank with him.

"The Choreography that we're learning now is actually for the video."

"Really?"

"Yeah, I'm sure a lot of it will also be used for live performances, but right now, it's all about the video."

"So did they tell you anything about the video?"

"Nah, I wish, but you know how Mr. D is, he goes from zero to a hundred in three seconds."

"Oh, I know!"

Sal and I laughed, as I rolled down my window, and peeked out.

"Hey Sal, make a left at the corner if you don't mind, I wanna check something out."

Though Mr. D's orders are always to bring me to and from without stops, Sal and I had gotten to know and trust each other pretty well, that we both pretty much did as we wished. I had never been through here when it was dark, but I was with Sal, so might as well.

After he made the left I told him to keep going straight, but to slow down. As he did, I stuck my head out the window and listened carefully... but nothing!

"Make a right, here." I said, and he did. Sal watched me through his mirror, trying to figure out what I was up to. Drug Dealers working the corners nodded as we passed, and a hooker walked up when we stopped at a light. "Looking for a date?" she asked, her voice deeper than mine, good thing the light changed.

"What's going on?" Sal asked, concerned about my sudden weird behavior.

"Make a right here!" I said, pointing in the direction I wanted him to go. As we drove through one of the blocks I stuck my head out the window and stared up toward the tops of the surrounding buildings, hoping to catch even a note of my song.

"Hey, look who's there?" Sal said as he pointed up ahead. It was Quenepa. I quickly rolled up my window, hoping he didn't see us. But Sal pulled up at the curb.

"What's up you fucking midget! Sal called up as he got out of the car. "How's your head?" He asked laughing with his hand on top of Quenepa's head playfully shaking it.

"Man, that shit wasn't funny!" He said, pulling out from

under Sal's hand.

So, wha'cha doing rolling around here like y'all Five-O and shit?"

Sal gestured toward my direction, though I wish he hadn't.

"Oh shit, you got Queeny-Boy up in there?" He said laughing. I just sat there behind the dark smoked window, just hoping he wouldn't come over…

And so, there he was, tapping on the window for me to open, and so I did.

"Wadup yo?" Quenepa said, cool and calm as he held out his hand. I was a bit hesitant and looked toward Sal who was looking back, and as much as I hated to do it, I took his hand.

"You still looking for that dude that was singing your shit?"

"Yeah, have you heard him lately?"

"Nah man, besides, I don't see what the problem is, it's not like he's gonna doing anything with it."

"The problem is, he stole it from me."

Quenepa looked at me and realized this was serious shit.

"What's going on?" Sal asked, so I explained

"I lost a note book that had a bunch of my raps in it, and then one day, I'm walking around here and I hear my shit."

"What do you mean, hear?" Sal asked.

"Some Spanish mother fucker, playing piano, and singing my shit!"

I still don't see what the big deal is," Quenepa insisted.

"The big deal is that it's my song. Not only that, he's not even rapping the shit, he's singing it! Fucking it all up!"

"So when you find this dude, wha'cha gonna do?" Quenepa asked. I looked at him, giving myself a moment to think about it. Then I answered.

"I'm gonna kill him!"

Sal and Quenepa both looked at me for a long moment before breaking out in laughter. I looked at them wondering what was so funny.

"King, listen to me." Sal began. "Let's just keep our eyes and ears open. We'll find this person, get back your shit, and tell him never to play your stuff again. You don't need to kill him."

"You guys don't get it." The song is called Yes Yes Y'all, and it's gonna be my biggest record ever, you watch."

'Does Mr. D know about this song?" Sal asked.

"Yeah."

"What did he say about it?"

"What do you mean?"

"I mean, is he using it for anything?"

"Well, not yet."

Sal looked at me, and felt that if Mr. D didn't want to use it, it probably wasn't worth much anyway.

"Mr. D is a control freak.' I said. "The only reason he didn't want to use it is because it wasn't his. But trust me when I tell you, Yes Yes Y'all is going to be a major hit.

Quenepa stood there, stroking his baby-like chin, just looking at me, until he broke out of whatever was going through his head.

"Check it out home boy, I got you!" Quenepa said, pointing a stern finger.

"What do you mean?" I asked.

"Imma find this dude for you." I didn't know what to say, because the way he said it kind of scared me. This kid was mental. Just as I was about to say something, my window when up. I didn't notice that Sal got back in the car.

CHAPTER 54

Bumps and Bruises

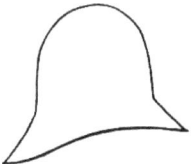

Sal placed the last of the groceries on the kitchen table, as Grams began putting everything away.

"Okay, you two, time for me to hit the road.

"Thanks for everything." I said as he and I shook hands.

"You're off tomorrow, right?" Sal asked.

"Yeah, thank God, I really need a break.

"I gotta give it to you, kid, you're doing it."

"Thanks."

Sal gave Grams a kiss, and then headed for the door. I followed to lock up behind him, but before he left he turned around and looked at me.

"King, I need you to listen to me carefully."

"Sure man, what's up?"

"Look man, I clown around with Quenepa and shit, but I gotta tell you, the guy's got issues."

"Oh, I already know that."

"No, I mean serious issues." I looked back at Grams putting away groceries, hoping she couldn't hear us.

"What kind of issues we're talking about."?

"He's from the streets… Literally!" He has no boundaries, no regard for law or life. Can never be trusted… By anyone! And when you think you're friends… that's when he slits your throat!" Sal stared at me, then turned and left.

"Everything okay, Grams?" I asked as I reentered the kitchen. She was still putting groceries away.

"Mijo, do you think this is a good idea?"

"What?"

"Taking these things every week from these people?"

"Grams, trust me when I tell you, these are not handouts. I worked for this."

"So why don't they just pay you and let you buy your own groceries?"

"Well, that's pretty much what they're doing."

"No Reynaldo. I mean pay you with money, so you can do your own shopping? Why do people have to know what kind of toilet paper we use?"

"I understand, but this is still all one big blur. I've done nothing but cost these people money, from my hair, wardrobe, trainer, choreographer, photos, driver, the list goes on."

"This Mr. D guy, who I haven't even met yet, he's kind of strange, you know, the way he does things."

"I know, and I promise, once I'm in a little deeper, I'll

bring all that up. Right now, let's just go along with it, I don't want him to think that I don't trust him.

"It's not about trust, it's about your life, and every moment wasted because you're playing someone else's game."

Grams got on her toes and gave me a kiss.

"Good night, Mijo." she said, before exiting the kitchen.

I continued putting groceries in the cabinet, thinking about what she was saying, and I have to admit, all her points were valid. I was just scared. I didn't feel like I was home free yet, or that any of this was even real. Every time Mr. D called me to his office, I swore it was to tell me that it's all over.

Suddenly, I heard a loud crash! I dropped what I had in my hands and dashed into the living room just to find Grams getting up from the floor.

"Grandma!" I yelled as I grabbed her from under her arm and helped her up.

"I'm okay, I'm okay." She said as she straightened up.

"What happened?"

"I don't know," She said, dusting herself off. "I tripped over something." I looked down and around where Grams had fallen and couldn't find anything that might've been the cause.

"Are you hurt? should we go to the hospital? Let me call Sal…"

"I'm fine! Reynaldo please, coño!" She said annoyed. "I'm tired and I just want to go to bed."

But when she took a step, a sharp pain attacked her leg. I

immediately grabbed hold of her.

"We're going to the hospital."

"If I had gone to the hospital every time I fell, they would've moved me in. It's no big deal!"

She was really annoyed, and I didn't know why. She tried walking, but couldn't hide the fact that she was in pain.

"Grams…" I started to say, but she threw up her hand and stopped me.

"Just help me to my room." I looked at her, and knew arguing would get me nowhere, so I grabbed on to her, and helped her to her room. Her face distorted as I sat her at the edge of her bed.

I stood there and watched her lean back and close her eyes. I was able to sneak a peek at her leg, and what I saw nearly killed me.

"Grams, your leg looks really bad, let me call Sal, he'll give us a ride to the…"

"I don't need to go to the hospital for a little bruise."

"But it's not a little bruise."

"You should've seen it when it first happened, this is nothing!"

"What are you taking about?" I asked. Grams thought about it before speaking.

"This happened a few weeks ago, in the bathroom."

"What happened?"

"The floor was wet, like most bathrooms, and when I

stepped out of the tub I lost my balance."

"Are you kidding me? Why didn't you say anything?"

"For what? so you can get all crazy, like you're doing now?"

"I don't tell you a lot of things because I am grown, and have been taking care of the two of us for many years. I don't need to answer to you, or tell you anything I don't want to!"

It's been a long time since she's yelled at me. So long in fact that it sounded weird. But maybe it's because it wasn't really about *me*!

CHAPTER 55

Pizza Guy

It's Wednesday morning and I'm off, so I decided to do something I never usually do, and that is... Do nothing!

I turned on the TV that sat up on my dresser, and one of those Morning talk shows were on.

"And joining us here in just a moment is Rap music sensation, Nemesis!" announced the female host.

"That's right and he will be performing his new hit, so don't go away!" added her male co-host.

I immediately jumped up from my bed, because no way was I about to start my day off watching that mother fucker.

I turned the channel, working quickly past the Soap Operas. It seemed like every other channel was doing something on Nemesis. I couldn't believe it, not even on my day off could I avoid that dude, so I decided to just get up, and get out.

"Good morning!" Grams sang, all bright eyed, and Busteloed up," morning Grams. I replied as I leaned down and kissed her. "How's your leg?"

"It's fine, Mijo," she said waving it off. "I'm sorry about last night. I was just tired."

"You had me worried."

"Trust me, I'm fine, you have nothing to worry about. So, I thought you were going to stay in today?" I looked at her, relieved that she was fine, but she obviously didn't want to talk about the fall.

"I tried, but didn't work." I said with a slight laugh. "You want breakfast?"

"Nah, I'll just grab some orange juice." I said on my way to the fridge. "Look I saved this for you." She said handing me a newspaper.

"What is it?" I asked.

"This guy sounds like he's doing I think, the same thing like you."

I looked at the ugly face that practically took up the entire page, and sighed.

"You should try and get in touch with him." Grams suggested. "He might be able to help you out." I closed the paper, and handed it back to her.

"Take it with you, so you can read the story, bendito, he went through so much.

"I'm really not interested, Grams." I said taking a sip of my juice.

"You know, both his parents died in a car crash."

"No. I didn't know that." I replied, looking at Grams as I gulped down the rest of my drink.

"Yes, it was so sad, he has a sister and she was in college, and they had no insurance or anything, so she had to quit school."

I continued listening, while studying the pulp at the bottom of my glass.

"He started working, and taking all types of odd jobs so his sister could go back to school. It worked out for a little while, but eventually she had to get a job too because they just weren't doing good."

"Well, I'm sure they're doing much better now," I so coldly replied.

"They are, they figured it out, but what I thought was so interesting was that without telling anyone, even his own sister, he would find time to go out on these meetings, with these different music companies. Almost like what you were doing. He said he went on hundreds of them before someone finally said okay, and now, he's really famous!"

"Yeah, Grams, I kind of know the rest" I said stopping her from continuing on.

"Oh, so you know about this guy?"

"Sort of," I said placing my glass in the sink. "Look, I gotta go okay? I have a few things I gotta take care of."

"Are you coming home late?"

"I don't think so, but If I do, I'll call you." I said, giving her a kiss, before leaving.

On my way to the subway, I heard that familiar voice call out my name. I immediately knew who it was, and tuned around.

"What's up, Junior, I said, as he and little chubby friend rolled up on their bikes. I slapped then both five, and then asked.

"Hey, why aren't you guys in school?" They looked at each, and then back at me shrugged their shoulders. "You don't realize it now, but school is very important." I looked at Junior. "What you wanna be when you grow up?" Junior scratched his chin while looking up into the air.

"A cop," he said.

"Really?"

"Yeah, a lot of my sister's friends are cops.

"Okay," I replied, shaking my head to myself.

"But do you know you have to take a test to become a cop, right?"

"Yeah."

"You do?"

"Uh huh… A shooting test, right?"

"Yeah, but before the shooting test, they want to see how smart you are, your reading and your math, can't have no dumb cops running around, you know what I'm saying?"

"My sister sometimes says they're dumb!"

"Well, I'm sure some of them are, but those are the ones that end up losing their jobs."

"What about you?" I asked Junior's friend. He did the same, scratching his chin while looking into the air. He had a huge smile on his jolly fat face, like he was happy that someone was even showing him any interest.

"A Pizza Guy!" He suddenly blurted out. I looked at him and laughed, totally taking the hint.

"A Pizza guy, huh?" I asked and he shook his head real fast. "Well that's a very important job, too."

"Is there a test for that?"

"Absolutely, you have to be able to read ingredients, tell time, temperature, and count money.

"And taste it to see if it's good?"

"Well, of course."

So you see guys, school's very important."

"I'm going back to school tomorrow!" Junior proudly said.

"Me too!" Said his friend, and *that* was my cue!

I dug into my pocket and pulled out three dollars, and handed them to Junior. The Chubby kid's face lit up, sort of reminding me of that image of the smiling moon.

"Okay guys, I got go, tell Sarge I said hi!"

"Thanks Rey!" Junior said, nudging his friend to also say thanks.

"Thanks Rey!" These were some funny kids, I would only hope that life treats them well.

"Oh, and Rey, check this out!" Junior said, and out of nowhere, he started to rap.

I Don't care what them other peoples say yo,'cause in my book, homeboy you okay bro!

"That was great, Junior, where you learn that from?"

"That's from the song, Starlight!"

"Starlight?"

"Yeah, that's that fresh new joint from Nemesis!" he yelled out, hitting me in the chest with what felt like a bag of bricks. I stood there, baffled, here I was giving them money for Pizza, yet they're going around reciting rhymes from Nemesis.

"We'll see you later, Rey." Junior said, as the other one just waved.

I didn't say anything, just watched as the two of them rode off.

I kept replaying the line Junior had rapped to me, as I made my way up to the station.

And as I was about to go through the turnstile this huge poster suddenly caught my eye. Ironically, it was an ad for Nemesis' new single called, Starlight.

I nearly damaged my goods when I forgot to put in the token before pushing through. I acted like I didn't hear those girls behind me laugh, and quickly dropped in the token, and hurried up the steps.

Standing on the platform, I couldn't believe what I was seeing. Every fucking billboard on both sides displayed that ugly mother fucker's face. I've never seen a campaign for a record like this before, let alone a *Rap* record. This shit had to cost a fortune, another reason to make me regret ever turning down those people at Frontline.

It was weird to watch how kids would just hang around his poster while waiting for the train, as if he was a part of their crew or something. One poster I noticed even had red lip prints on it. *What the fuck!*

When the train finally arrived, I felt a little relieved, as this scene was becoming extremely tortuous, little did I know, that the scene I was *about* to encounter, was even worst.

I just about lost my mind, when the car I stepped into was lined tight with nothing other than ads promoting Nemesis' new record. I quickly turned to exit the train, but it was too late. The doors had closed.

Side by side, posters featuring a different close-up of Nemesis took up all of the display areas above the seats, and on the walls of the car. Everywhere I looked, there he was. I just couldn't take it, and this dude was making me dizzy.

Apologizing as I pushed my way through the car I made my way to the next, only to find myself in the same scenario.

Subway car after car, I found, saturated with these ads. I had never seen a campaign as big as this one, and when I got to the last car, and there was nowhere else to go, I stopped.

Standing against the very back door, I turned around and looked at the people sitting down, baffled by how many of them were intrigued by the campaign.

Girls sat, reading issues of Right On, and other teen magazines that also featured articles on Nemesis.

Mr. D had to see this shit for himself. All the ads, and magazine covers. The TV interviews and the fact that Nemesis was able to make a fan out of not just one of the youngest kids on my block, but also one of the oldest... My Grandmother!

But I despised even talking about him. I felt that if I acted as though Nemesis didn't even exist, just maybe, he wouldn't! But I would only be fooling myself, because as far as the rest of the world was concerned, Nemesis *did* exist, and he was becoming one of the most famous people of our time.

I got off on 34th Street and decide to walk a bit, and though his ads didn't take up the entire city. There were enough to make a solid point, and the point was, Nemesis was the new kid in town. New York City's Golden Boy of Rap.

Every other block pretty much had its only newsstand on the corner, and I couldn't help but notice that everyone was taking advantage of his success. On the side of every stand was a huge poster of Nemesis, to help boost the sales of the many magazines he covered.

I made my way first to the Library to check out Charlotte, but she wasn't there. I decided to sit down, hoping that maybe she was on a break. I tried to hide from Ms. Crumble, but she spotted me and of course, gave me her puss face.

After flipping through the Voice several times, waiting to see if Charlotte would walk in, I decided to give up. Ms. Crumble stopped what she was doing and watched as I gather my things, and though she wore her usual Stone-face, her eyes on the other hand, seemed to be laughing.

I decided to walk uptown through 10th Ave, in hopes of catching the guy who's been fucking with my song, not surprised when I ended up running into Quenepa.

"Wadup yo?" he said, slapping me an unnecessarily hard five.

"Just walking through,"

"Nobody just walks through here, unless they're copping drugs or hoes."

"You know why I'm here," I replied.

"How that shit go again?" He asked. And though I really didn't feel like rapping, I did need the help, so I gave him a bit.

I had no doubt that he was feeling it, because he closed his eyes and began bopping his head. After just the first verse and hook, I stopped.

"Yo, that shit is fresh!" He said, sending a multitude of playful jabs into my chest until I covered up. "So that's what it *supposed* to sound like!"

"Yeah, so you see now, how he butchered it?"

"Hell yeah! wait till we catch that mother fucker, we're gonna butcher his ass too!" I laughed for a quick second, until I noticed Quenepa acting really weird.

"I just wanna find out, how he got my lyrics, and what made him wanna do what he did." I said, trying to dilute the situation, just a bit.

"Nah, fuck that! That nigga gonna pay. First with his tongue, and I got just the tool for that."

Oh, this dude was out his mind. I'm watching him bouncing up and down. His hand holding what seemed like an invisible knife, he starts stabbing and slicing the air.

"Hey man, you're getting me a little nervous here. I mean, we don't wanna hurt him or anything."

"What? Man, you gotta teach this dude a serious lesson. I'm telling you, man. You don't do this shit right the first time, mother fuckers will be hi-jacking your shit all week!

Damn, what did I do? I thought as I watched Quenepa jump around like a maniac. He always seemed off to me, but now I was convinced.

"Don't worry yo, I got you. Imma find this mother fucker and make him pay royalties. How you want them?"

I had no idea what he was talking about. But then... He made it clear...

"You want them in hands? Feet? Oh, I know balls! I'm gonna make him pay with his balls!

The Story Continues with Book 2

An Excerpt From Yes Yes Y'all Book 2

The stagehands hurried off with scaffolding and other equipment used to build the set. I had no say in any of its design, though I did know what it would look like from the many drawings and architectural meetings I was allowed to sit in on.

"Sunshine!" yelled the choreographer, waking me once again from my constant daydream. His long, lanky hands gave a succession of claps just beneath his chin, as he rustled the dancers up on stage and into place.

"Are we ready?" He asked. I took a deep breath and exhaled with a nod. He then cued the light man to hit the switch. And in total darkness, I stood.

What seemed like an eternity was in fact only a few seconds when suddenly a loud clank echoed throughout the empty arena, and the blinding spotlight knocked me back.

"Okay," said the choreographer… "from the top!"

Dear Reader

I just wanted to take a moment to personally thank you for reading Book 1 of Yes Yes Y'all, and though the dream of many authors is to one day have a Best Seller, and move a million copies, mine on the other hand is simply to move you!

Whether my stories make you laugh, cry, scream, or just allow you to share with my characters, their incredible journeys, I pray that you could find in them, something just for you. It could be the answering of a long grueling question, making you think about something you've never before given thought, or just remind you to tell that special someone, that you love them.

Though none of the books so far are autobiographical, they do however run a parallel dimension to my own life, and therefore knowing them is in fact, knowing me!

I intend on writing until life's last page, when God finally says, The End! But until then, it would mean so much to me, if we could stay connected.

By logging on to Latifmercado.com, and subscribing to my mailing list, you'll receive my Newsletter, alerts of anything new coming out of the La' Camp, Freestyle events headed your way, and of course exclusive gifts and offers just for you!

Thank you again, and I'll see you soon

Your friend

Latif

About The Author

Latif Mercado has been a part of the Freestyle Music scene for well over 25 years, and though his role in the beginning was minimal, the role he's been playing ever since, has been massive, and a major force behind the genre's continued success.

As a Booking Agent with a who's who roster of Freestyle Legends, as well as his managerial involvement with such industry icons as Lil' Suzy and The Cover Girls, rarely would you find a Freestyle event happening without Latif somewhere in the mix.

In an attempt to make people aware of the fact that Freestyle isn't just a music, but rather a culture, La' began writing books, in hopes of reaching fans through a medium they would never expect, and in 2011, his debut novel, FREESTYLE FOR LIFE, did just that!

Since then, Latif has released several books that, not only feature Freestyle as part of its overall theme, but also its main characters of Latin decent.

Though born and raised in New York, Latif currently resides in North Carolina with his wife, two grown children, four grandkids and a dog named Coco.

Latif loves hearing from his readers, answering questions, and sharing whatever advice he possibly can, whether it be on writing, or maybe something Freestyle related, so be sure to reach out, even if it's just to say hi.

For more information on Latif, or to connect with him on the various platforms, please go to LatifMercado.com

Books By LA'

FREESTYLE FOR LIFE

FEASTYLE

FREESTYLE PROMOTIONS
And the 7 Simple Steps To Getting Started

HOW TO BOOK A FREESTYLE ARTIST
IN 5 EASY STEPS

YES YES Y'ALL Book 1

YES YES Y'ALL Book 2

YES YES Y'ALL Book 3

www.ingramcontent.com/pod-product-compliance
Lightning Source LLC
Chambersburg PA
CBHW070216260626
47160CB00002B/575